A Waste

Born in 1950, Jim Lusby is a former Hennessy Award winner for his short stories and has also written for the stage and radio. He lives in Dublin.

Also by Jim Lusby

CRAZY MAN MICHAEL

MAKING THE CUT

FLASHBACK

KNEELING AT THE ALTAR

A WASTE OF SHAME

Jim Lusby

ORION

First published in Great Britain in 2001 by Orion Books
an imprint of The Orion Publishing Group
Orion House, 5 Upper St Martin's Lane, London WC2H 9EA

A CIP catalogue record for this book is available
from the British Library

ISBN 0 575 07186 9 (hardback)
ISBN 0 575 07187 7 (trade paperback)

Typeset by Deltatype Ltd, Birkenhead, Merseyside
Printed and bound in Great Britain by
Clays Ltd, St Ives plc

To Séamas and Margaret Ryan

PART ONE

january, 2000

It was still dark when the boy was woken. Just eighteen minutes past five according to his Adidas Chrono watch, which he'd synchronized with the speaking clock the night before and which he'd checked again for accuracy a little after midnight. Because it had been a last present from his dying father, he relied on the watch as one of the few sources of certainty in his life. He thought of it as his guide. In a world where almost everything else had become treacherously unreliable, he trusted it as a talisman.

When he found himself sitting upright in his bed, screaming wildly and drenched with his own sweat, he knew that no one would come to calm or comfort him. He sensed immediately that he was alone again in the cottage. The previous night, on New Year's Eve, his mother had left at ten o'clock with Michael Slade, the man who took her out at weekends, every Friday and Saturday night. She never stayed at home those nights. Not even when the boy was sick. She hadn't believed him when he'd told her about the limping man with the No. 1 haircut who was hanging around the village harbour one night before Christmas, accusing him of inventing scares and trying to blackmail her. Last night, she'd said they were going to join a house party in a nearby town, about twelve kilometres north of the village, and she'd promised to return by one, if only to check that he was sleeping. But he hadn't believed her. She had no transport of her own. No one would want to drag themselves away from the party to drive her back to the village. And besides, she wouldn't ask them to. When she was with Michael Slade, she always forgot about the boy.

On the small screen in his darkened bedroom, he'd watched the television coverage of the New Year celebrations. But he had no interest in the pleasures of strangers. His attention was driven by terror. For almost a year his mind had been darkened by prophecies of disaster on this day, of blood-soaked accidents and gory chaos, as the western world lurched from one millennium to another, slipping its tenuous hold on its own technology. This was why he'd obsessively checked the accuracy of his wristwatch after midnight. And this was why he'd left the warmth of his bed a minute later and stood shivering on the damp flagstones in the kitchen, testing the cooker and the fridge, the microwave and the VCR.

In the end, as at the close of so many other nights, it was disappointment that finally exhausted him. Nothing happened. None of the appliances in the cottage refused his instructions. No aircraft fell to the earth from the skies outside. No stock markets around the world were sent dizzily crashing. And his mother didn't come home.

At one-thirty-six, propped up by sponge pillows in front of the still flickering television, the boy had fallen asleep.

He didn't ask what woke him so savagely almost four hours later. Nightmares were too frequent an experience for him. Shivering violently as the sweat cooled on his skin, he quickly switched off the television and slipped from the bed. But killing the light so suddenly was a mistake. In the darkness, as he groped towards his mother's bedroom, he stumbled against his own furniture, painfully stubbing his toes. He cursed but didn't call out, because he hated the sound of his own unanswered voice echoing through the empty cottage. And because he was so drained of hope that even his instincts were stunted.

As he'd expected, his mother's bedroom was still empty. The bed, unmade since it had been abandoned the previous morning, was cold, and untidy, and uninviting. The boy sat on its edge, his body slumped forward, exhausted, but too terrified of dreams to give in easily to sleep again. In that position, fighting to keep his eyes open, he heard what might have been a woman's scream in the distance, cutting through the stillness of the night. He paid no attention to it. He knew that the dark was full of strange, distorted sounds and that most of them came from inside his own head.

By morning, waking at the foot of his mother's bed, the boy had forgotten about the scream. He felt cold. The untidy covers had kept falling away from him through the night and the disrupted pattern of his sleep had left him dull and slightly disorientated. He had no appetite. He drank a carton of orange juice, because his mouth was dry and sore, and then he dressed, pulling on the same tracksuit and rain jacket he'd been wearing the last few days. The morning was damp. Through the kitchen window he could see that a heavy mist had come in off the sea. But he needed to escape the deadness of the cottage, although he knew that he'd find nothing livelier or warmer beyond it.

He had no friends to call on any more. One by one, the other kids had vanished from the area over the last few years, migrating to the cities with their parents, until he was the only child still living in the village and there was no one left to play with. Some of the abandoned houses had been sold to foreigners, who used them as holiday homes. But most of them were still unoccupied.

It wasn't so lonely during school term. The school bus collected him early in the morning and dropped him home in the late afternoon after a crowded day. But he dreaded the rest of the year. Sometimes, at the weekends or during holidays, he still climbed the garden walls of the empty houses and sat alone in the long wet grass, spearing ants or woodlice with a penknife and bitterly remembering the games he'd once shared in.

He couldn't understand why they didn't leave as well. There was nothing to keep them in the village. No friends for him. No social life for his mother. Not even a shop to buy their groceries. He knew that his mother was an artist and needed seclusion for her work, but it was unfair to make him a freak as well. They should live where there were other people. And football pitches. And cinemas. And shopping centres.

The boy hated the dying village.

It had only three streets, for instance, a total he found intensely embarrassing whenever he was asked to describe where he lived. Pier Road ended at the reconstructed harbour to the west and Beach Road, running parallel to it, gradually disappeared into the sand to the east. When the tide was out, it was possible to walk from one street to the other along the stony beach. Otherwise the only link between them was Main Street, a curved and narrow strip that dropped suddenly down from a third-class road to the north and then hurried back up there again. Long ago, the boy had noticed that if the village was drawn as a street map, it looked like the mathematical symbol for pi. Now it struck him as stupid that a place that kept shrinking all the time should be represented by a constant.

There were fifty-two houses in the village: thirteen on Pier Road, eleven on Beach Road and twenty-eight along Main Street. The boy knew this because he counted them every day, always adding some extra details to his store of knowledge about the buildings and noting any further deterioration in their appearance. Thirty-three of the houses were vacant. Ten had been bought as holiday homes by outsiders, mostly by German and Dutch families who sailed their yachts into the harbour every summer and hung around for a few short weeks before going home again. Sometimes they came for Christmas and the New Year too. But not this year. All the foreigners had stayed in their own countries for the millennium.

The rest of the village's houses were owned by locals. The boy himself lived with his mother in the last cottage to the east of Main Street. At the opposite side of the village, a strange and angry man named Carthy lived by himself. Two childless old couples were on Pier Road and another couple, with grown-up children who had left, were on Beach Road. Back on Main Street, on either side of the boarded-up post office, three of the houses were occupied by single men who worked at the local creamery. And finally, in no. 9, right in the centre of the street, there was the old woman who was said to be a witch, but whose only friend, apart from the boy's mother, was a nervous young priest with sweaty hands and sticky sweets.

When he stepped outside his home that New Year's morning and casually looked west, along the length of Main Street, the first thing the boy noticed was that there was no smoke coming through the open front door of the old woman's house. This was a sign that he had often been warned by his mother to look out for. The old woman burned turf and wood in her grate. Because her chimney was blocked, the heavy smoke came back down the flue and into her front room again. Regardless of the weather or the time of day, she always left the street door open, simply to avoid suffocating herself. The yellow smoke, billowing into Main Street, was a constant reassurance that she was active. Its absence threatened an emergency.

The boy knew that he had to go and investigate, but although he didn't like to admit it, he was still frightened of the old woman. When he was younger and had actually believed that she was a witch, her shrivelled face and cackling laugh had haunted all his dreams and nightmares. He realized now that these were only fairy tales, of course. But he still found her scary. He felt a cold shiver down his spine whenever she looked at him. Her milky, bloodshot eyes and her humped back, as if she was carrying a rucksack under her black dress, still disturbed him.

The boy crossed the road and walked slowly along the narrow footpath, past the junction with Beach Road, until he was standing directly opposite the old woman's house. The buildings on either side had all been abandoned and neglected for more than a year, but hers was still the shabbiest in the row. The plaster had crumbled from the outside walls, exposing the brickwork underneath. The door and window frames were badly rotted. The few surviving gutters were choked with weeds and litter, and the roof, pock-marked with gaping holes and broken slates, sagged inwards where a joist had weakened in the centre.

In five minutes, the boy decided, if his mother didn't come home from the party, if no one else woke up in the village and if he hadn't caught sight of the old woman through the open door, he'd cross the road again and look into the old woman's house. He set the timer on his wristwatch. Knowing that time moved slower if it was watched, he stared at the display as it counted off the seconds. His nervousness tempted him to cheat, first by changing the rules and then by imagining movement in the crumbling house, but he resisted both. When the wristwatch bleeped at him, telling him that his wait was over, he took a deep breath and jumped from the footpath.

There was no electric bell or metal knocker on the old woman's rotting front door. The boy picked a wet stone from the street and used it to hammer loudly on the wood, remembering that the old woman was almost completely deaf. When he called out afterwards, he tried to get the same power into his voice as well. But his throat was dry from nervousness. And at the last moment, it occurred to him that he didn't even know the old woman's name.

His summons came out as a limp squeak. 'Hello?'

And it wasn't answered.

The boy stepped warily inside. He took only a single step, but he felt immediately as if he'd entered a different world. The house was in darkness. The only sound was that of water dripping steadily. Cold and damp and heavy with the sense of some hidden danger, the place had the eerie stillness of an isolated cave.

Too frozen by fear to call out loud again, the boy stood rigidly inside the draughty doorway, waiting for his eyes to adapt to the darkness.

The scene only gradually became clear to him.

There was no carpet or linoleum under his feet, just a bare concrete floor, covered with dust and strips of dirty paper and small stones. In front of him, over to his right, an open grate held powdery grey ash from the fire the old woman had kept. But there were no embers and the flames had obviously died a long time before. There must have been an attractive fireplace here once. A few of the coloured tiles and bits of the wooden surround were still in place. But nothing else had survived and now the grate was really just a blackened hole in the chimney breast. On the sloping mantelpiece above it there was an open greeting card, unsigned, but carrying a message printed in large black type. WELCOME TO THE NEW MILLENNIUM, it read. Beyond the grate, in a shallow alcove, there was a ragged cardboard box, holding a few sods of dried turf, some wooden logs and a worn, old-fashioned poker.

Close to this tattered cardboard box, the old woman was lying on the floor. She seemed to have slipped or fallen, possibly from the stained floral armchair that was pulled up to the fire. Her tiny feet, their toes pointing towards the boy, were covered with layers of black and grey woollen socks, but had no shoes. The heavy black dress she had on, entangled in an old-fashioned knitted shawl, was stained and badly torn. Above it, the boy thought at first that she was wearing a red blouse or vest and that a red necklace hung around her scrawny neck. But as he shifted sideways to allow more light from the street behind, as he noticed that the old woman's face was heavily bruised and that detached clumps of her thin white hair were snagged under a leg of the armchair, he realized that he was mistaken about this. The old woman was actually naked from the waist upwards. What was biting into her shrivelled flesh wasn't a beaded necklace, but a knotted cord that had been used to strangle her. And the colour on her frail chest and shoulders didn't come from dyed material. It came from her own blood.

For a long time, unable either to step forward and confirm that the old woman was dead or to turn away and run for help, the boy stood shivering inside the open doorway, trying to locate the source of the blood. It was only when he succeeded in doing this, two or three minutes later, that he finally screamed and fled from the house. To the left of the corpse, beside a faded milk carton where two wet rats were scurrying, a section of the old woman's right breast, nipple upwards, was lying on the dirty floor.

one

By the morning of 3 January, when he was ordered to travel south and join the local investigating team, McCadden had been kicking his heels in Dublin for almost two months, waiting for confirmation of his new posting. For all his eagerness for change and his fear of settling for routine, it seemed as if he'd left the familiar comforts of his job in Waterford at the wrong moment. Savage political wrangling had held up the launch of the new national homicide squad he'd been assigned to. Hastily proposed by the Minister for Justice in response to a public outcry about the level of unsolved murders in the state and cautiously backed by the Garda commissioner, the squad was now the victim of second thoughts and revised priorities. Four months on from the initial announcement, it still had no official status, no formal title, no resources and no leader. In his worst moments, woken at night by the pain from his wounded shoulder and drifting restlessly around the gloomy basement flat he was renting in Dublin, McCadden was convinced that the entire unit consisted only of himself. Detective Inspector Robinson Crusoe, he mocked himself. Another victim of Irish fondness for confusing talk with achievement.

He had no enthusiasm for the investigation into the brutal murder of an old woman in a remote southern village. He was a stranger to the area, the case was already three days old, and he was uncertain about the nature of his role. Possibly, he thought, this was just a temporary assignment to keep him busy on the sidelines. He accepted that his idleness was making him a nuisance in Dublin. Possibly, he was expected merely to go through the motions and kill some time. But he suspected another, more devious agenda. The village was in West Cork, part of the division controlled by one of the commissioner's most bitter internal enemies, Chief Superintendent Pat Foran. After recent successes against local drug barons, Foran's reputation was at its height. By contrast, the commissioner was under pressure. His aggressive crackdown on organized crime in the capital had brought him rapid promotion at a young age; but in the highest office, as so often happens with the talented, his virtues had suddenly become embarrassments. His personal profile was far too high for the comfort of his minister's ego. And his fierce belief in the justness of what he was doing had left him open to accusations of arrogance and unaccountability. As the commissioner's man, McCadden was entering hostile territory and risked being treated as a spy.

To avoid being confronted by the entire investigating team in an unfamiliar incident room, he'd arranged to be met by a single officer at the scene at two o'clock that afternoon. But his heart wasn't in the journey. On the country roads past Cork city he contrived to get lost and had to stop on several occasions to check directions. He was an hour late when he finally reached the village. Following the instructions he'd received by email, he turned right immediately after passing the road sign at the entrance to the village. He half expected his contact to have left, but as soon as he cleared the junction he saw that a yellow Volkswagen Golf was parked at the end of the pier, facing the rough grey sea. The driver was resting against its bonnet, looking out at the choppy water. The man's shoulders were hunched against the cold and his hands were stuffed into the pockets of the green ski jacket he was wearing. Smoke from the smouldering cigarette in his right hand was being blown behind him by the wind.

It was only when the man turned, pushing himself away from the Volkswagen and flicking his cigarette into the harbour as he heard a car approaching, that McCadden realized that the waiting officer was a young black. He had no time to conceal his surprise. As he braked, the other was already passing quickly in front of the bonnet of his own car and striding impatiently across to open McCadden's door.

'Inspector McCadden?' the man checked. He extended an arm for a handshake, withdrew it to perform a more correct salute just as McCadden was about to accept it, and then offered an open palm again while McCadden was gesturing acceptance of the formality.

'Right,' McCadden acknowledged. 'Who do I have?'

'Detective Garda Joseph Curtis, sir. Chief Superintendent Foran sends his apologies. He has a press conference this afternoon.'

'Well, I wasn't expecting the man himself.'

'I'm to show you around. I tried to contact you to let you know, but your mobile seems to be switched off.'

'I left it at home,' McCadden claimed.

'Would you like me to arrange a—?'

'No.'

McCadden stepped from the car. He tried to keep the smile off his lips, in case Curtis misinterpreted its meaning and felt aggrieved, but he had to accept that he was already struggling here. Assigning a black officer as his liaison in a conservative rural area was a subtle opening thrust in what was obviously going to be a nasty campaign. It invited him to consider his own involvement as worthless and unwanted. At the same time, it would force him to reassess his own liberal credentials if he ever caught himself equating black with useless. It cut off any prospect of easy integration with the local detectives. And instead of easing his burdens, it added another one to the pile. It was a neat move, not least because its hidden instigators were publicly blameless. What could he accuse them of? Racism in Ireland was like the Irish sense of humour: so natural a part of normal life that it went unquestioned until it isolated you as a victim.

He wondered if Curtis was aware of any of this, but then quickly decided that the question was dangerous. Posing it would only be jumping enthusiastically into the trap that had been set for him.

McCadden moved away from the car and walked to the unprotected edge of the pier. The harbour struck him as overambitious for such an isolated spot, an impression intensified by the fact that it was totally empty. Nothing was moored there. The narrow inlet offered natural protection, but a lot of money had recently been spent fortifying and prettifying it.

'Who paid for the restoration?' he wondered.

Behind him, Curtis coughed to clear his throat. 'The harbour? I don't really know, sir. The local authority, I suppose. Mostly. Maybe with some lottery funds from central government as well.'

'Any fishing done here?'

'Fishing? No. There's no fishing fleet.'

'What's it used for?'

'Wealthy peoples' yachts, mainly.'

McCadden sighed and turned. His shoulder was starting to ache a little now. The cold and dampness were seeping their way through to the wound, adding to the stiffness from the long hours behind the wheel. And he wasn't seeing the humorous side of things any more. 'I don't suppose there's anywhere I can get a cup of coffee around here?' he risked.

Curtis shook his head. 'You can't get anything here, sir. There are no shops. No cafés. Not even a pub. Only a few people actually live here.'

McCadden looked forlornly past the young detective, back up the slight hill he'd descended to reach the pier. The place had the feel of an abandoned movie lot, he decided. The exteriors of the houses were variable: some neglected, some well maintained, a few carefully renovated in traditional rural style, with whitewashed walls and thatched roofs and brightly painted doors and windows. But there were no people.

You could *imagine* its life, he thought. A slow dissolve, say, into the bustle of pedestrians, a market, flower sellers, fishermen, the occasional car inching its way through the merry throng. But all the sounds and movements were inside his own head.

It was eerie. Post-apocalyptic stuff, without the fun of having witnessed the big bang. Three days into the new millennium, and he could almost convince himself that one of the dreaded bugs had just struck here. No nuclear power plants seizing up. No businesses going to the wall. But a seaside village in south-west Ireland mysteriously emptied of its folk.

'Where's the house?' he asked.

Curtis gestured vaguely along the line McCadden was already staring at. 'In Main Street. We can walk. It's not far.'

They passed between the two cars and climbed away from the pier in silence, McCadden slightly hunched from the discomfort in his shoulder, and Curtis, much taller anyway, so stiffly erect that he towered over him. McCadden wondered if the other played basketball. But he didn't ask. His curiosity flirted too dangerously with stereotypes. All black men are naturally adept at shooting hoops. And white men can't jump . . .

It was going to be tough, he accepted, negotiating a working relationship while burdened with such a paralysing level of self-consciousness. But then, that was exactly the strategy of the jokers who had assigned Curtis.

At the old woman's dilapidated house in the centre of Main Street, Curtis used scissors to cut the crime-scene tape. When he also slit the adhesive seals across the crumbling front door, the door itself started tilting away from him and he had to reach out quickly to prevent it from falling.

'The front door was never closed,' he explained. 'I don't mean that it wasn't locked. I mean, the wood holding the hinge screws had rotted away. At night she just placed what was left of the door in the gap, pushed a table behind it to stop it falling, tried to cut out the draughts with old clothes, blankets, that sort of thing. It's been like that probably a year or more.'

'She lived here alone, obviously.'

'Yes.'

'Tell me about her.'

Curtis placed the door against an interior wall. Searching along the wall for a switch, he grimaced as the light came on. 'I don't know if I'm the best person to ask about that, to be honest, sir.'

'Why not?'

'Well, I'm not actually part of the team investigating the murder, you see.'

'So why did they send you to meet me?'

Curtis took a breath. 'Probably, because I'm not the best person to ask, sir.'

McCadden stepped inside and had a quick glance around the ramshackle hovel. 'Do you play basketball, Curtis?' he asked.

'What?'

'Basketball.'

'Basketball? No. Table tennis. I play table tennis, sir.'

'Right.'

'And chess. I also play chess.'

'Right.'

'I don't quite see . . .'

'Tell me about the woman, Curtis.'

'Well . . . nobody had much to tell, really,' Curtis admitted. 'Her name was Hannah Fraule. She lived alone in this house for as long as anyone can remember, but no one knows for sure when exactly she came.'

'She's not from here?'

'She's not from the village. She's not from the surrounding area, either, apparently. Not originally, anyway.'

'How old was she?'

'Past ninety, we believe.'

'What about relatives?'

'None that we know of.'

'Neighbours?'

'The mother of the young boy who found her sometimes looked after the old woman. Her name is Elizabeth Cole. I don't think anybody else bothered much. There's not many, anyway. The village is almost deserted.'

'Social services?'

'She refused to consider a nursing home or hospital. The health nurse visited regularly to check on her. A social worker called on a weekly basis to help her with shopping and other necessities. They did their best. There was also a Catholic curate who visited her regularly. Verscoyle. Father Verscoyle.'

'What about the greeting card that was on the mantelpiece? WELCOME TO THE NEW MILLENNIUM. How was it delivered?'

'Not through the post, so presumably by hand.'

'Before or after the old woman was killed?'

Curtis blinked. 'How could you tell?'

McCadden gestured impatiently. 'She burned turf to keep herself warm and the chimney was obviously blocked. The fine dust from the turf must have settled on everything. Including the mantelpiece. If the card arrived a few days before her death, it would've accumulated dust on the top edge. Probably enough either way to help a guess. Did anybody check?'

'I don't know.'

'Why not?'

Curtis swallowed hard and stared into the gloomy interior of the house. 'I've already told you, sir. I'm not part of the investigating team.'

'Have you had access to the file, Curtis?'

'No.'

'Have you seen the crime-scene photographs or read the pathologist's report?'

'No.'

'But you've been briefed on the victim's background.'

'Yes.'

'And I'll bet you have a theory covering what happened on the night she was killed.'

Curtis struggled to control his breathing. 'The investigating team think that some time after midnight on New Year's Eve Hannah Fraule was sitting in that chair by the fire when intruders came through the front door. The intention seems to have been robbery. They left this room and the scullery behind pretty much untouched, but they ransacked the bedroom in there.'

'Did they find anything?'

'I don't know.'

It was possible, of course, McCadden thought, that the old woman had kept her life savings under a frayed mattress in the bedroom. Possible that some odd combination of circumstances or prejudices helped her to endure a miserable existence while simultaneously hoarding for a fanciful future.

The front room told only of debilitating poverty and radical neglect. About fifty years of it, McCadden calculated, judging from the style and condition of the few remaining pieces of furniture.

Nothing matched in the room. And nothing was really intact. A chipped mahogany sideboard, close to the bedroom door, had both its front legs missing and was tilted forward, like a stunned cow sinking to its foreknees after being shot in an abattoir. The surface of a rough pine table was split into two uneven sections. Another armchair, unrelated to the one the old woman had preferred, was just as grimy and dilapidated. The more recent items weren't even standard pieces of furniture. There was a wooden fruit box, for instance, between the two armchairs. And a plastic display stand for holding paperback novels leaned unsteadily against the scullery door.

Except for a single framed photograph, the walls were entirely bare. No ornaments. No baubles. Not even a religious icon.

The photograph was hanging above the stricken sideboard. Its heavy wooden frame was too ornate, too large for the size of the print. It hadn't been varnished or painted for a long time, but it *had* been recently cleaned. So had the protective glass over the print itself. And both meticulously. So that there was no dust clinging to its surfaces, no dirt lodged in its crevices.

Intrigued, McCadden picked his way across the concrete floor for a closer look. He had to stoop a little, to keep the reflection from the electric bulb in the glass from dazzling him. But when the image clarified he tapped the glass with the fingernails of his right hand. 'Do you know what this is?' he asked.

Curtis was still stiffly resentful. He seemed to take the question as a test he wasn't up to and muttered bitterly, 'No.'

McCadden was too absorbed to respond to the petulance. He was thinking about history. Distant history. All the way back to 1932, when ninety-seven per cent of the population was Roman Catholic, when other voices were far too weak to trouble the majority, and when Ireland hosted the Eucharistic Congress, a huge symbolic celebration of its own institutionalized religious ethos. Because the cherished photograph on the wall of the old woman's hovel captured a moment from the high point of that Congress: the open-air mass in Dublin's Phoenix Park, which was celebrated by the papal legate, attended by a million ordinary citizens and thousands of church dignitaries from around the world, and sung by the famous Irish tenor John McCormack.

The photograph must have pre-dated the first furnishing of the room, of course. It must have been carried from elsewhere to here and was possibly the only object from that distant past that the old woman had considered worthy of preservation.

Or possibly not, McCadden decided.

To the photograph's left, at the same level above the sideboard, there was evidence that a companion had once hung there. The plaster was chipped where a nail had been driven in. The hole was mostly sealed with grime now, but its location was still visible. Around it there was a rectangle, roughly the shape of the nearby picture frame, where the old paintwork was a slightly brighter shade, suggesting that it had been covered and protected at some stage. But whatever had once hung there had also been absent for a long time.

What would make a companion piece to the Eucharistic Congress? McCadden wondered. Why should it have fallen into disfavour? And where was it now?

'Did they recover any of the old woman's personal papers?' he asked. 'Any correspondence? Any other photographs?'

Curtis doggedly shook his head. 'I don't know.'

McCadden straightened, again ignoring the other's resentment. He turned slowly and glanced around the room once more, over the stricken sideboard and the fractured table, over the pathetic containers of cardboard and plastic, past the spot where the mutilated corpse had lain, until he settled on the mantelpiece where the card had been placed. WELCOME TO THE NEW MILLENNIUM, it had jeered. In the crime-scene photographs, the rest of the sloping mantelpiece had been bare. No knick-knacks. No personal items. Not even a clock or a box of matches. Something had lain there once, beside the greeting card. The photographs clearly showed a smudged pattern in the dust, something long and narrow, roughly arranged in the shape of an S, along with the mark of the gloved hand that had grasped and removed it. No fingerprints had been lifted from that section of the mantelpiece.

By now, Curtis was looking anxiously at his watch. 'If you don't mind, sir . . .'

'What?'

'There are a couple of other places I have to bring you.'

McCadden smiled. 'They gave you a *schedule* for me?'

'The chief superintendent wants all areas of the investigation covered in your briefing, so that—'

'So what's next on the agenda?'

'Martin Curran, sir. He's a farmer. He lives along on the other side of the bay. On Dunowen Head.'

'Maybe in the morning, Curtis,' McCadden said wearily. 'Right now I'm tired from the journey. I need to eat and get some rest.'

'The chief superintendent has arranged accommodation for you at—'

'The cause of the old woman's death was either strangulation or heart failure, Curtis,' McCadden interrupted. 'The autopsy was inconclusive. If the case ever comes to trial, the uncertainty may be decisive. But that's not the most *engaging* aspect of the pathologist's report. The most *engaging* revelation is that, before she died, someone stripped the old woman to the waist, partially severed her right breast with a hunting knife, then took the dangling flesh in their mouth, bit off the nipple and spat it into the dirt on the floor. Your investigating team clearly has someone in the frame. Does that fit the profile?'

Curtis cleared his throat. 'I told you, sir. It's not my case.'

'It's not really mine, either,' McCadden admitted. 'So what do you suggest we do? Jump enthusiastically through all the hoops they've placed for us?'

'That's your call, sir.'

'Right.'

Suddenly irritated, McCadden moved quickly across the cold concrete, towards the open doorway. He stepped outside and stood on the footpath. And while he was checking the grey skies and calculating the closeness of the rain that was threatening, he had a curious experience. Like everything else in the abandoned village, it struck him as slightly unreal, almost a parody of life. A motorized wheelchair, driven by a toothless old man in a sparkling white mackintosh, droned towards him from the west along the broken white line in the centre of Main Street. When he was opposite McCadden, the old man manoeuvred the wheelchair so that he stopped beside a shallow pothole, directly opposite the house. He said nothing. He gave no indication that he was aware of McCadden's presence. He sucked his slack cheeks between his toothless jaws, making a fish-mouth with his lips, and he stared impassively for about half a minute. When he had enough he worked the buttons on the arm of the wheelchair, swung sharply to his right and continued his journey along the faded marking in the centre of the street.

Watching him recede, McCadden heard Curtis stumbling through the open doorway behind him and called back absently, 'Put the door in place.'

Curtis was formal. 'Yes, sir.'

'Refix the seals and the crime-scene tape.'

'Yes, sir.'

'I'll let you know where I'm staying and when to call me in the morning. Not too early.'

'There may be a problem with—'

'And turn out the light before you leave.'

two

The irony was, McCadden would never graduate to the corridors of power simply because he was such a lousy subordinate. What he lacked as a careerist was the virtue of unquestioning respect. Standard instructions he could take. Strategic orders that placed him in a location and on a case. But being told where to look, what to search for, what to note as significant, what to eat and where to sleep . . .

Of course, he was also aware that there were *two* little wanton demigods out there, trying to reduce him to an instrument. The district chief superintendent needed him contained. Caged, preferably. Locked up and under constant supervision, like a stray dog who might otherwise worry the local livestock. The commissioner, on the other hand, saw him as a fly on the walls of his enemies' bunkers, only as valuable as the information he carried out, and ultimately distasteful and disposable.

He was on his own, McCadden accepted. Curtis was unreliable. The young black man's obvious resentment at being set up on his job, which was probably only an extension of his frustration at the casual rough treatment the colour of his skin attracted, made him seem a likely ally. But Curtis's nerve was uncertain. At any moment, he might cut out and run back to the comfort of his desk. He had the confused bitterness of a potential double agent. And the instability. The source of his loyalty was exactly the same as the source of his betrayal. His own pain.

The clever thing, McCadden decided, would be to notice only what he was shown in West Cork and let the Director of Public Prosecutions take up the slack if someone later found the investigation inadequate. But McCadden wasn't blessed with an admiration for cleverness.

Still irritated, he swung west after collecting the car from the pier and leaving the village. Once he was certain that Curtis hadn't followed him, he drove the short distance along the coast road to the nearby town of Clonakilty and checked into a hotel in the main square. Too hungry to enjoy weighing the options, he settled quickly on the town's only Italian restaurant. The food was fine, but the place was swarming with young couples. Some of them affectionate. Some fractious. And all noisy.

When he took refuge in the complimentary tabloid supplied by the restaurant, the news coverage only sharpened his irritation. A front-page item, dripping with affected outrage but wallowing in sensation, covered a controversial television interview given by a former terrorist the previous day. Convicted of bombing British seaside resorts in the early 1980s, the man had recently been released from a high-security prison in Northern Ireland under the terms of the peace process. Although christened Pius Eugene in his native Donegal, he now sported the cuter handle of Baker Shanahan. Nobody seemed quite sure whether the nickname was a tribute to his culinary skills or to his talents for incinerating holidaymakers. But the lead story in the tabloid, complete with a colour photograph of the miserable animal, featured a Jack Russell bitch which had been strung up by its hind legs and beaten with sticks, before being doused with petrol and set alight. Three county councillors, two government ministers and a bishop were quoted. The word *outrage*, in a range of cases and tenses, was employed fifteen times.

The murder of Hannah Fraule, and the ongoing investigation into the crime, was awarded a two-sentence paragraph on page five, close to a lurid photograph of a leggy blonde whose ambition was to bed a famous soccer player, and even closer to an advertisement for health insurance showing a sparkling, white-haired old lady surrounded by generations of her adoring offspring. On a separate page, in an unrelated column that gathered stories from around the country, two other attacks on old people living alone were casually mentioned. Both victims were named. One of them, Martin Curran, was the farmer Curtis had mentioned.

McCadden asked a waitress for a local map. Dunowen Head, where Martin Curran lived, was only ten kilometres to the south. But even though he had time on his hands and had left himself nothing else to fill it with, McCadden decided to defer the visit. It had been dark for almost two hours by now. A shaken old man, living alone on an isolated farm and recovering from a recent attack, wouldn't welcome a stranger pounding on his door. In the morning, after breakfast, would be more appropriate.

three

At eight-thirty the next day, McCadden woke to find that the rain had settled in from the west. Gloomy grey skies and a steady, depressing drizzle that never varied, never burst into a downpour or lifted to let a little sunlight through. Within fifteen minutes, despite a vigorous shower and heroic resistance to looking out on the damp grey streets, McCadden was overcome by the monotony of it all. Trudging below to the breakfast room, he could see that the weather had had the same crushing effect on the staff and the other guests. Even one of the young couples from the restaurant the previous night looked too beaten to resume the argument that was their life.

McCadden wasn't particularly hungry. The unrelenting rain killed the appetite for everything and the sight of unfinished eggs and bacon cooling in congealed fat on other people's plates did nothing for him. He tried the coffee and a few slices of toast with marmalade and then went back to his room to contact Curtis.

The young detective had obviously been stewing in pique overnight. 'Where are you, sir?' he demanded.

'Morning, Curtis!' McCadden addressed him cheerfully. 'I've got a few things I need to get out of the way the next few hours. Personal stuff. Nothing you can help me with.'

'The chief superintendent has arranged a briefing for you at the station in Bandon at two o'clock this afternoon.'

'That's okay. I'll be through by then. Anything urgent?'

'No, sir.'

'Anything you need to tell me?'

'Where are you, sir?'

Funny, McCadden thought as he broke the connection without responding. Curtis seemed to have gone off the idea of hurrying him towards the old farmer.

Which, from McCadden's point of view, made a visit even more attractive.

The farm itself – named 'Glenties', according to locals, after the birthplace of the owner's grandfather, five hundred kilometres away – was easy enough to find. The last dwelling on the last stretch of a pock-marked winding lane, it stood on a bleak patch of the headland, a bright, whitewashed cottage whipped by the winds off the Atlantic and drenched by the interminable rain.

When McCadden pulled up, his tyres skidding in thick mud by the farmyard gate, the place seemed deserted. There were no fowl in the yard, no livestock in the adjacent field. The only sounds were the wind whistling through the gaps in the low stone wall and a distant helicopter patrolling the coast.

McCadden stepped out of the car. As he put his hand on the metal gate to swing it open, an invisible dog started barking furiously. Seconds later, the animal came scurrying from the barn that was attached to the house, so desperate to start a scrap that its hind legs kept losing balance on the wet surface and skating from one side to the other. As a deterrent, it should really have stayed under cover. Apart from the distinct lack of style, it was also too puny to induce anything better than laughter. It was an uncertain mix of breeds, all of them squat, and none of them reared for fighting. Its only weapon was its bark. And it knew it. Bouncing up and down on its hind legs, it yapped incessantly, until McCadden stooped to pick up a stone. Then it whimpered in mid-air, turned tail as soon as it landed, and scampered back to the barn.

Despite the noise, there was still no movement from the house itself.

McCadden opened the heavy gate and let it swing back on its creaking hinges. The path to the doorway was uneven and overgrown in places with sodden weeds. Although he sensed that someone was inside watching him, no one responded to his first knock. His second wasn't louder, but over to his left a curtain moved in the nearest window and a shadowy face peered at him through the gap.

He walked across and held his ID to the glass, noting as he stood there that the crumbling wooden frame had no security locks and was so weak that it would hardly resist the efforts of a child. It made a mockery of the three heavy bolts that had to be drawn to finally open the front door for him.

Inside, in a neat little hallway, a tall, dark-haired old man, dressed in striped blue pyjamas and a navy dressing gown, stared at him blearily, painfully scrunching up his bruised face to protect his eyes from the light. He didn't wait for introductions. 'Did you get them?' he demanded immediately.

McCadden was surprised, as much by the old man's intensity as by his dress. He couldn't help glancing quickly at his watch. But it wasn't that early. And certainly not for a farmer. It was already past ten o'clock.

'I'm sorry,' he apologized. 'I've disturbed you. Were you taking a nap?'

'I was asleep,' the old man growled. Already disappointed, he swept quickly into anger. 'I told your fellas from Bandon, I sleep in the day now, until five o'clock anyway, not to call here before five, unless you caught them. And you haven't caught them at all, have you?'

McCadden shook his head, mentally making a few sad calculations. If the old man slept all day, he obviously stayed awake all night. It was a security measure. Robbers didn't come by daylight. They struck in darkness, their approach unnoticed through the nearest village, their arrival unseen by the scattering of distant neighbours. Merely to be certain of staying alive, this vulnerable old man had relinquished everything except base existence. His work on the farm. His animals. His visits to friends and neighbours. Probably the occasional evening in the pub.

McCadden felt uneasy. His sympathy was worthless, his presence just another intrusion, his motives questionable. Compromised by the commissioner's order to look after the big picture, he still couldn't find the necessary detachment from the small stories of the little people involved. The old man's plight saddened him.

'I'm not from the local station, Mr Curran,' he explained. 'I'm from Dublin. My name's McCadden. Detective Inspector Carl McCadden. I'm helping with the investigation into a number of attacks on elderly people. Yours is one of the cases. I'd like you to describe for me what happened, but if you prefer I can come back later this afternoon to talk to you.'

The old man wearily shook his head. His nerves mightn't take the strain of another disruptive visit, the surge of another empty hope. Better finish with it now. He whistled softly for the mongrel, which came sliding frantically from the barn to skate between McCadden's legs and jump into the old man's arms. It was a kind of comfort. And a welcome distraction. Something to maintain the distance between himself and McCadden.

Inside the cottage – a plain, neat interior that was almost entirely functional – McCadden worked for a while to warm the relationship.

From the old man's reluctant descriptions of the portraits on the walls and mantelpiece and sideboard, he learned that Martin Curran had been born here, in 1930, the third in a family of three boys and one girl. He was the lucky one, the white-headed boy, the son chosen by his parents to inherit the family farm. His sister married a farmer living in the north-west of the country and his two brothers emigrated to America, one to become a cop in New York, the other to make a modest name for himself as a props buyer in the movies. Martin had never married and had no children, so his prize for winning the family lottery all those years ago was to get to sleep alone behind inadequate barricades during daylight and to sit up all night grasping an iron bar and waiting for the barbarians to come hurtling at the gate again.

He couldn't have shared his grim story with anyone for a long time. Towards the end of it, his eyes welling with tears and his voice catching in his throat, he covered his loss of control by suddenly rising from the armchair he'd settled in and hurrying towards the kitchen. 'Would you take a cup of tea, inspector?'

'I'd love one,' McCadden lied.

When he came back, balancing cups, teapot and a plate of plain biscuits on a tray that was being threatened by the snapping jaws of the mongrel bouncing up to it, the old man had recovered his composure. But his reserve had dropped away, and a little of the chatty, feisty bachelor he must have been before the recent assault was creeping back.

'They had to be watching me for a while,' he explained. 'The ones who robbed me. At that time, I'd have a set routine. This hour to be walking the dog there, another one to stroll to the village for a pint, and so on, like. I was after bringing Jess there out, down the lane, like we did every night at ten o'clock. They were waiting for me when we got back. The dog started barking at the gate. But I didn't pay any heed. Sometimes it barked at the chickens, sometimes if one of the neighbours or the priest had called in. But it wasn't a neighbour waiting for me inside the house that night. The first thing I noticed was I had no light at all. I tried the switch inside the door. But they'd taken all the bulbs out.'

'How did they get in?'

'The guards, the fellas from Bandon, they said it was through the back door. They drove a van down the lane and hid it. They waited until I was past them with the dog. Then they went and broke into the house.'

'Did they do much damage?'

'They ruined the place, boy. Nearly everything in it. It's only the last few days I'm getting things back together, though it'll never be the same as it was. Nothing'll ever be the same as it was again. Do you take sugar?'

'What?'

'The tea's ready there.'

'No, no sugar, thanks. A little milk.'

The old man poured, the china rattling slightly in his trembling hands. He handed McCadden a cup and drank himself, savouring the taste over a few leisurely sips. 'This'll keep me awake now,' he muttered. 'I used to think it was a great man for getting you to sleep, but it only keeps you awake.'

'My fault,' McCadden accepted.

'Maybe it's better. But I couldn't sleep any more at night, not after they broke in here and robbed the place. Every little noise outside had me up, peeping out the windows. The dog was the same, barking out there in the barn. And if things went quiet and there was no sound at all for a while, sure that was only worse.'

McCadden tested the tea. A useless exercise. He couldn't tell good from bad. He drank only to be polite. 'How much did they take?' he asked.

The old man grimaced. 'There wasn't anything to take. A bit of loose change lying around. Maybe a few pound coins. That was all. I never kept money in the house, always in a bank. They must've had the wrong information. Or the wrong man. Or something.'

'Information? From where?'

'Someone from around here, God forgive them. Someone who knew I wasn't short, after selling a bit of stock at the mart there a while back. They wouldn't have known that themselves. They were strangers.'

'Did you see them?

'I saw enough of them. They were here long enough. And your eyes get used to the dark.'

'Their faces weren't covered?'

'No.'

'How many were there?'

'Just two. Young fellas. About eighteen or nineteen, I'd say.'

'Would you recognize them?'

'They were tinkers.'

'Tinkers?'

'The two of them. Tinkers.'

McCadden sat back in his chair, still holding the steaming cup of tea. The old man's term was old-fashioned and out of date, even considered abusive in certain quarters, but it was obviously the word he'd grown up with. He was referring to Travellers, a cultural minority of about twenty thousand migrant people.

Nobody denied that a Traveller's existence was harsh and unforgiving. Their average life expectancy was struggling to reach fifty, a grotesque figure in a prosperous western country. Most lived in cramped mobile homes on unofficial sites, where there was no sanitation and no electricity, and where their children played on or near their own rotting rubbish heaps. Alcoholism was widespread, and its related diseases were rampant. Violence was a common means of settling even trivial disputes. The arguments flew about the reasons for such degradation, though. Bigots castigated the Travellers themselves as vermin, a problem that needed to be addressed and eradicated. Idealists dumped the blame on an uncaring, racist society.

One of the few things McCadden knew for certain was that a nineteen-year-old Traveller didn't look or sound much different from any other rural youth, so he was interested in the source of the old man's certainty about his attackers' identities.

''Twas what they said,' Martin Curran explained. 'You could tell from that. They were drunk and talked a lot. But I think they meant to leave me for dead anyway, you know. They didn't care what they said or what I heard. Something disturbed them. The guards from Bandon said they thought someone drove down here after taking a wrong turning in the village and that frightened them so much that they panicked. But I don't know. They had me unconscious by then, after beating me to tell them where I'd hidden the money. They didn't believe I hadn't got it. 'Twould've been better for me if there had been some money in the house that night. A hundred pounds or so. They could've taken that.'

'Probably not,' McCadden disagreed.

'I would've told them. I would've told them anything to stop the pain.'

'But they wouldn't have believed that a hundred was everything. They would've held out for more.'

'Maybe you're right, I suppose.'

'How badly were you hurt?'

'Three or four nights in hospital. I forget which. They grabbed me as soon as I was in the front door there. They hit me a couple of times with something, a club or something, just to keep me quiet. One of the knocks broke a couple of my ribs. I lost the use of my legs. While I was lying on the floor they stuffed a rag into my mouth to keep me from screaming. A dish rag, that was after lying in the sink for the day. You could still taste the onions off it and the dirty dishwater. They dragged me up and put me sitting in that chair you're in yourself there. They were looking for something to tie me with. One of them got the cord from the TV there. They used that, around my wrists. The other one cut the telephone cable too and they used that on my ankles. But they couldn't find anything long enough to go round the chair itself and tie me to that. In the end they took down all the curtains and used the cord we had in them, that was there from my parents' time.'

'What colour was it? The cord.'

'Red. Bright red.'

'Did they take any away with them?'

'Some of it was missing when they were gone, all right. Some they put round my neck to choke me with.' The old man lifted his head and felt with his fingers along the ridges where the cord had cut and burned the skin.

'Did they tie knots in the cord?'

'Knots? No. They just had it around my neck and around my chest, tying me to the chair. They hit me in the face, then in the stomach, with their fists. I got sick. I still had that rag in my mouth. They had to take it out. When they stuffed it back in again, you could taste the vomit on it . . .'

Their persistence made sense, even if they couldn't turn up any substantial cash in the cottage. A lot of old people living alone still either distrusted banks or feared having their pensions cut if they were earning a little interest on savings.

'How are you now?' McCadden asked gently. 'Are you recovering? Physically, anyway.'

'Things won't ever be the same again, inspector,' the old man lamented. 'Never again. I used to love a neighbour or the priest calling in to chat, you know. Even the odd stranger who'd lost their way and was looking for directions. But the worst thing I can hear these days is the sound of another person. Like yourself there when you knocked first. All I want now is the dog. They won't bite you if you're only halfway decent to them.'

four

McCadden had a couple of hours to spare after leaving Martin Curran. He could have checked out the incident room at the station in Bandon, met some of the local detectives working on the case and trawled through the notes they'd accumulated. But he had the feeling that this would have been a waste of time. About as useful, in fact, as a committee of well-heeled spinsters visiting a prison on a tour of inspection. He wasn't welcome enough to be shown the important stuff.

In heavy mist, he drove slowly away from Dunowen Head, hugging the coastline all the way round to the opposite side of Clonakilty Bay, where he turned south again, back towards the village. Mostly, he had the narrow roads to himself. He didn't enjoy the freedom, though. And not only because the local sights and scenery were almost invisible through the rain. He was thinking about the stupidity of the ordinary criminal, decent or otherwise. He was thinking about the profile of the average inmate of every prison in the country: young, poor, uneducated, almost invariably from a broken community and broken home. The contrast between this and the myth of the wealthy master criminal was almost as depressing as the weather. The evil genius, he scoffed, and the notion of an admirable, stable society that had to be protected from his schemes. Pure popcorn.

McCadden had no *particular* reason for revisiting the village. It was just that the lifeless place seemed to have an odd hold on him. He found it as fascinating as a graveyard. The same unquiet stillness. The same sense of mute history. *More* fascinating, really, because the scale was larger. The empty houses were its gravestones, and the neglected public buildings its memorials. And its spooky caretaker seemed to be a gaunt old man who patrolled its sepulchres in a motorized wheelchair.

Entering the village from the west, McCadden caught sight of the wheelchair in the distance, holding a characteristic line along the central marking in the middle of Main Street; but by the time he reached the spot, the thing had turned down Beach Road and vanished again. He assumed that the old man was one of the local residents and had simply returned to his home. It surprised him. He'd heard that the older people had moved out after the murder of Hannah Fraule, so fearful for their own safety that they'd abandoned their lives and their possessions and gone elsewhere to live with relatives. As far as he could tell, the boy who'd discovered the old woman's body and the boy's mother were still living in the village. But when he drove to the east end of Main Street and called at their cottage, there was no answer to his knock.

McCadden was disappointed. No one other than the boy's mother seemed to have bothered to look out for the old woman. She'd given no indication that she was familiar with Hannah Fraule's shadowy history, but it was always possible that some shared understanding, some casual intimacy, had passed between them. For McCadden, the old woman's past had already become a problem. No relatives had come forward to claim the body. No resources had been put into tracing any relatives, or into explaining the old woman's extraordinary lifestyle. Such neglect allowed only a single interpretation. The case was about to be neatly wrapped up.

Turning away from the empty cottage, McCadden sat back in the car and decided to pay another visit to the harbour at the base of the village. Again, for no particular reason. Or perhaps because he was certain that at least there was *something* living in the sea beyond it. He pulled up, cut the engine and stepped out from behind the wheel. Pulling on a rain jacket, he strolled to the end of the pier and stood there, thinking again about good and evil geniuses. Holmes and Moriarty. Father Brown and Flambeau. Contemporary serial killers and their celebrity hunters. But after a while, as he became conscious of a sound being carried to him on the wind, his attention slackened. It seemed like music, he thought. But it was faint. And intermittent.

Almost convinced that the noise, like his reflections, was inside his own head – a kind of ghost soundtrack to accompany his eerie return to a ghost village – he turned away from the sea and walked away from the pier up the slight hill facing it. At the T-junction, he turned left on to Main Street, following the source of the noise, back along the approach road he'd just driven through. As he went, his pace quickened. Because the music grew louder with every step. Until it was finally loud enough for positive identification. It was The Doors, he recognized. From 1967. Jim Morrison's desperate urgency. And Ray Manzarek's wild assault on what sounded like a church organ. The opening track of their debut LP. *Break On Through.*

The house where this extraordinary injunction was coming from stood by itself on the outskirts of the village, slightly detached from the end of the row that formed the main street. It had a revealing name. According to a crudely carved plaque on the outside wall, it was called 'Astral Weeks'.

McCadden rang its electric bell and stood there entranced, wiping rainwater from his eyes and wondering what type of character might be playing The Doors at full volume in a deserted village at one o'clock on the fifth afternoon of a new millennium. An ageing hippie? An aspiring young rock musician searching for inspiration? A contemporary mystic?

The guy who finally opened the door was none of these. If he'd managed to emulate his mentors and break on through, then the other side of the sixties revolution looked remarkably like any other man in late middle age. The music buff was small, balding, paunchy, dressed in a black T-shirt and a pair of blue-jeans that were too tight around his spreading waist. There was one variation on the standard model, though. He was obviously stoned. His blue eyes were unnaturally wide, glassy from too many recent cannabis hits. And the vaguely amused expression of a cat who'd coolly opted out hung around his slack lips.

'What can I do for you, man?' he drawled.

McCadden showed his ID. 'My name's McCadden. I'm a Garda officer.'

The smile dropped from the other's face. He struggled to focus. 'This another bust?' he demanded angrily.

McCadden shook his head. 'No, it's not a bust.'

'What, then?'

'I'm interested in the old woman who was killed.'

'Don't know anything about it, man.'

'Do you mind if I ask you a few questions anyway?'

'What's your chosen subject?'

'What?'

'For the questions. Hannah Fraule? I told you, I don't know anything about her. I haven't spoken to her for twenty years. And there's a reason. Okay, I mean, nobody wants to see anybody attacked and hurt, but Hannah Fraule was a sanctimonious old bitch. That's all I know. It's enough for me. If you want to know more, don't ask me. Ask her priest.

Right? Ask her postman. Ask her social workers. Ask the limping man with the No. 1 haircut. Don't ask me.'

'Could I ask your name?' McCadden wondered.

'Ciaran Carthy. Do you have a search warrant or something?'

'Have you noticed any members of the Travelling community around the village lately, Mr Carthy?'

'How do you recognize members of the Travelling community? They wear a yellow star on their clothes or something?'

'What was your dispute with Hannah Fraule?'

'She had the problem, man, not me.'

'Were you playing your music too loud?'

'She isn't exactly next door. She's fifteen, twenty houses away.'

'I was standing on the pier and I could hear it.'

'Today I've got the whole village to myself.'

'Except for me.'

'You didn't warn me that you were visiting.'

'What was Hannah Fraule's problem?'

'I told you. She was a sanctimonious old bitch.'

'Do you know who her priest is?'

'Some young enthusiastic fucker who thinks he's hip. Ronan Verscoyle. What a fucking handle. Father Ronan Verscoyle. You'll find him at the local parish church.'

'Do you feel vulnerable here?' McCadden asked.

Carthy folded his arms and leaned his shoulder against the door frame. The clouds had dispersed from his eyes. They were sharp with dislike now. 'Is that a threat?' he challenged.

McCadden shrugged. 'It's a question. I mean, you might like to imagine yourself otherwise, but the reality is, you're old and you're living alone in an isolated rural area. I'm part of a team investigating attacks on the elderly.'

Carthy sneered. 'Listen, mate, the only time I was ever threatened here was by geeks who thought that God, the law and the moral majority were all on their side. I've had this place searched more often than you've made mistakes. I've been arrested even *more* times. But never convicted, man. You got that? I've never been convicted. I've had health inspectors in here. I've had drugs squad officers in here. Customs officials. Representatives from a local community that doesn't even fucking exist. Representatives of foreign landowners who shit here once a year. What's everybody's fucking problem? I don't bother anyone. What's *your* fucking problem?'

'Hannah Fraule,' McCadden admitted honestly.

'Fuck Hannah Fraule!'

McCadden nodded. 'It'll probably put a dinge in your self-esteem,' he confided, 'but that seems to be the popular position. Welcome to the new millennium.'

'Fuck off,' Carthy muttered.

He stepped backwards and slammed the door.

As McCadden turned and strolled away, the music came back in behind him, even louder than before, drowning what was left of Carthy's tenuous contact with the rest of the world. He'd changed the record. Or the CD. This time is was Crosby, Stills, Nash & Young, with Joni Mitchell's *Woodstock*. Ironic, he thought. So much of the music of that period seemed to be about the buzz of making great journeys and significant connections.

He glanced at his watch. It was one-thirty. He was so wet, he decided he needed to get back to the hotel in Clonakilty and have a shower and a change of clothes. Which meant he was probably going to be late for his appointment with the chief superintendent at Bandon.

Should he ring and warn him?

And risk being ordered to report immediately, still steaming from the rain?

five

McCadden had never met Chief Superintendent Pat Foran, and he had to wait a little longer for the pleasure. Reaching the station in Bandon almost thirty minutes late, he found a doom-laden old desk sergeant who kept wringing his hands and foretelling obscure recriminations while directing him to the offices at the rear. Apart from Joe Curtis, though, the detectives' room was completely deserted.

Curtis was pacing between the desks and glancing at his wristwatch every time he made another turn. When he saw McCadden standing in the doorway, he pulled up sharply. But he was clearly so choked with irritation that all he could release was the absurdly obvious, 'You're late, sir.'

'Tell the chief superintendent I got lost,' McCadden suggested. 'I'm not on familiar territory.'

'The chief superintendent is not here any more, sir. He couldn't wait.'

'Right.'

'But you can tell him yourself. I have to bring you to him.'

Curtis waited for McCadden to step out of the doorway, then he swept past and silently led the way back through the corridors. As they collected the bright yellow Volkswagen from the rear car park, McCadden wondered whether the splash of colour was an aberration or an irresistible bargain from some relieved dealer. Or if the dullness of Curtis's clothes was actually a self-conscious effort at restraint. It wasn't the occasion for banter, though.

Without any idea of where they were going, or any notion how they could get there if he *did* know the destination, McCadden quickly lost interest in following the route. They left Bandon, travelling west on the N71 to Skibbereen, but then turned north on to a minor road and started climbing into the mountains. After that, a fog obscured almost everything. They came upon villages without warning, having missed all the road signs, and passed through them without seeing any of the houses. Past a sharp bend, the ruins of a high round tower loomed at them menacingly out of the mist, making Curtis brake nervously. The wheels locked and the car skidded, its rear getting the worst of a tangle with some roadside brambles and coming out with a few scratches to the paintwork.

The incident seemed to loosen Curtis. 'Could I say something, sir?' he asked.

'Please,' McCadden encouraged. 'Give it a try.'

Curtis took a breath and tightened his grip on the steering wheel. 'I've applied for a transfer to the new homicide squad, sir. I don't know its official name.'

'It doesn't have one yet.'

'I do know it's being formed at the moment. And I know you're probably vetting the applicants. But while I'm waiting for a decision, I'm still attached to this district. You're not making it any easier for me to do my work, sir, if you insist on keeping your movements a secret from me.'

'Well,' McCadden answered. 'Two things. I'm not sure I'd make my *own* work easier if I *did* tell you my movements. And secondly, I'm not your responsibility. You were told to liaise with me. If I refuse, you can't do anything about it except report my refusal. Which I suggest you do. And while we're on the subject of movements, where the hell are we going?'

'We're going to a christening, sir.'

'A christening? What are we going to a christening for?'

'I can't tell you any more.'

'Under orders?'

Curtis shook his head. 'Because I don't know any more, sir.'

'Right.'

Five minutes later Curtis slowed, peered out at the signposts and took another left; and two hundred metres down this narrowing lane they hit a roadblock. Two squad cars were drawn across the width of the lane, manned by uniformed guards and armed detectives. Curtis pulled over on to the grass margin and got out to talk to someone. Stiff and bored from the long mystery tour, McCadden started to follow him, but then suddenly veered left, over to where he caught sight of two more detectives. Both of them were wearing bullet-proof vests and both of them were carrying Uzi sub-machine guns. Behind them, on a mound of earth, was the most extraordinary stockpile of weapons McCadden had ever seen. There were no firearms, but almost everything else. Knives, hatchets, machetes, slash hooks, knuckledusters, batons, baseball bats, billiard balls . . .

McCadden was on the point of asking for an explanation when Curtis's voice interrupted him from behind. 'We have to walk from here, sir. It's not far, about three hundred metres up the road, around the next bend.'

They took their rain jackets from the yellow Volkswagen and pulled them on. Curtis had also brought a spare pair of wellington boots, which McCadden swapped his shoes for. They squeezed between the two squad cars at the roadblock and trudged up the lane.

'Who's getting christened?' McCadden wondered. 'The chief superintendent's grandchild?'

Curtis didn't answer.

Beyond the bend, the scene reminded McCadden of a staged tableau from a film shoot. A plain old church stood in its own grounds a little back from the intersection of four roads. It was a simple rectangular building, without a tower, mounted with a cross at each apex of the roof, adorned with eight pointed windows and surrounded by old headstones in the graveyard, most of them in the form of Celtic crosses. The junction itself was no longer passable. It had been turned into a huge car park and was crammed with parked vans, whose drivers and passengers were obviously inside the church attending the christening. But the building was also ringed by uniformed guards. And among the trees and hedges off the side roads, the occasional armed plain-clothes officer was visible, holding a walkie-talkie as well as a firearm.

Near the end of the lane, on a raised piece of ground that overlooked the entire battlefield, the command post had been located. The chief superintendent, a tall, gloomy-looking character with a military bearing, stood with his hands clasped behind his back, surrounded by his senior officers. He turned when he heard the newcomers approaching, silently endured Curtis's faltering introductions and explanations, silently accepted McCadden's greeting and then silently returned to staring across at the church.

Three minutes later he said, 'I hear you've taken to exploring our countryside by yourself, inspector.'

McCadden, standing slightly behind him, only nodded, so of course the chief superintendent had to turn again to check if his opener had registered. He had a face built for disapproval. It was thin and angular, without the promise of softness that a little excess flesh might offer. There was simply no slack to shape itself into a smile. His blue eyes were cold and unfriendly.

He said, 'Initiative is a great thing in a police officer. Self-reliance. Not taking anything on trust. The man who has to test everything himself will always go far.'

McCadden didn't respond. He didn't want to. But he didn't need to, either. And he probably wasn't expected to.

Foran seemed an arrogant character, not used to competition when he spoke. The weight of what he said didn't have to come from any insights of his own, from any careful thought or any detailed research, or even from any relevance to the particular situation. It was supported only by the power of his rank. To challenge him, to baulk at feeding his ego, was to risk making your job a much more consistent pain in the ass than it should've been. Like most senior brass, he'd already decided on the solution to a problem before he consulted you. The more honest ones just barked out their decision as an order. Some, like Foran, loved to maintain the illusion of interaction by generously offering your side of the argument as well as their own.

'Of course,' Foran went on, 'what you're going to miss are all the subtleties. All the little things that the local man takes for granted and that are invisible to a stranger. It's all too easy to get a distorted picture. That's why the local knowledge is vital. And that's why this proposed new squad is going to fail.' He turned again, looking casually over his shoulder. 'You *are* attached to this new squad, aren't you, inspector?'

McCadden nodded. 'That's right.'

'Not a good idea,' Foran announced. 'A gang of strangers descending on some small community, trampling the evidence into the mud with their heavy boots. Oh, it's expedient, I know. I can see the political pressure for it all. So many unsolved murders in the files. It must be some small comfort to the public to know that a team of dedicated officers like yourself is working around the clock on the cases. But it won't last. The shine will wear off. You won't get the resources. You won't get the support from local detectives. And you'll be forgotten about when you don't produce the results.'

Below them, the church door opened and a squat, middle-aged man in a brown jacket and navy trousers came out. He showed no reaction to the ring of policemen facing him. He didn't hesitate. He walked straight down the gravel pathway through the graveyard, passed by the cordon at the church gate and headed across the intersection towards the command post, weaving his way through the layers of parked vans. The chief superintendent moved forward to consult with him, out of McCadden's hearing. When he came back, he left a bustle of activity behind him, and a perceptible tightening of the cordon as the men braced themselves after the order was passed on.

Foran returned to his former position and stood there, his hands clasped behind his back. 'Do you know what's happening here, inspector?' he asked.

McCadden shrugged. 'I've no idea.'

'Have you ever had any trouble with Travellers?'

McCadden had never arrested a Traveller for murder. He'd put away unemployed factory workers, career criminals, a cleric, and even a member of the force itself, all of them from what was ironically known as the settled community. But there was no point in being glib. He hadn't come here for an argument. He'd come to observe. 'Not much,' he said.

The chief superintendent managed a thin smile, possibly of pity. 'For the last ten years,' he explained, 'I've had two rival Traveller families in this district, sometimes camped just a mile or so apart, sometimes jostling for the same official or unofficial halting sites. Do you know how big a Traveller family is, inspector?'

McCadden knew. The extended family was the most important thing in most Travellers' lives. 'Pretty big.'

'Pretty big,' the chief superintendent agreed. 'There's a blood feud between these two families. Nobody knows how it started, of course, not even the Travellers themselves. It could be as much as fifty years old. The battles between the factions go back that far. But one man was actually killed in an argument some years ago and that intensified the thing. Whenever the families meet now, there's extreme violence. The running total to date is two deaths, three severed limbs, and an awful lot of non-fatal injuries. A lot of blood. A few years ago there was a juvenile boxing tournament in Cork. My son was expected to be crowned national champion in his age group. Some Traveller children were competing as well, from both these families. There was a riot outside the stadium. I couldn't be there, unfortunately, but my wife and son got caught up in it. The boy's elbow was shattered so badly, by a manhole cover some lunatic was using as a weapon, that he never boxed again.'

In revealing the personal source of his prejudice, the private pain that drove it, rather than just declaiming his bigotry, the man suddenly became more human, more attractive. But also more dangerous,

McCadden thought. He was beyond persuasion, beyond conversion to a more rational or sensitive approach. He was motivated by his own loss and no political or moral stance could restore to him what he'd been deprived of. It was a family matter, and probably not much different in kind to the blood feud that had provoked it. Unfortunately, Foran had the power to turn his pain into a public issue, to meet a social problem with as much subtlety as the manhole cover had met his son's elbow.

But McCadden also guessed that the show of force wasn't intended just to keep warring factions apart. Something else was on the agenda here. He waited.

The chief superintendent unclasped his hands and gestured with his right down the lane. 'Inside that church,' he said, 'at this moment, there's practically the entire complement of both Traveller families. Sitting on opposite sides of the aisle, no doubt. They're there to celebrate a christening. The child is the result of a relationship between a seventeen-year-old boy from one of the families and a sixteen-year-old girl from the other. You'd think the happy event might've brought them together, wouldn't you?'

McCadden had a fleeting, irrelevant inspiration. What a project for an amateur drama producer, it occurred to him. The entire cast of *Romeo and Juliet* at his disposal, and all of them released from the need for background notes.

A mass audition wasn't the purpose of this complex police operation, either, of course. McCadden reluctantly killed off the idle fantasy and waited again, but the chief superintendent kept his mouth shut and his hands firmly clasped behind his back and didn't elaborate any more.

The explanation would come with the spectacle, McCadden understood, along with the unfolding action. In the meantime, he'd have to suffer in the dark. It was a practical demonstration of Foran's thesis that the outsider was blind, the local man blessed with perception. A small addition to the chief superintendent's corner in his fight against the commissioner.

A dreary five or six minutes passed, during which the wind shifted and started carrying the rain into their faces, before anything happened. Then the church door was opened again. Slowly. And carefully. A young cleric in vestments slipped cautiously through the narrow gap and stood uncertainly on the single step at the entrance to the building. Gathering up his soutane to save its hem from the mud and the water, he stepped down on to the gravel pathway and walked uncomfortably towards the gate, his movements restricted by the way he'd clasped the cassock tightly around his legs. The effect was unintentionally comic.

'It's Father Verscoyle, sir,' an officer reported to the chief superintendent.

The unusual surname immediately alerted McCadden. 'Anybody know his first name?' he asked.

Curtis stepped forward from behind. 'What, sir?'

'Father Verscoyle. What's his first name?'

'I'm not sure. Roger? Ryan? Something . . .'

'Ronan,' someone else supplied. 'Father Ronan Verscoyle.'

By now, the priest had reached the cordon and was negotiating with the uniformed inspector in charge of the men on the ground. His comments and requests were being relayed to the chief superintendent.

'He wants us to withdraw, sir. He says that such a heavy police presence is adding to the tension. He insists that the two families have settled their differences, with himself as broker. If we leave them alone, he'll guarantee there'll be no trouble.'

The cold expression on Foran's face didn't change. 'Has he finished the service?' he asked.

'Yes, sir, it's over.'

'Then tell him to send his congregation home, with his blessing.'

Even at a distance, the crushing effect of this blunt dismissal was obvious on the young cleric's soft face. When he turned to trudge back to the church with the message, he didn't even bother raising the hem of his vestments from the dirt.

His flock seemed reluctant to leave him, though. They trickled out after he'd thrown the doors wide open. The women and children came first, among them the new young mother, cradling her baptized infant. Whether or not this was intended as a ploy was unclear. The surreal scene certainly had some unsettling biblical echoes. Although they'd obviously dressed up for the ceremony, the women's clothes were dull and worn and ill-fitting. By contrast, the baby's christening robes were magnificent. They were of Irish lace, handcrafted and brilliantly white. Obviously a treasured family heirloom.

The women didn't talk. Even more unusually, their kids were silent. In fact, the only sound was the forlorn wailing of the infant itself, whose early experience of the world, confronted by a line of hostile policemen, more than likely set the tone for the rest of its life.

Eventually, the men shuffled out after the women and kids, awkward, their hands stuffed in their trouser pockets and their shoulders hunched, apparently not knowing what to do with themselves.

Apparently, because it was at this stage that it struck McCadden that the chief superintendent's careful strategy was actually going haywire. These were supposed to be two warring families, riven by a blood feud. But there were no battle lines. There were no divisions within the crowd. They mingled as one. And they didn't leave the church grounds. Instead of trooping as expected down the gravel path to be filtered quietly through the gate by the waiting police and sent quietly on their way, they suddenly dispersed about the graveyard surrounding the church, until they filled every corner, occupied every plot and leaned against every headstone.

Beside McCadden, the chief superintendent tensed with anger. He didn't get a chance to adapt his strategy. As he hesitated, a fist fight broke out in the graveyard below, an explosive confrontation that torched off other disputes nearby and then quickly spread through the entire crowd, dragging in the women and kids as well. But there was something almost choreographed about the violence. The blows were real and blood was spilt, but very few fell, and of those who did none stayed down.

It was obviously a diversion. And it worked. As the superintendent furiously snapped out an order to break it up, a cluster of brawling Travellers made rough contact with the police cordon, sucked in other officers to help their colleagues and thereby fractured the ring that had been held around the church. Immediately the gaps opened, they were exploited. Two youths, concealed until now in the centre of confusing scraps, suddenly broke away from the fight, jumped over the low stone wall, slipped past the preoccupied officers and made a run for it through the fields in opposite directions.

The excitement with which they were identified by the officers near the chief superintendent suggested that the fugitives were the real focus of the operation. From what McCadden could gather out of the babble around him, the two youths were brothers and one of them was the father of the newly christened infant. Both were black-haired and small and wiry. Both were dressed in denim jeans and check shirts. And both were fast on their feet.

The contours of the landscape did for the youth on the left. A low-lying field with poor drainage, levelling out at the bottom of an incline, it had not only held all the day's rain on its surface but also gathered all the water running off the hill.

Glancing behind to check the advantage he'd gained, the youth didn't see that the ground was waterlogged in front of him. He lost his balance as he hit the pool. Pitched forward, he fell face downwards into the water, thrashing wildly. When he struggled to his knees, he was dazed and soaked and blinded. He took too long to recover. Within seconds, he was overtaken by four officers. He was struck from behind, winded by a blow between his shoulder blades. His face was pushed violently back into the water and his hands twisted behind his back to be cuffed. When he was dragged up again, spluttering and gasping for breath, he was still kneeling in the pool of water. One of the officers stooped to whisper something in his ear. It must have been a threat, a warning that he'd be submerged again, or at least a question backed up with this threat. The youth screamed in fear – so loudly that McCadden heard the cry distinctly – and then started nodding his head, desperate to co-operate.

The other one, the father of the baptized infant, looked as if he might make it. His escape wasn't spotted so quickly by the officers on the right of the church and he got a much more generous start. By the time he reached the hedge, his pursuers were only starting from the graveyard. He was also more intelligent than his mate. The angle of his run took him uphill. The ground under his feet was yielding, and slippery in places, but it hadn't retained the water.

Beyond the hedge he vanished for a time, obviously running parallel with the hedge itself and concealed behind it. A little later he broke on even higher ground. By then, he'd stretched the distance between himself and the chasing pack. Unable to find the gap in the hedge that had been exploited, the officers were running crazily up and down, searching for an entrance to the next field, like dumb but eager hounds who'd lost the scent of the fox.

The next field was narrower than the first. On firmer ground now, the youth headed straight for the stone wall on the other side. But beyond the wall was one of the roads that fed into the intersection where the church was located. Like all the other approaches, it held a couple of police vehicles forming a roadblock. The youth didn't see them. And he didn't seem aware that they must be there. Possibly he'd been smuggled to church, bypassing the roadblocks on foot, and his relatives had intended spiriting him away by the same route, a plan scuppered by the chief superintendent's ring around the church.

Without hesitating, the youth vaulted over the stone wall, straight into a crouched detective who'd been positioned there over his radio. The two went down from the contact, both surprised by the collision. The youth recovered first. The detective had broken his fall and been winded. But the fugitive was injured, too. He tried to sprint away, but his right leg immediately crumbled. He didn't fall. He managed to stay on his feet. But his pace was gone. Limping pathetically across the road, he was swamped by officers before he'd even reached its centre.

Curtis, who'd been following the chase through binoculars, suddenly gave a grunt of disgust and looked away as the youth disappeared under the scrum. McCadden borrowed the glasses. They were already focused for the distance. The first image they magnified was the youth's face, bloodied and torn and contorted with agony. As McCadden watched, another fist landed in the boy's cheek, smashing the nose to a wretched angle and forcing another spurt of blood through his swollen lips and broken teeth. This mistreatment would be concealed by the circumstances of the arrest, of course. The flight. The youth's horrific fall. The collision between the stone wall and his face.

They had him cuffed by now, but they didn't bring him to his feet. While he squirmed uncomfortably on the ground, his hands secured behind his back, one of the detectives slit his jeans to examine the damaged leg. Through the glasses, McCadden could see that there were extensive cuts on the youth's thigh where he'd caught the stone wall or the road at speed. What had lamed him was the damage to his muscles, which had been deadened by the blow. There was nothing fractured or broken.

They offered him no support when they dragged him to his feet. He hobbled along between them, crying wretchedly, and was brought to a waiting police van and locked in its rear. Not an enviable conclusion to the christening of your first child.

The drama faded quickly afterwards. The mock battle had already petered out in the graveyard. There was no point to it any more. For a while, the Traveller women argued furiously with the guards, screaming into their faces. The young mother, the girlfriend of the captured youth, was particularly vehement, particularly distressed. But that, too, exhausted itself. The men drew their women away, knowing from experience that nothing could be won from the uniforms, not even compassion.

In small groups, mostly family units, they were allowed to leave the graveyard, reclaim their vans and drive away from the scene in defeat, wet and beaten. The system of roadblocks and traffic filtering ensured that there were no further clashes, but it was doubtful that they had the stomach for any more struggle. Some of the police cars left with selected groups of the departing Travellers, monitoring their journey, until finally there were only the satisfied chief superintendent and his immediate staff still occupying the battlefield.

'There you are, inspector!' Foran gloated as he left. 'I'll see you back in Bandon, then.'

Curtis also turned to go, but McCadden stopped him with a hand on his arm. The others had already walked out of earshot, and they weren't interested anyway, too animated by their own excited discussion to attend to anything else.

'Wait for me for a few minutes, will you?' McCadden requested. 'I want to go down to the church.'

'There's nobody there any more,' Curtis objected.

'There is,' McCadden said. 'I'll only be a little while.'

six

Father Verscoyle was kneeling at the altar rail in front of the tabernacle, deep in prayer, with his hands clasped and his head bowed. After a while he became conscious of being watched and looked around to where McCadden was standing in the shadows by the baptismal font just inside the front door of the church.

Although he couldn't see who was there, Verscoyle smiled benignly. He stood up, genuflected and walked briskly down the aisle, still smiling. Up close, he looked even younger than he had from a distance.

His face was too smooth under his shiny blond hair to have endured much personal suffering, McCadden thought. All the pain he had experienced came at second hand, from the troubles of others. And that didn't cut into your good looks with the same brutality. His cheerful manner was practised, a self-conscious style of engaging with the world.

His hand outstretched in greeting, Verscoyle said breezily, 'How are you? Can I help you at all?'

But after the handshake, McCadden's ID tested his self-control.

For a moment or two, the young priest's indecision betrayed his predicament. He didn't want to condemn. He wanted to *save.* His natural sympathy was with the poor and the underdog. But he had no history of revolt, a horror of being branded radical, and only a martyr's longing to take the world's sins on to himself and cleanse them away with his own suffering. So conflict made him miserable, because it forced him towards making a choice. He was the anguished spectator.

He said, 'If you're looking for Travellers, inspector, I assure you they're all gone. There aren't any hiding in the confessional boxes or under the altar. They have far more respect for the temple than that. But you're welcome to search in these places, if you want to.'

It was probably as close as the young man had ever come to fighting. A little surprised, McCadden shook his head. 'Actually, I wanted to talk—'

'You realize what you've done, don't you?' the priest swept on. 'What chance do these poor people have of peace if you talk to them only with a gun in your hand? What chance do they have of self-respect if you treat them only as a social problem that needs a final solution? You castigate them as dirty, but deny them basic amenities and force them to live in squalor on the sides of the road. You condemn them for drinking in public, but refuse to serve them in bars and hotels.'

McCadden held his patience, waiting for the sermon to run out of steam. There was no point interrupting, nothing to be gained from explaining that he wasn't a barman, a social worker or a member of a commission on itinerancy. Overwound from the drama of the arrests, the young priest wasn't capable of listening.

Still agitated, Verscoyle threw his hands up in a gesture of despair and walked quickly away towards the open church door. 'Come with me,' he ordered.

McCadden sighed and ambled after him.

Outside, ignoring the rain, Verscoyle jumped to his left from the front step on to the narrow path under the walls of the building, and walked to a section of the graveyard, behind the church, that McCadden hadn't been able to see before.

The corner was dominated by six huge memorials, gigantic slabs of light-grey stone with prayers and valedictory verses and the names of those buried in the plots underneath carved on their surfaces. A life-size sculpture towered at the centre of each tablet. They'd all been chiselled by the same artist and they depicted various scenes from the crucifixion and resurrection of Christ. They were so elevated, on top of the headstones, that they dwarfed everything else in the graveyard. They even threatened the scale of the modest church building itself.

These were Traveller graves. Four of the memorial stones bore the surname of one of the feuding families. The other two belonged to their rivals. The most recent names on the lists of the dead included the two men killed in the ongoing feud.

Verscoyle stood in front of the graves. He blessed himself, then joined his hands in front and bowed his head in silent prayer.

McCadden waited by the corner of the church, considering the scene. The memorials were certainly impressive. They were obviously expensive, way beyond what the families would've spent in a single gesture on any of the living. They testified to a faith that genuinely considered the next life more worthy of attention than this one. They aspired to the grandeur and magnificence that were God's gifts to man and that were denied the

Traveller by all those bigoted little barmen and social workers and commission members.

It was a personal view, but McCadden didn't think that they realized this aspiration. He was an atheist, of course. And his taste inclined towards the more subtle, the more understated. He found the memorials too loud.

When Verscoyle turned and walked back to him, the young priest had obviously calmed himself. He wasn't any less emotional, but he'd swung now from agitation to sadness. 'Their faith is so strong,' he said admiringly. 'So strong.'

McCadden nodded. 'I was just thinking that myself,' he confided.

'People don't seem to realize this. Their faith. Their sense of family. All the things that were always so valued by the Irish. Why is it that people can't see this any more?'

It was a rhetorical question. McCadden let the implied answer enjoy a few moments' silent appreciation before he asked, 'I may have this wrong, Father, but isn't your parish further south, somewhere down around Seven Heads?'

'Yes, that's right. I'm actually based in Clonakilty. But I work a lot with the Travellers in the area, and as you can see, this is their church. It's only a matter of seeking permission for a christening, burial or a wedding here. It's very common.'

'I believe you knew Hannah Fraule, the old woman who was killed on New Year's night. Is that true?'

Verscoyle blessed himself again. 'Poor Hannah,' he muttered. 'Yes, I knew her. I have her funeral tomorrow morning. God rest her.'

'I'm part of a team investigating her murder, Father. That's really why I'm here. Anything you could tell me about her would be helpful.'

The priest looked up at the unbroken grey sky and wiped the water from his damp blond hair. 'Maybe we should go back inside, inspector.'

They returned and stood again by the font in the baptistery.

'What do you want to know about Hannah?' Verscoyle wondered.

'Have you already given a statement to the investigating detectives?'

'They were made aware that I knew her. They noted that. I wasn't interviewed. Not until now.' He looked dubiously at McCadden. 'Shouldn't you already be aware . . . ?'

'I'm from Dublin. I'm working with the local team, but not attached to it.'

'Ah! You're not under the command of Chief Superintendent Foran, then?'

'No.' A plus, obviously, McCadden noted. He pressed home the advantage. 'How well did you know Hannah Fraule?'

'I hardly knew her at all, to be honest. Not in any real sense. I visited her twice a week. I did what I could for her. She didn't ask for much. A little company. A little comfort in prayer. I sometimes organized transport to bring her to mass. When she was unable to travel, I said mass for her in her home. She was very distressed if she thought she'd miss mass.'

'When did you last see her?'

'Christmas Day. I said mass for her in the morning. No. I also said mass the next morning as well, because it was Sunday. Christmas was on Saturday. She was poorly. She'd taken a fall the previous night. Christmas Eve, I mean. I could tell she was shaken by it. She bruised her face. I tried to persuade her to go to hospital, but she wouldn't listen to me.'

'She had a photograph of the Eucharistic Congress on her wall.'

'Yes. You noticed that, did you?'

'Do you know why she hung it there?'

'She was a devout woman.'

McCadden shook his head. 'It's more than that. There were no religious statues, no holy pictures, no other icons. The Eucharistic Congress had some personal meaning for her.'

'I'm not a detective, inspector. I'm not allowed to probe into the private lives of those who don't want to talk about them.'

'Right. Did she ever talk about the past?'

'Never. She hardly talked at all.'

'How long had you been visiting her?'

'Since I came here, more than two years ago.'

'Did she have any relatives?'

'She never mentioned any.'

'Any other visitors?'

'The health nurse. The doctor occasionally. Although she was quite healthy, I suppose, her age made her vulnerable. But she refused to be transferred to a hospice or hospital. She was a very independent old woman. There was also a young neighbour, Mrs Cole, who was kind to her.'

'Have you any idea how she ended up living alone in such a neglected house in an almost deserted village?'

'You have to remember that when she first came here—'

'When?'

'What?'

'When did she first come here?'

'A long time ago. Some time in the 1950s, I believe. You have to remember that it was an ordinary fishing village then. It's only lately that her neighbours moved away and that some of the houses around her were bought as holiday homes and left unoccupied for most of the year. The deterioration of her own house dates from that time as well.'

'Surely she could've sold the property?'

'Perhaps. But she preferred the discomfort she knew to the risk of change. She was very resilient, a very independent old lady, as I've said. Even though she had no wanderlust at all and was very different from them in that respect, I often held her up as an example to the Travelling community.'

McCadden, who'd been looking down at the floor where he was pushing damp pieces of coloured confetti around with the toes of his shoes, suddenly went still and felt a familiar tingling sensation along the back of his exposed neck. He didn't look up at Verscoyle. Not yet. 'An example?' he asked. 'In what way?'

'Well, her self-sufficiency, I suppose. Travellers are often the victims of discrimination, as are the old. She never paid much attention to the ignorant opinions of others. She knew what she wanted from life. She knew what God had asked of her. That was all that was important.'

'Did you ever ask any of the Travellers to help her out? Tidy her house, maybe? That sort of thing?'

Verscoyle laughed. 'I'm not naive, inspector.'

'No, I didn't mean that you were.'

'Apart from Hannah's dislike of strangers around her house, I know that things aren't as simple as you suggest. It's not simply a matter of the settled and travelling communities cheerfully giving each other a hand. The distrust is still too great for that.'

McCadden went on staring at the shredded confetti by his feet. He didn't want to be a *cynic*. And he didn't think he was one, really. He just wished at times that he didn't see so much and that so much of what he saw wasn't dark.

He'd thought earlier, standing beside Foran in the lane, that the chance discovery of Father Ronan Verscoyle with the hunted Travellers was a lucky coincidence. He should've known better. There are few coincidences in life. What looked like one is usually just a failure to spot the connections. Everything Verscoyle said about prejudice against Travellers was accurate. His defence of them was justified. His work with them was admirable. The priest was a genuine Christian.

And yet . . .

McCadden looked up. 'Do you know Martin Curran, down on Dunowen Head, Father?'

Verscoyle sadly furrowed his brow. 'Ah, poor Martin. He's had a terrible ordeal.'

'Do you visit him?'

'Of course. More so now than ever. I try to get around to all the old people living in the area. It's not always possible, not every week. But we can only try.'

The awful truth was now obvious to McCadden. This cherub-faced young priest, with his evangelical idealism, his desire to think the best of every soul, his zealous struggle to break down the barriers between humans . . . this lethal innocent had unwittingly passed on crucial information about the habits and property of vulnerable old people living alone in isolated rural spots.

'Do you know what the two youths were arrested for today, Father?' he asked.

Verscoyle was baffled. 'What youths?'

'The point of today's operation by the local guards was to arrest two youths from one of the Travellers' families.'

'Why couldn't they arrest them at their own halting site?'

'I'm not certain. Possibly because they couldn't be found otherwise and it was known that they were going to be here. Possibly the intention was to arrest them *en route*, before they reached the church. Possibly it was considered too dangerous to enter the halting site. But do you know the reasons for their arrest?'

'No, of course not.'

McCadden felt slightly ill. He was wet and cold. His wounded shoulder had ached all day from the dampness. His distaste for Foran's excesses had already turned his stomach. And now this sorry innocent was adding a bitter twist at the end of a bleak day. But he knew that Verscoyle's sensitivities were irrelevant. He knew that he'd have to be brutally honest. The security, the health, possibly the lives of the cleric's elderly parishioners depended on it.

The priest probably considered the two suspected murderers as no worse than untamed youths. The news that they were wanted in connection with the grotesque killing of an old woman and the brutal attack on an old man would inevitably test his optimism. But how he'd take the order to present himself at the incident room in Bandon Garda station to be grilled as an unwitting accomplice was anybody's guess.

McCadden looked again at the soft young face in front of him, with its patient smugness, its slightly superior expression of a man who had elevated himself above the worldly and who was now looking down on one who was still unhappily stuck in that mire.

It would almost be more humane, he decided, to just smash it with a fist.

seven

The kindest thing that could be said about Hannah Fraule's burial the following morning was that it was hurried. Indecent would probably be a more accurate adjective, though. It was held in a remote country graveyard, exposed to a biting wind that was whipping in off the Atlantic Ocean. There were no relatives at the ceremony. In fact, there were no mourners at all. A faltering young cleric, now paralysed by doubt, seemed to discover only God's judgement in his own foolish vanity in each of the prayers he read out. A shivering altar boy held a sodden incense burner. A quartet of bored undertakers, so anxious to get on with it that they were always a move ahead of the dreary priest, lowered the coffin before a decent silence was observed and shovelled the clay before the holy water was sprinkled. And throughout it all, the rain persisted. The same weather front that had kept the previous day so depressing was still squatting over the south-west, slowly smothering the energy from everything.

McCadden, watching the sad spectacle from his car at a discreet distance, began to regret his presence. An hour earlier, plotting his route through the narrow country roads, he'd been encouraged by optimism. Something in the old woman's life must illuminate its awful end, he'd thought. Somewhere among the mourners at her funeral, he'd hoped, there must be someone who had known her in the past. More than hoped, really. *Believed.* But as it turned out, it didn't seem the occasion today for the renewal of faith.

Parked outside a bungalow on the road above the graveyard, he sat through the brief ceremony. He watched the undertaker's men hurriedly roll the cover over the open grave, briskly collect their harnesses and spades and hasten towards the relief of the idling hearse. He saw the dismissed altar boy scurrying through the headstones and coming from the church a few minutes later in a heavy jacket to run home along the narrow road. He waited for Verscoyle to finish the final few prayers and leave.

But the priest lingered by the edge of the grave, although he clearly wasn't praying any more. He seemed disturbed. Convinced that he was alone and unseen, he turned his face to the sky and while the rain fell into his staring eyes he called upwards. If he got any answer from the heavens, it didn't appear to comfort him. He stayed for a long time afterwards, his head lowered again now, very still. Finally, wet and bedraggled, he made his way unsteadily towards the church, sometimes colliding with a headstone and lurching away at an odd angle.

McCadden might've worried more about him, if he hadn't discovered that someone else was also watching the priest.

Leaning forward to turn the key in the ignition, thinking of giving himself the option of checking again on Verscoyle while he was driving towards the church, he caught a glimpse of the front tyres and dented bonnet of a blue Nissan Micra that was parked behind a wall on the opposite approach to the graveyard, where there was no house, no farmyard, no entrance to a field. It hadn't been there earlier. It hadn't even been there when the hearse pulled away and the altar boy skipped off home to warm himself.

McCadden released the ignition key without starting the engine, so alert now that he unconsciously prevented the other keys on the ring from jangling together as he removed his hand. He couldn't see the cabin of the other car. It was always possible that it was empty, that the car's presence was incidental, that some daft tourists were just taking a stroll around a quaint rural church. But he hung on, although more out of hope than with any optimism.

Twenty minutes passed.

Father Verscoyle, looking more composed, even a little sheepish now, came from the church, checked his wristwatch and drove away in his own car.

After that, for a minute or so, McCadden heard rather than saw the movements. The opening and closing of a car door that needed to be slammed to stay properly shut. The inward push on the creaking iron gate at the entrance to the graveyard and the quieter scraping as it slowly swung closed again after it was released.

The character who came into view afterwards, picking his way carefully through the graves while clearly looking for one in particular, was a small, thin man, dressed in a tight navy overcoat and a dark soft hat. He was cautious. He quickly saw McCadden's car. He stopped and stared up at it. But he must have decided that it was empty. He couldn't see inside because the windows were clouded, and its location outside the bungalow probably convinced him that it belonged to a local.

He moved on, taking only one more suspicious glance upwards. When he came to the freshly dug grave, he stopped again, removed his hat, and stood, staring down at the plot. He was middle-aged, McCadden saw now. Possibly fifty years old. Almost completely bald. With stern little features.

He stayed for five minutes, a long time to hold a single position, and during that time he never gestured, never shifted on his feet, never varied his expression. At the end, he replaced the hat and walked quickly away.

McCadden let him go, listening to the reverse sequence of the earlier sounds. The creaking gate. The car door. When he heard the engine starting, he was on the point of firing his own ignition. He hesitated only because he was waiting for the other driver to engage reverse. He expected him to turn the car on the narrow road and drive back home the way he'd come. Instead, moving quickly up through the forward gears, the Micra kept coming straight for him, forcing McCadden to slip hurriedly down in his seat and out of sight until it passed.

Rising again, he had time to glance through his rear-view mirror at the registration plate before the car disappeared around a bend. He hurried to catch up with it. He scribbled the registration number on a pad. He started to negotiate his own three-point turn, but as he reversed and prepared to swing back on the final leg of the manoeuvre, a yellow Volkswagen Golf came roaring over the hill by the church and bore quickly down on him, screeching to a halt directly in front of his bonnet and blocking his path. From behind its cloth-covered steering wheel, his face brightened by relief, Curtis looked across and nodded.

McCadden gestured frantically. Curtis frowned. With anyone else, McCadden might've thought that the other was pretending to be obtuse and deliberately blocking his pursuit. Realizing that Curtis was simply bewildered, he stepped from the car and started swearing to clarify his request. But it was too late, of course. By the time Curtis had reversed and McCadden had finally swung by and reached the next junction, there was nothing in sight any more. The roads ahead of him were clear. And he knew that he'd already lost the Micra.

When he drove back, he found that Curtis had pulled in off the road and parked at the entrance to the church. The young detective was waiting in the rain, leaning against the bonnet of his Volkswagen.

McCadden swung over alongside him and lowered his window. 'How did you know I was here?' he asked irritably.

Curtis shrugged. 'You mentioned it yesterday.'

'Did I? Right. So. What did you want?'

A car horn sounded sharply to McCadden's rear. Checking his mirrors, he noticed that one of his back wings was still jutting slightly on to the road. It clearly wasn't enough to obstruct any traffic, but he pulled forward a few metres anyway. Behind him, a red Mercedes came into view and snaked through. Its driver was an extremely nervous middle-aged woman. But in the front passenger seat beside her was a toothless old man in a white mackintosh whose folded wheelchair was visible on the rear seat and who was staring aggressively across the driver at the pair outside the church gates.

McCadden stepped out of his own car and walked across the gravel to the edge of the road, looking after the retreating Mercedes and noting its registration. He waited for Curtis to join him. 'Do you know those people?' he asked.

'Who, sir?'

'The disabled old man in that car. He was in the village the other day. Yesterday, too.'

'No, sir.'

'Is there anyone living in the village who's confined to a wheelchair?'

'No.'

'Are you certain?'

'In so far as I can determine, sir, with my limited access to the file.'

'Right,' McCadden accepted. 'You didn't tell me. What do you want me for?'

'The chief superintendent wants you.'

'What for?'

'He didn't actually *say*, sir.'

eight

The chief superintendent was no longer in his office by the time McCadden and Curtis reached the station in Bandon. He wasn't even in the building any more. In fact, the whole place seemed curiously deserted, as if the occupants had just learned of some impending disaster and cleared out, leaving behind them a slightly tense atmosphere and a resentful rearguard.

The lugubrious old desk sergeant received McCadden's greeting with a doleful look. Unrelated to anything that McCadden was saying, he suddenly started to explain that the two young Travellers arrested the day before had just been charged with the assault on Martin Curran, who had positively identified them. The pair's lawyer, a young Legal Aid attorney appointed by the court, was still with his clients, trying to explain to them that the lesser charge was only an easy method of keeping them in custody and that the more serious one of murder would inevitably follow.

The sergeant paused. He found a stray sheet of paper to his right that immediately needed to be restored to its proper place and he laboriously set about locating where it should be. When he was satisfied, he looked back at McCadden over the rim of his heavy glasses and slowly delivered the unexpected invitation, 'You can talk to them, you know.'

McCadden stared at him, taken by surprise. 'Talk to who?'

'The two lads,' the sergeant explained. 'While their lawyer is still here, like. You can talk to them.'

'Who says?'

'It's the chief superintendent's orders, sir.'

'Are they being interviewed at the moment?'

'No, they're back down in the holding cells.'

'But what? They're being interrogated again shortly? I can sit in on the session?'

'No, you can talk to them all by yourself. Or with Detective Curtis there.'

'About what, sergeant?'

'I don't know. Anything you like, I suppose.'

'That's the chief superintendent's instructions?'

'That's it.'

'So he won't mind if I see him for a minute to clarify the orders.'

'I'm already after telling you. He's out.'

'One of the officers from the investigating team, then.'

'There aren't any of them here right now.'

'You're joking, aren't you?'

'No, sir.'

'Let's think about this, sergeant. I have no idea what ground has already been covered. I have no idea what the pair have already admitted to or denied. I'm going to be wasting my time. And everybody else's time.'

'But I have the transcripts from the earlier sessions ready for you to read.'

'You have transcripts of the interviews?'

'Didn't I already mention that?'

'I don't think you did, sergeant.'

'The chief superintendent's orders as well, sir.'

McCadden was wary. The previous day, when he'd requested permission to monitor the interrogation of the two young Travellers, his application had been scoffed at and bluntly refused. Something had clearly changed. And he had no idea what it was. He went on staring at the desk sergeant, hoping to discover clues in the old man's dull expression. But it was like trying to eyeball a Friesian heifer, he decided. There simply wasn't enough happening back there to make the effort worthwhile. He turned to glance at Curtis, who was standing behind him. But Curtis only gestured his ignorance.

Wary or not, McCadden decided that he couldn't afford to turn his back on the offer. He took the transcripts to Curtis's desk in the abandoned detectives' office and, with Curtis's ambivalent co-operation, started to work quickly through them. The tale he extracted was depressing. Over a ten-day rampage that stretched across Christmas and towards the New Year, the two Traveller youths, fuelled by alcohol and rocks of crack-cocaine they'd picked up in Cork city, had broken into the homes of six elderly people within a radius of fifty kilometres from Bandon. Three of the pensioners had the good fortune to be out when the pair called. Martin Curran, Hannah Fraule and a spinster named Betty

Foran hadn't been so lucky. The youths had stolen only cash. Most of this had been blown on yet more alcohol and drugs. A stash of ancient money, in pre-decimal currency, had been taken from a mattress in Hannah Fraule's bedroom. The useless notes and coins, no longer legal tender, had been recovered from the youths' caravan at the Travellers' halting site. They'd also left something behind them, linking them to the crimes, at almost every location, apart from the crude signatures that were their fingerprints. A ring had slipped off in Betty Foran's cottage. A shop receipt was abandoned somewhere else. And of course the length of red curtain cord taken from Martin Curran's house had been used to strangle Hannah Fraule.

The forensic evidence was clear-cut, but the youths themselves, their brains corroded by substance abuse, were horribly confused. They couldn't even remember the sequence in which they'd attacked the old people. They had no idea of dates or times. In separate interviews, they repeatedly contradicted each other. One thought they'd robbed Hannah Fraule *before* waylaying Martin Curran in his own home. He couldn't explain how the red curtain cord from the latter ended up in the old woman's house. The other insisted that Hannah Fraule hadn't been their final victim, although they clearly hadn't had time between New Year's Day and their arrest to attack again and no other assault was reported for that period. The entire episode was clouded for them. Events had passed them by in a haze. And the only apparently reliable chronology was the sequence provided by the investigating officers.

McCadden wondered if he had the entire transcript. He noticed, for instance, that no one had mentioned Father Ronan Verscoyle during the interviews. Nobody wondered why the youths had specifically targeted Hannah Fraule and Martin Curran, or whether any of the other pensioners were known to the priest. The natural assumption, that the victims were picked at random while the youths were travelling the countryside in their van collecting scrap metal, was reasonable enough. But Verscoyle had made a statement the day before. He wanted to atone. He practically *demanded* penance. He needed to take the guilt upon himself, to cleanse away the sins of others with his own pain. He was also desperate to demonstrate, of course, that very few Travellers were criminals, that the vast majority were decent and that the two youths were tragic exceptions. In terms of a criminal investigation or a court case, he was probably a potential menace. So perhaps the decision to exclude him, at least for the moment, was only an aid to clarity.

But McCadden gradually noticed a second, and much more significant, omission. Once he'd established its absence, not only from the early interviews but from the entire investigation, he immediately asked Curtis to have one of the youths brought up to the interview room. He became restless as soon as Curtis had left. His impatience brought him to his feet, away from the desk and down the corridor a full three or four minutes before one of the youths and his lawyer were ready to join him and sit opposite him. When they finally arrived, escorted by Curtis, who stood by the door afterwards, McCadden switched on the video recorder and quickly introduced himself and the others for the record.

'What do they call you, son?' he asked the youth. 'Michael? Mike?'

The youth's face was so bruised, so obviously sore, that he had trouble talking comfortably. They'd taken him to hospital after his arrest the day before. Nothing had been broken or fractured, but the injuries were severe enough to need extensive treatment. They'd given him a painkilling shot which had obviously worn off a long time ago.

'Mika, sir,' he said.

'Mika,' McCadden repeated. 'Right. Do you read, Mika?'

'No, sir. I never learned to read.'

'Do you go to films in the cinema? Do you watch television?'

'Yeah, I'd do that all right.'

'You'd know about the Mafia, then?'

'The Mafia?'

'In Italy. And America.'

'I would've heard of them, sir.'

'Right. Do you know what kidnappers sometimes do as part of their demand for a ransom?'

The youth was getting more painfully confused. 'How do you mean, sir?'

'They cut off part of the victim's body,' McCadden explained. 'An ear. A finger. They send it in an envelope to the relatives. Partly it's to prove that they have the victim. Mostly it's to scare the relatives into coughing up the ransom money.'

'Yeah, I suppose I would've heard of that.'

'Good. Can you think of any other reasons why a part of a body might be severed, Mika?'

'How do you mean, like?'

'Severed. It means cut off.'

'Why it would be cut off?'

'That's what I'm asking you.'

'I'm not sure, sir.'

'A religious ceremony, maybe?'

'I never heard of that.'

'A medical operation? Even for the purposes of judicial punishment? They chop off the hands of thieves in some countries.'

The young lawyer leaned forward to interrupt. 'This is rather gruesome, inspector.'

'Yes,' McCadden agreed.

'Can you give us some indication as to where it might be heading?'

'I'm not sure. That really depends on Mika's answers, here. What I can tell you is that there's an unexplained gap in the investigation which will go harder on your client if it's *left* unexplored. Do you want to continue?'

The lawyer nodded. 'For the moment.'

'You said in an earlier interview, Mika,' McCadden resumed, 'that you and your brother wanted to force Hannah Fraule to tell you where her money was, that you meant only to frighten her. Is that true?'

'That's as true as I'm here, sir.'

'What was she wearing underneath her dress?'

'What?'

'Hannah Fraule. She had on a black dress. Right?'

'I'm not sure. I don't remember.'

'You told one of the other detectives that she was wearing a black dress.'

'Then it must be so, I suppose.'

'What did she have on underneath?'

'How would I know that, sir?'

'What did you mop up the blood with?'

'What blood?'

'Come on, Mika, don't mess me around now.'

'I'm not, sir. I wouldn't, sir. Honest.'

'What did you clean up the blood with?'

'I don't remember. Honest. I don't remember.'

'This is not the sort of thing you forget, Mika.'

'I don't remember, sir.'

'Even with your mind blown by crack, you couldn't forget this.'

The door opened behind McCadden. Someone came noisily in and spoke to Curtis, who stepped forward and stooped to whisper into

McCadden's left ear, 'The chief superintendent is back, sir. He needs to see you. Immediately.'

McCadden sat back in his chair and stared across at the bewildered youth. 'The Mafia,' he mused. 'Kidnappers. Ransoms. Severed ears and fingers. Underclothes and blood. You have no idea what the hell I'm talking about, do you, Mika?'

nine

During McCadden's short absence, while he was preoccupied inside the interview room, life had miraculously returned to the station around him. The sharp tension in the air hadn't quite been lifted, but at least there was bustle again and the sense of normal business. Even the chief superintendent's office seemed to have been reclaimed. More or less abandoned less than an hour before, it was now remarkably overcrowded. Apart from Foran, who was sitting rigidly behind his desk, there were seven others in the room. Six were local officers, veterans of the elaborate campaign to bring in the two Traveller youths. The surprise exception was the Garda commissioner, sitting close to the chief superintendent on his left, and more relaxed than any of the others. A vacant chair had been placed for McCadden, directly opposite the commissioner. Curtis wasn't invited.

McCadden sat down. No one welcomed him. No one explained the purpose of the gathering. For about a minute, the same stilted atmosphere that seemed to hold the entire building in its grip kept the occupants of this room tight-lipped as well. And then the silence was finally broken by the commissioner.

'What do you think, inspector?' he addressed McCadden. 'What are our chances of carrying a conviction for murder against the two young Travellers?'

McCadden recognized that the question had been carefully framed. He said, 'Conviction? That will depend almost entirely on the abilities of their legal team. If they're represented by an indifferent lawyer, they'll be found guilty. And the odds are, being poor and outcasts, that'll be their fate.'

'And if not?'

'Competent counsel would tear the present case to shreds, simply by insisting on DNA testing of the victim's severed breast.'

'In other words, you don't think that the youths killed Hannah Fraule.'

'No.'

'Why not?' The chief superintendent, already sitting upright in his chair, drew attention to himself by squaring his shoulders a little more impressively. 'Hannah Fraule was robbed and beaten by the two suspects.'

'Yes, I accept that.'

'Then are you trying to suggest, inspector, that immediately after the robbery, when the youths had left, she was attacked a *second* time, by some person unknown, and strangled and mutilated? That would be too implausible a coincidence.'

McCadden shook his head. 'No. I believe that the sequence of events proposed by the investigating team is inaccurate. We know that one of the burgled houses was entered on December 22nd and that Martin Curran was attacked the following night. I think that Hannah Fraule was robbed and beaten on Christmas Eve. She never reported this. The youths didn't return to her house. They had no reason to. They'd already cleared her out. Seven days later, on the night of New Year's Eve, she was mutilated and murdered by someone else. Someone, I would suggest, with a motive more personal than robbery.'

'Have you any evidence for this?' the commissioner wondered.

'For the motive?'

'For the view that someone else killed Hannah Fraule.'

'The two youths know nothing about the mutilation,' McCadden pointed out. 'They're obviously not intentionally concealing anything. They don't have the nerve or the guile. It's unlikely that they both suffered identical blackouts, regardless of what dope they were on. As I've already mentioned, DNA tests should confirm that neither mutilated the old woman. Since they didn't witness the mutilation, either, it follows that they weren't present at her death. Two other things. Father Verscoyle has stated that when he visited Hannah Fraule on Christmas Day, she was badly shaken from a fall the previous night. He accepted her story. I don't. I believe that she had been attacked and robbed, but not seriously injured. The youths discovered her money too easily, and too quickly, to inflict much damage before they fled. And finally, one of the crime-scene photographs clearly shows that the greeting card on the mantelpiece was placed on to a layer of dust that had accumulated from the burning of fuel in the fire below and that some other thin, winding object, put on the mantelpiece some time previously and so making a different indentation in the dust, had been removed. I believe now that the person who placed the greeting card also removed the object beside it at the same time.

Because of the shape of the indentation in the dust, I also believe that the object was the length of red curtain cord taken from Martin Curran's house and left behind in Hannah Fraule's house by the two Traveller youths when they robbed Hannah Fraule on Christmas Eve. The rope had been lying on the mantelpiece for seven days while the dust settled around it. And clearly, the person who placed the greeting card must also have cut Hannah Fraule's nipple before biting it off and spitting it on the floor.'

There was another silence when McCadden had finished. It should have been appreciative, or at least reflective. Instead, it was mostly resentful.

Once again, it was the commissioner who broke the silence. He lifted the flap on the breast pocket of his uniform, reached in with two fingers and extracted a folded sheet of paper, which he straightened and handed across the desk to McCadden. 'Read it,' he instructed.

McCadden read, guessing from the reactions of those around him that the others had already studied the paper, that in fact this must be the real purpose of the conference. It was a photocopy of a letter. The original had been run off on a laser or ink-jet printer, presumably from a computer file. It was dated the previous day, Wednesday, 5 January 2000. The sender's name or address wasn't included. The intended recipient was Jason Scott, a well-known crime correspondent for one of the major tabloids, a man whose popular books on turf wars and gangland killings, based entirely on material released by the police from their files, had done more for the image of the force than the Garda press office.

> Welcome to the new millennium, Scotty. I bet you don't really understand the significance of that greeting, do you? And yet, I see you're reporting on the murder of Hannah Fraule. Shouldn't you ask your friends in the guards what they're holding back from you? Ask them to keep you a breast, Scotty. They'll understand. They have one to spare. Ask them. And then print the truth. But do it quickly. If you're not successful by Friday's edition, I'll let one of your female rivals have the full treatment. Imagine her delight. When she helps to expose you as a worthless tool. Of the police. Welcome to the new millennium, Scotty.

On a separate line, aligned with the right-hand margin as if it was a signature, the exclamation *DOH!* was printed in upper-case letters.

'Any idea who wrote this?' McCadden wondered.

Opposite him, the chief superintendent gave a nasty little laugh. 'We all thought *you* might be able to help us answer that, inspector.'

McCadden looked up, across the desk, into Foran's hostile blue eyes. 'Are you implying that I leaked confidential information?'

'Who else knew those details? They haven't been released.'

'The boy who discovered the corpse knew them. It's unlikely that he was the source of this letter, of course. The investigating officers and pathologist's assistants knew them. Also unlikely. Which doesn't leave me. It leaves the lunatic who actually killed and mutilated Hannah Fraule.'

The commissioner coughed lightly to break up the spat. 'It seems obvious to me,' he said, 'that the inspector's theory about a gap between an assault on Hannah Fraule and her murder must be correct. The book of evidence against the Traveller youths can therefore be quickly finalized. Otherwise, the investigating team should immediately redirect its energies. It also seems obvious to me that Inspector McCadden's expertise and experience in this area must be better employed. He will take charge of the continuing murder investigation. Operational control, of course, under the supervision of Chief Superintendent Foran. Any questions?'

As surprised as the others by this sudden development, McCadden looked quickly around the circle of sullen, hostile faces and knew immediately that he was in trouble. He'd just trampled all over their investigation. And once the commissioner wasn't offering him shelter any more, they would inevitably piss on his. That's how it went. And he had no option but to grasp the nettle with apparent enthusiasm.

'Could we meet in the incident room for a briefing in thirty minutes?' he suggested cheerfully. 'There are a few new directions I want the team to work on. Otherwise, everybody's going to be doing much the same job as before. I want to keep disruption to a minimum. Also . . .' McCadden needed assistance. He thought of requesting Curtis as his aide, initially as a mischievous gesture, but then for more practical reasons. Whichever way he leaned, towards McCadden to further his own career or towards the local unit to court acceptance as a spy, Curtis would have to be diligent. But while his abilities were probably impressive, his nerve was variable. So McCadden went for more experience, more reliability and more protection for himself. 'I'm following a line of enquiry of my own at the moment,' he continued, 'and if it's possible, I'd like to have a colleague of mine from Waterford seconded to the team to help me with it. Detective Sergeant Frank Ryan.'

'Is that all right with you, chief superintendent?' the commissioner enquired.

Foran silently gestured his helplessness. Whether or not he was comfortable with the idea was irrelevant. He could do nothing about it. He clearly felt that he'd been outmanoeuvred and he obviously resented what he saw as abuse of power, but in reality it was his own prejudice that had betrayed him and the mute loyalty of his officers that had confirmed his blindness.

When the conference was over, McCadden was the only one to accompany the commissioner to his waiting car. He was also the only one to receive a handshake or a valediction, presumably because he was a safer bet than any of the others to quietly accept either.

The commissioner nodded briskly at him. 'Good luck, inspector.'

'Thanks.' McCadden accepted ironically. He held the car door open, but not quite wide enough for the man to escape him quickly. 'That letter, by the way . . .'

'The original is with the Technical Bureau. But they're not very hopeful.'

'Is it genuine?'

By now, the commissioner had forced the door wider and stooped to sit into the front passenger seat of his car. The question stopped him. He looked upwards, then stood upright again, his hands resting on the top of the open door. 'In what sense?'

'Chief Superintendent Foran is clearly convinced that its sole purpose is to compromise his position. He can't accuse you of inventing it, but his insinuation that I did so amounts to the same thing.'

'You answered him, inspector.'

McCadden shook his head. 'I answered only for myself.'

'And now you're asking me to answer for myself?'

'Yes.'

The warmth drained out of the commissioner's eyes and his breathing became a little more strained. 'You don't make things easy for yourself, do you, inspector?' he observed.

'That's not a consideration,' McCadden insisted.

'Would you seriously expect me to tell you the truth if I *had* fabricated that letter?'

'Yes. Other people's lives probably depend on it.'

The commissioner took a long breath. It gradually turned into an exasperated sigh. He said, 'The letter is genuine. And I agree with you. It was clearly written by the lunatic who murdered and mutilated Hannah Fraule. If it makes you feel any better, it's so genuine that we've assigned armed protection to three female journalists to counter the implied threat in it. I'll let you know, of course, if there are any developments in that area.' And then he sat sharply into his seat, slammed the passenger door and ordered his driver to move out.

PART TWO

january, 1948

Since the war, the river had become a sanctuary for me. When my sister Penelope, worried by my increasing reclusiveness, asked me why I spent so much time on that narrow stretch of water, I told her that it was because it perfectly captured my present mood: I could look backwards in one direction and touch my own boyhood and I could turn and reach towards the future in the other direction, while all the time staying becalmed in the centre. My language struck me afterwards as rather too florid, but I was satisfied with the accuracy of the image. And of course, Penelope knew exactly what I meant. The river flowed through adjoining estates, linking two ancient families with a bond that was fluid rather than rigid. Something that now suggested the grace and softness of a ribbon on a bridal bouquet or the tenderness of a malleable wedding band. For the expectation was that Penelope, only daughter of the Etchinghams, would soon marry Albert, our neighbours' only child.

I could eagerly list the reasons why this prospect delighted me. Not least, there was the individual happiness of two people I loved. There was, as well, the comfort it offered to both sets of parents and of course the increased security it granted the families in difficult times. But I was less anxious to explain why it also saddened me. I had no doubt that I would suffer some personal loss from the union. It would surely be impossible to sustain the old intimacy between myself and Albert when one of us was still single and the other newly married.

I was thirty-three years old, a veteran of the Second World War, wounded near Dunkirk on the retreat from mainland Europe in 1940. Apart from Albert, however, I had no friends. My emotional life revolved around my neighbour. Just as Albert's had always depended on me. We were outsiders. Even as boys, although in the vague, muddled way of children, we had known that we were awkwardly different. We didn't attend the same schools as the village boys. We didn't worship at the same church on Sundays. We rarely mixed. And even when we did, the outcome was usually violent. Once, led by Cheevers, the bloated son of the local butcher, in his offal-stained shirt and his unbuttoned short pants, the village boys had even invaded the river. I was rowing the small boat we called Excalibur. *Albert and Penelope were stretched on the other seat, enjoying the sunshine. As we were drifting past the hazel trees that marked the boundary between the two estates, we suddenly came under attack. A hail of missiles – mostly stones and tree branches – rained down on us. The boat might have capsized. All three of us were excellent swimmers, but under such pressure, a fatal accident was always possible. The situation was dangerous. And it was Albert who retrieved it. Telling Penelope to shelter behind him and ordering me to steer towards rather than away from the ambushers, he stood upright in the boat, ignoring the hits he was taking himself, and used a catapult to slam rounded pebbles into the wobbling flesh of the butcher's fat son with such frequency and precision that the slob turned tail and fled from the onslaught. Albert said afterwards that he only aimed for the boy because he offered an unmissable target. It was typical modesty. I knew that my friend had instinctively grasped the essential thing. Without their behemoth, the village boys were cowards.*

There are many such memories, most of them episodes in the long, precarious siege that seemed to have been our childhood. But the most extraordinary recollection I have is of a June day in 1934. I was eighteen years old at the time. Albert, a few months older, had already passed his nineteenth birthday. Sent on an errand of some sort by my mother, we walked together to the village and found it eerily empty. All the shops were closed. The houses were locked, and the streets were deserted. The only sign of life in this ghostly, abandoned landscape was a little seven-year-old girl named Emily Fraule, who was skipping by herself on the footpath outside the entrance to her parents' public house. Partly for amusement and partly for information, Albert started talking to her. It was she who explained to us that the villagers had left on some sort of pilgrimage connected with the religious feast of Corpus Christi. But in return for this information, she also wanted to know why we weren't in the procession as well. 'We're different,' Albert told her. 'From now on, I'm going to be different, too,' the little girl claimed.

I was nervous about Albert talking to the girl. I didn't trust the deserted village. I was convinced that we were being secretly watched and I feared an ambush at any moment. When the girl's father, a sullen giant of a man, appeared at the door of the public house and glared at us, I hurriedly tugged Albert away, pleading with him to return to the familiar comforts of the river. By then, at eighteen, I knew just how precariously different our families were. We were Protestants. Hundreds of years earlier, our ancestors had been granted the land by some grateful English monarch in return for loyal service. While the British had continued to rule Ireland, we had prospered, apart from the occasional upheaval caused by agrarian agitation or republican insurrection. But with the establishment of the Irish Free State in 1922, the tide had started to turn against us. The mildest of our troubles under the new nationalist government was being shunned and now allowed equal trading conditions. The most severe were attacks from the Irish Republican Army, sometimes leading to murder and the burning of ancestral homes.

Even then, back in 1948, more than two years after the end of the war that had so radically changed our world once more, I still felt safest on the river. My happiest memories were of waiting there for Albert on warm summer evenings, perhaps with a good wine from my father's cellar cooling in an ice bucket and the season's most talked-about novel, borrowed from Penelope, waiting to be lampooned. It wasn't summer that night in 1948, however. It was winter, a bitterly cold evening in early January. I was wrapped in a heavy greatcoat and wore a lined hunter's cap to keep my head warm. Brandy, not wine, was in the flask I kept in my right-hand pocket. And although I was again waiting on the river for Albert, my mood was one of determination rather than anticipation.

We had been through so much together. And in every crisis, Albert had always seemed the stronger and the more resourceful. That pitched battle with the village boys, for instance, had only been playful preparation. In a forest in Belgium almost twelve years later, as commissioned officers serving with the 2nd Inniskilling Fusiliers, we had encountered the real thing. With the outbreak of war between Britain and Germany in 1939, many of the Protestant Irish had naturally seen Hitler as the enemy, even though southern Ireland had remained rigidly neutral. For Albert and myself, it was a simpler choice. Our families had a long tradition of service in the British Army. My uncle had died at Gallipoli in 1915 with the Inniskillings. Albert's three uncles had been at the Somme with the regiment in 1916. Only one had survived.

In May 1940, on the retreat to Dunkirk, the Inniskillings had pulled out of our temporary headquarters, leaving Albert in command of the rearguard. In the night, we had clashed with forward patrols of the advancing Germans. We were quickly encircled. I was wounded in the shoulder. Several others were also hit. Albert had refused to leave anyone behind, however. We held our fire at one stage and moved location in an effort to elude the pursuing troops. In the early hours of the morning, we managed to slip through one of their camps as the enemy slept. Unfortunately, we stumbled on two forward machine-gun posts on the other side. Albert led a small raiding party to disable the first. They did so silently, with knives and bayonets, taking the Germans completely by surprise with the angle of their approach. But they were spotted by the other nest. Once this opened up, of course, it alerted the sleeping troops behind. We were trapped again. The two men with Albert were quickly hit. He decided that he had no option if we wanted to escape. He charged the machine gun single-handed, killing all those manning the post. His courage and his leadership eventually brought the men safely through to the British lines and evacuation at Dunkirk. And they also saved my life.

After that, however, our paths had diverged for a few years. I was invalided out of combat duties and assigned to a desk in London. Albert eventually went back to the European mainland with the invading force in 1944. Until the war ended and we both came home, our periods of leave never seemed to coincide.

Roused from these memories by a rustling in the hazel trees where I was moored, I looked at my watch, struggling to illuminate its face with the moonlight. It was eight-fourteen, I saw, and Albert was already almost thirty minutes late. Although I was cold by then and my flask had been emptied of brandy, I was also patient. Albert was in trouble. For so long the stronger and the wiser of the two, he now needed my help. And since I was still carrying a debt that I had waited nearly eight years to start repaying, I was eager to stand and struggle once more beside my friend.

When we were boys, we had built a little jetty by the hazel trees as a kind of memorial to commemorate our rout of the villagers, and it was along the remnants of this platform, after squeezing through the overgrown trees, that Albert finally approached the boat. He was breathing heavily and seemed excited.

'Let's go downstream, Richard,' he said as he stepped in. 'I have something to tell you.'

one

The registered owner of the blue Nissan Micra that McCadden had lost at Hannah Fraule's funeral had an unfamiliar surname. It was Siggs. McCadden looked it up, expecting an English origin, and learned that it was the diminutive of the Scandinavian personal name Sigrior and had been common in northern England in the twelfth century. There was no explanation for its appearance in a suburb of Cork city on the south coast of Ireland eight hundred years later. A subsequent search through Garda records was just as inconclusive, but less entertaining. The owner of the Micra had no history. Born on 1 August 1948, Mr Siggs was previously unknown to the police. His motor tax, vehicle insurance and driving licence were all current and clean.

His environment reinforced the sense of greyness. He lived alone in a sleepy, prosperous estate of three-bedroom semi-detached houses. Most of the other houses seemed to be rented by young professionals. There were few families. When McCadden took a quick tour around it, during one of the day's sunnier spells, he saw only four children out playing. And that was on Saturday morning, a little after eleven o'clock.

The driveways were full of BMWs, 4-wheel drives, Audis and Mercs. By contrast, Siggs's modest Nissan Micra drew attention to itself. But that was the only thing remarkable about the house. It had dull paintwork, subdued curtains that were closed across all the windows and an unpretentious front garden with a neatly mown lawn, three rose bushes and a discreet shrub.

McCadden rang the doorbell.

When Siggs answered, he was holding a hardback book in his right hand, with his index finger between the pages as a marker. A pair of heavy reading glasses made his tight little features look even more severe. The bald head added to the sharpness. He was wearing a white shirt, grey slacks without a belt and black shoes. The impression was of gradations of monochrome.

'Mr Siggs?' McCadden established. 'I'm Detective Inspector McCadden, from Garda headquarters, in Dublin.'

Siggs nodded. 'Is it about the damage to the car?'

'No,' McCadden told him. 'What damage to the car?'

'It was vandalized in town last week. The bonnet was badly scratched. I reported it.'

'I'm sure the local guards are following that up.'

'I see. It's something else, then, is it?'

McCadden stared at him. It was obvious that Siggs didn't recognize him, had no apprehensions about the police calling to his door and therefore probably had nothing to conceal from him. Was it possible that the man's apparently suspicious behaviour in West Cork was nothing more than preoccupation or distraction?

Just in case the man was stringing him along, though, McCadden decided to skip the preliminaries. 'Mr Siggs,' he asked abruptly, 'why did you wait until the service was over and you were sure that the graveyard was deserted before you went to visit the grave of Hannah Fraule?'

There was a silence. But no perceptible reaction from Siggs.

'You know what I'm talking about, don't you?' McCadden prompted.

Siggs nodded. 'Yes, I know what you're talking about.'

'And?'

'You'd better come in, inspector.'

Siggs had been reading in the front room, immediately to the right inside the hallway.

It hadn't been furnished for visitors. The walls were lined with books. A heavy old mahogany writing desk had been placed in the alcove to the left of the chimney breast. There was one comfortable leather armchair and the only other seat was a swivel chair by the desk. A small coffee table, its surface covered with books, was the only other item of furniture. The reading material indicated a taste for English philosophers. Russell, Ayer, Locke, Hobbes . . .

When McCadden was settled in the armchair, Siggs slowly inserted a bookmark in the volume he'd been reading, left the book on the writing desk and sat in the swivel chair. He said, 'I visited the grave only after the funeral because I didn't want to be noticed.'

'Why not?' McCadden wondered.

'Because I didn't know how far I wanted to take my interest.'

'Your interest in what?'

'Hannah Fraule.'

'And what *is* your interest in Hannah Fraule?'

'I think she could be my grandmother, inspector.'

'Could be?' McCadden echoed.

'Could you wait there a moment?' Siggs requested. 'I mean, you don't mind if I . . . ?'

'No. Go ahead.'

Siggs stood up and smiled apologetically before he left. McCadden heard him climbing the stairs and entering the room directly above, where he moved a piece of furniture before retracing his steps and descending the stairs. When he came back in he was carrying a sepia photograph that was elaborately mounted in an ornate old wooden frame that had once been painted gold. Without comment, he offered this to McCadden.

As far as McCadden could judge from the clothes and appearance of the subjects, it seemed to have been taken in the 1930s. It showed a prosperous, well-dressed couple, probably in their early or mid-thirties, with a ten- or eleven-year-old girl beside them, standing outside the entrance to a large public house with the title FRAULES in old-fashioned lettering above. Something in their expressions and their postures made it quite obvious that the pub was theirs and that they were thriving. In fact, they seemed to have it all. The woman, dark-haired and sparkling with a haughty self-confidence, was quite beautiful. The man was tall and strong, handsome, and aware of it. The child glowed.

The only unusual aspect that occurred to McCadden was the *position* of the child. She wasn't placed between the adults. She stood beside the man, holding his hand, and he in turn separated her from the woman. In fact, on a second look, although she clearly enjoyed the attention of the lens, the woman seemed slightly self-conscious, humorously resisting the pose, almost on the point of turning away and going back indoors.

Siggs was sitting again in the swivel chair. He wasn't watching McCadden, wasn't waiting for any response to the photograph or any queries about it. He seemed lost in thoughts of his own.

'The past is lighter when it's only a burden,' he said suddenly. 'Don't you think so, inspector?'

'In what way?' McCadden wondered.

Siggs gestured vaguely. He was silent again for a while. Then, like a cork that was released after being submerged under water, his reflections popped up in another location.

'I was born here in Cork,' he explained. 'In 1948. But not in this area.

We lived in the slums of the inner city. Just my mother and myself. She wasn't particularly pious and I was spared the drunken Irish father, so I've been unable to make a fortune out of publishing my memoirs. She worked in a clothing factory, for a Jewish couple who were very kind to us until they emigrated to America. We were poor. But honest, as the ballad goes. Whatever I have now I owe to my mother's understanding that education was the only way out of our poverty trap. Not knowledge, inspector. And not information. Education. Certainly not information. She concealed an awful lot from me. I suppose it was meant for my own good. She wanted me to look forward, not back. For as long as I can remember, that photograph you're holding hung against the peeling wallpaper on the damp walls of our tiny house in our cramped lane, in the centre of our ghetto. You become so indifferent to the familiar, don't you? It never occurred to me to wonder what an image of such opulence was doing in the middle of such deprivation. If I thought about it at all, I assumed that the image, the world it captured, just appealed to my mother. A sort of fantasy of hers. A life to dream about, along with our boat coming in. The thing was so distant and so familiar at the same time, I just ignored it. But I know now, inspector, that the little girl in the photograph is actually my mother. The two adults must be my grandparents.'

'The woman is Hannah Fraule?' McCadden guessed.

'I believe so.'

'And the man?'

Siggs shook his head. 'I don't know. Mr Fraule?' he suggested.

'The woman's hands are concealed,' McCadden pointed out. 'But the man is clearly wearing a wedding band.'

Siggs was unimpressed. 'I don't know,' he said again, stressing it this time as if the admission itself was important to him. 'You see, my mother always maintained that my father deserted us when I was an infant. This is what I meant by the past being a burden. A creative burden. The sense of injustice spurred me on. The reluctance to have my mother disappointed again, abandoned for a second time, made me work all the harder. But I doubt now that this was the truth. I'm not certain any more. The past has become a problem instead of a burden. And it's paralysing. My mother died three years ago, a few months after her seventieth birthday. She lived here with me. She brought that photograph with her from one home to the next as we moved up the ladder. Apart from the time we lived in the slums, she always had it hanging in her bedroom.

Out of sight, it bothered me even less than before. I remember asking her about it once. She was casual about it. "Oh, that. It's only something your father had. I don't know who the people are. It's the only thing I kept of him." Of course, when she died . . . When you lose a parent, you not only have to go through their effects, but you also mentally sum up their life. A sort of private obituary. There was nothing among her papers or belongings that gave me any clue to her past. But last year – and I still don't know why this occurred to me; something on television, I think, the discovery of a valuable artwork hidden behind a common print – last year I slit the brown paper backing on that frame. There was a newspaper article pasted to the back of the photograph underneath. At least, a section of an article. Nothing else. Just one brief cutting from a newspaper. Turn it around. You'll see.'

McCadden turned the frame over. The original paper backing had been replaced by a sheet of thin cardboard held in place by small clips. He released the clips, let the cardboard fall backwards towards him and held the frame to the light to read the item within.

Protected from the air for so long, the clipping had been preserved in almost perfect condition. Someone had written the name of the newspaper, the *Wexford Chronicle*, and a date, 11 February 1937, in ink in the upper margin. There was no headline. The small section had been cut from the centre of the article. Under the sub-heading 'The Suit' the piece continued:

> Mrs Fraule's versatile suit is of mid-grey flannel. The short jacket is the latest thing in casual wear. The skirt is slim and straight, but has a pleat in the centre front and back for ease of movement. When travelling from their home and business in Naune, Mrs Fraule and her delightful daughter, ten-year-old Emily, both wear a scarlet tailored blouse and a simple scarlet beret with comfortable flat heeled shoes.

And that was it.

The article had been cut quite deliberately, not between paragraphs, but between sentences. It was so insubstantial that it was unsatisfying, frustrating. It seemed a pointless keepsake. And yet it had been selected and attached and concealed with great care, so that only the collector knew of its existence and its relevance to the photograph on the reverse side.

McCadden read it twice. And he didn't feel any more enlightened after the second helping.

'Ladies' fashions,' he muttered. 'Not one of my stronger points. Maybe not geography, either. Where's Naune?'

'It's a village in County Wexford near the east coast,' Siggs told him. 'About a hundred kilometres south of Dublin.'

'Whose is the handwriting?'

'Almost certainly my mother's. It's that of a child, obviously, but there are substantial similarities that she retained throughout her life. I'm not an expert, of course . . .'

'And your mother's name?'

'Emily. But Emily Siggs, of course. She was born in Dublin, on January 15th, 1927. She was ten years old when that article was written.'

'Have you been to Naune?' McCadden wondered.

Siggs shook his head, smiling slightly to himself. 'I've been thinking about it.'

'For a year?' McCadden asked.

'Almost.'

'Are you frightened of what you might find?'

'No, not really. The truth, I suppose, is that I'm sorry I slit the brown paper backing on that photograph. My entire life has been built on a few certainties. My mother was deserted as a young bride. My father abandoned us. When I was growing up, struggling out of the slums, there were days when I could remember only betrayals. They were probably my happiest days. I had someone else to blame for my misfortunes. Now I don't know. The past is not so simple any more. I've lost touch with it. It makes no sense. It's as if I've lived too long or things have changed too rapidly. Things can never stay the same, of course. But if you're certain of the past, at least you have the illusion of *continuity*. As you suggested, I've been haunted by that little cutting for almost a year now. When I heard the reports of the old woman who was murdered in West Cork over the New Year . . . Hannah Fraule. The surname is too unusual, isn't it? How many do you think there are in the telephone directory? I've never found any. It's listed in dictionaries of Irish surnames, but it's very rare. How many with the personal name Hannah? And her age. Calculating backwards from my mother's date of birth, my grandmother must've been born before 1912 or 1913. It's too much to be a coincidence, don't you think? The name. The age. Too much.'

'Did your mother ever give you any indication of her own background?'

'She always maintained that she had no surviving relatives. I started life with a clean genealogical slate. It's what everybody wants, isn't it? Wipe away the false starts, the imperfections of previous generations. Start again.'

'You obviously had a close relationship.'

'Yes.'

'And she talked to you a lot.'

'But not always truthfully.'

'Can you remember *anything* she said that you might understand better now?'

'Oh, yes!' Siggs said with a kind of sad enthusiasm. 'I remember. I remember one summer, one hot afternoon, when two women neighbours were visiting my mother. I was sitting on the floor in the room with them, playing with pieces of cloth, offcuts of the material my mother worked with. I was probably eight or nine years old. The women were looking out on the lane through our window when a young girl passed. I knew her. She was seventeen or eighteen. A very kind girl, very fond of children. I remember the exchanges exactly, but I don't remember seeing the girl again. She disappeared from the neighbourhood. "Do you see her?" one of the neighbours said. The other asked, "Did you see her yesterday?" and my mother said, "Wait until you see her tomorrow." That was it. And I had no idea what they were talking about. I had no interest, either. I probably would've forgotten about it, if it hadn't been for the bitterness in my mother's voice when she said those words. "Wait until you see her tomorrow." I have never, ever known my mother to be so vicious, so hostile, so caustic as when she said those words. That's why the puzzle has stayed with me down through the years. Do you understand what it means, inspector?'

McCadden shook his head. 'No, not straight off.'

'Think about it,' Siggs encouraged. 'And if you have to go to Naune, as I suppose you must now, think about it there as well. Carefully. It's my past, after all, that you're going to alter.'

two

Without a permanent office to hang his hat in, McCadden spent the early part of the following week in the National Library in Dublin, searching on microfiche through old issues of the now defunct *Wexford Chronicle* for further references to the Fraules. He found quite a number, stretching across two decades and almost thirteen years, from the mid-1930s to the late 1940s. But the most astonishing thing he found was that there were no published photographs of any members of the family.

These were important business people, at least in the small world of the village and the surrounding parish. The couple owned the liveliest pub and the largest grocery store in Naune. Between barmen, clerks, shop assistants and home helps, they employed at least ten others at any given time. And being central to the parish economy, of course, they became at times influential in matters that stretched to the borders of the county.

It was a distinctly shadowy influence, though.

They seemed never to have dabbled in local politics, for instance, although rooms in their public house were frequently used for branch meetings of Fianna Fáil, the party that came to power in 1932 and stayed there until the post-war years. They seemed never to have served on voluntary committees, although their support for cultural and charitable organizations was often noted. They seemed never to have featured as religious activists, although they were always described as devout Catholics and pillars of the parish. And such were the confusions of the time in a poor, insular, rural society that, as well as being respected as staunch Christians, they were also admired and imitated as a fashionable couple.

And yet, no one had ever published a photograph of these engaging, attractive people. Not at a dog show or a race meeting. Not at a dance or a dinner, a religious procession or a St Patrick's Day parade. Even the item in the fashion pages on Mrs Fraule's versatile suit, which McCadden located first because he already had a date for it, was illustrated only by line drawings and sketches of the clothes discussed.

The group photograph outside the pub that Siggs had inherited from his mother had been taken by a local photographer. His name and address were stamped on the rear of the print. John Carberry, Main Street, Naune. McCadden eventually came across his obituary. Already an old bachelor at the time the photograph was taken, without children, without even an apprentice or an assistant, he'd died in late 1939, a couple of days before the German Army invaded Poland. And the business seemed to have died with him.

Stitching together the rest of the items that featured or referred to the Fraules, McCadden arrived at a tentative narrative.

It was a story of rapid integration, unusual in such a close-knit rural community. Hannah Fraule's husband, for instance, originally known as Harry, had quickly improved to Harold and shortly afterwards graduated to Mr Harold.

The couple first arrived in the village some time before April 1934, along with their daughter Emily. Where they'd come from was never mentioned or questioned, although Hannah first came to local attention because she was famous for being elsewhere. In 1932, during the week of the Eucharistic Congress, she had formed part of the official welcoming party for the papal legate, Cardinal Lauri. She had also been received at a State Reception in Dublin Castle, had been a guest of the Irish Hierarchy at a garden party and had sat five rows away from Count John McCormack while he sang Franck's *Panis Angelicus* to a million people at the open-air mass that brought the Congress to a triumphant close.

Like every other village in Ireland at that period, Naune was predominantly Roman Catholic. There was a dwindling Protestant community, long settled there but now squeezed to the margins and no longer of any social significance. That crowd at the mass in Phoenix Park, estimated at a million people, represented a third of the entire population. One in three of Naune's inhabitants had been there. Most would have travelled by the special trains that brought the faithful to the city and they would have stayed in the special hostels constructed for the pilgrims. The poorest, and the most penitent, would have walked the 150 kilometres to the city and slept outdoors.

Hannah Fraule, carrying the Hierarchy's imprimatur, would have been deeply respected by these people.

And the connection had obviously lubricated the cogs when it came to trade.

She and her husband bought the public house in April 1934, almost three years before that family portrait was taken for the album. Unlike some of their rivals, the premises were never in trouble under the licensing laws, its owners never summoned to court for allowing after-hours drinking. A year later, they also opened the grocery store.

Throughout their rise to wealth and respectability, McCadden noticed two other recurring patterns. The husband, Harry, was always in the background. And the girl, Emily, was invariably in the shadows. In fact, the only time the child was mentioned by name was in the item cut from the fashion pages of the provincial newspaper.

In its way, this was almost as extraordinary as the absence of photographs. And almost as extraordinary, McCadden thought, as the contrast between the fashionable young publican and the impoverished old woman killed in West Cork.

In that fall, he was convinced, that descent from sociability to seclusion, must lie the explanation for the grotesque mutilation to her body.

Searching for a link, he worked again through the material.

During the years of the Second World War, he noticed, from 1939 to 1945, Hannah Fraule seemed to have paid an unusual number of visits to Dublin. Ireland was neutral in the conflict, its location was of some, but not major, strategic importance, and so the capital city, full of part-time spies, had become the centre of limp intrigue. The writers Elizabeth Bowen and John Betjeman both reported from there to the British Ministry of Information. Eduard Hempel, the German Minister in Dublin, served the Third Reich as an analyst; and a small group of Nazi sympathizers formed an ineffective fifth column.

Was it possible that Hannah Fraule had dallied with either side?

If she had, she carried no taint of it back to her adopted village. In the austere post-war years, she settled again to the old routine, running the public house and the store, expanding into the clothing trade at one stage, and clearly thriving.

Until, most intriguingly of all, after several mentions in the preparations for Christmas 1947, she simply vanished from the pages of the *Wexford Chronicle*. There was no further *personal* reference to her after 19 December 1947.

An item from late January 1948, followed up a week later by reports of a court appearance, described the arrest of two men, Robert Hannifin and Joseph Mary Rudican, for the attempted robbery of Fraules public house. But even then, the owner of the pub – 'who was on the premises at the time', according to the reporter, and 'able to raise the alarm' – was not mentioned by name. It wasn't clear if Hannah Fraule *was* still the proprietor at the time of the incident. She may already have left the village.

McCadden searched for logical terminations, all of which would inevitably be reported in a provincial paper. The sale or failure of her businesses, for instance. Her departure from the village to another location. A death in her family. Emigration. Illness.

There were none.

The name Hannah Fraule simply never occurred again.

three

Copies of a printed note, despatched by someone who called themselves 'Eccles', landed on the desks of three female crime correspondents on Thursday morning. Each copy was accompanied by an illustration on a separate sheet. The graphic, downloaded from standard software, adapted on a PC and produced by a common ink-jet printer, showed a grotesque Amazonian warrior. It violently mixed religious and military images. The warrior was entirely naked. Consistent with the Greek legend, her right breast was cut off to improve her archery, but the ribcage underneath was taken from a different source. Lifted from standard representations of the crucifixion, it showed the gash in Christ's side where the centurion's lance had pierced. Above the severed breast and muscular shoulders, the warrior's shrunken head was that of a decrepit old woman, with blistered, wrinkled skin, blackened teeth and sparse grey hair. The note offered no explanation for the montage, although it clearly suggested that there was one. Addressed individually from a mailshot run and using diminutives of the three journalists' surnames, it taunted the recipients. The first read:

> There's a reason for everything. You know that, don't you? But I'll bet you don't understand the connection between my masterpiece here and the execution of old woman Fraule in West Cork. Better ask your friends in the guards. Ask them what boob they've been keeping to themselves. But don't ask them why the old woman was killed. They don't know. Maybe you can find out, Smithy, and let the people in on it. Eccles.

The three envelopes had been posted from Dundee, in Scotland, the previous Monday.

Two of the editors whose newspapers were selected handed the material over to the police. The third, running a tabloid that was rapidly losing a circulation war, went for broke. Time was against him, though.

Despite throwing massive resources at the story, he succeeded only in confirming that Hannah Fraule's breast had been severed by her killer. But this was enough to supply him with a sensational front page the following morning and to have him credited with the naming of society's newest psychopathic monster, Amazon Man.

On Friday morning, on his way south to visit the village of Naune and to meet Detective Sergeant Frank Ryan for a briefing, McCadden picked up a copy of the tabloid, along with updated reports from the Technical Bureau. Two photographs illustrated the newspaper story. One was of Hannah Fraule's dilapidated house in West Cork, the other, bought from a provincial paper which had covered the original attack, showed Betty Foran's heavily bruised face after she was robbed and beaten by the Traveller youths. SICK BEAST TAUNTS COPS, the headline screamed. It was followed by a sub-heading that was even more sensational, and even less accurate: 'Ritual mutilation of Irish women'.

The technical reports from Garda headquarters weren't encouraging. There were no prints on either the note or the envelope sent to the crime correspondent Jason Scott the previous week, apart from those of the journalist himself and the postal workers. There were no traces at all of the author, who had obviously taken meticulous precautions in preparing and handling the item. The paper, the printer that was used to run off the note and the software that created it were all mass-produced and untraceable. Preliminary examination of the new notes and their attached graphics indicated that the same findings would emerge from these.

Two possible directions were indicated by the technical crew. It was suggested that the graphic, or parts of the graphic, may have been downloaded from the Internet and that a search in this area might be worthwhile. And secondly, since the first note had been posted from Dublin and the next three from Dundee, those who had travelled from Ireland to mainland Britain in the interim should be checked out. While such a list was going to be long, and certainly not exhaustive – there were too many ways of getting from Dublin to Dundee without appearing on it – it still might throw up something interesting, particularly when compared with a list of those who had travelled in the opposite direction after the second batch of notes had been posted. McCadden, who already had a small team in the metropolitan regional headquarters searching through the records for previous attacks involving mutilation, wondered if he should pass the new tasks on to the local unit in West Cork. He had little hope of either avenue showing results and nothing to lose by trusting them to Chief Superintendent Foran's men.

When he left Dublin, McCadden was in uncertain mood. He was looking forward to meeting Frank Ryan again. They hadn't seen each other since McCadden was in hospital recovering from the gunshot wounds. But the ignorant self-interest of the tabloid editor depressed him. Whoever had written those notes craved publicity. They clearly enjoyed being the only one who knew why they had killed and mutilated Hannah Fraule. They experienced this secret as a form of power, as something that attracted and impressed others. Denied a means of advertising their superiority, they might have become more careless in the search for one and taken risks. But now that they'd so quickly gained an audience, they'd have to sharpen the performance to hold the interest. Purely as an encore, they might kill and mutilate again.

Despite McCadden's urgings, Frank Ryan hadn't applied for a transfer to the new homicide squad, and he hadn't been recommended for the assignment by the chief superintendent in Waterford. Overweight, overqualified and underwhelmed by the talents of his masters, he was bored by the compromises needed to advance his career. Critics dismissed him as a slug who lacked initiative. McCadden admired his honesty and his reliability. But Ryan wasn't the most sensitive of men. He was too extrovert. When they met for lunch, he was so pleased that he kept pounding McCadden's aching shoulder enthusiastically. He was also the only person McCadden knew who was physically incapable of having a working lunch. For Ryan, the phrase was a contradiction. Food demanded exclusive attention.

They met in New Ross, a short drive north from Waterford and just ten kilometres to the west of the village of Naune. A frumpy old port, now well past its prime, New Ross had little to offer the gourmet. Reduced to steak and chips in a grill room, McCadden was left with a lot of time on his hands to discover the inadequacies of the coffee after picking at the main meal. Finally, when his friend's plates were perfectly clean, he produced copies of the graphic and the killer's notes from a folder and passed them across the table.

Ryan studied them carefully, arranging the pages in a neat row on the surface of the table. 'Desperate for a bad press,' he observed eventually.

'And someone's obliged,' McCadden regretted.

Ryan gazed wistfully at a good-looking waitress passing their table. She was carrying a Black Forest gateau and a baked Alaska. 'It bucks the contemporary trend, though, doesn't it?' he said. 'Everyone else is eager for a good press. Sports manufacturers tear up the contracts of athletes exposed as drug cheats. Even the IRA are on their best behaviour for the American media. When was the last time you came across anyone who was so anxious to get a bad press?'

'I don't know. Left-wing terrorist groups in the seventies, I suppose.'

'That's what I was thinking.'

'But apart from *execution* – which might be terrorist, might be military, might just be a favourite word – there's no sign of any *political* context in either of the notes. No analysis. No programme. No complaints.'

'Maybe *people.* That's a political concept. *Let the people decide.* Most of us would use *public,* wouldn't we? *Maybe you can find out and let the public in on it.*'

McCadden was dubious. 'It's probably more a personal thing.'

'Then why is this character so desperate for publicity?' Ryan wondered. 'There has to be some social dimension. A point is being made. The killer is not satisfied with private revenge, if that's the motive. They want an understanding audience.'

'The commissioner had a pair of bright psychologists working on it.'

'They'll get back to him next year,' Ryan predicted caustically, 'and persuade him we're dealing with someone who's disturbed.'

'Right. We'll keep a profile in mind, obviously, Frank. We'll keep the technicians analysing the evidence and the team in West Cork doing the footwork, but I've decided that the two of us are going to approach it from the opposite direction for the moment, through Hannah Fraule's life. Did you come up with anything on the surname?'

'Something.'

'I knew you would. I still remember you rebuking me a few years ago for getting two different Sullivan clans mixed up.'

'Septs,' Ryan corrected again. 'In Ireland they're not clans, they're septs.'

'There you are,' McCadden acknowledged. 'So what do you have?'

'The name is Irish.'

McCadden was disappointed. 'Irish? I thought it might be German. If the final e was enunciated at some time.'

'It's actually the same origin as O'Farrell, Carl, just a variant spelling. It's not a very common variant, but that's all it is. Once upon a time they were all O'Farrells.'

'Right.' McCadden took another batch of papers from the folder which had held the graphic and the killer's notes. He handed them across. 'This is everything I've discovered so far about Hannah Fraule's life,' he explained. 'It covers only the years from 1934 to 1948 and it's confined to a village called Naune, which is a short distance down the road from here. That's where I'm going for the afternoon. I need you to go to Dublin.'

'Dublin?'

'You can stay in my place. I've got a spare key for you. Read this stuff when you get there. After that, you'll have to get your hands on a few things quickly. I need a birth certificate for Harry Fraule. You'll see from the notes that he was Hannah's husband.'

'Should be easy enough.'

'I also need his marriage certificate, the maiden name of the woman he married . . .'

Ryan had started a checklist on the back of one of the pages. 'Of Hannah Fraule?' he asked.

'Uh-huh. Of Hannah Fraule. Her maiden name, her place and date of birth, and also a birth certificate for their daughter, who was called Emily Fraule. I actually have a date for Emily's birth, according to her son. You'll find it in the notes. Starting with a public house in this village of Naune, I'm also interested in any property the Fraules bought or sold. You'll need some help, so pull a few of the uniforms off the team I have in Harcourt Terrace and redeploy them for the day. The sergeant there is expecting you. I'll see you back in Dublin tonight. Okay? I shouldn't be too late.'

four

Ten kilometres to the east of New Ross, the village of Naune straddled a third-class road whose only function was to link two other remote settlements to each other. A sign on the approach to it read:

NAUNE
A TIDY TOWN
3rd in its category, 1997
2nd in its category, 1998

Its reputation for neatness was unlikely to spread. Even when you were looking for it, the village was difficult to find. The nearest post office was eight kilometres away. The nearest Garda station was back in New Ross. The nearest primary route was somewhere to the south through a labyrinth of what the Ordnance Survey maps knew as 'other roads'.

Unfortunately, McCadden wasn't working with anything as detailed as an Ordnance Survey map. Without it, and without a navigator, he got lost. Repeatedly. It was late afternoon, and already dark, when he finally reached Naune. He didn't catch the place in its most favourable perspective. Even so, as might be expected from a multiple winner in the national tidy towns competition, it struck him as a pretty and quite prosperous village. A neat, nine-hole pitch and putt course lay on the outskirts, although it was closed for the winter months, of course. A compact village square, with a discreet memorial to the Roman Catholic casualties in the 1798 rebellion, provided an attractive centre. All around it there were well-kept flower beds and grass margins and brightly painted shops.

McCadden parked and strolled through the main street and up and down the residential side streets. There were five public houses. Three of them were far too small and the fourth occupied a corner site. Unless there had been radical changes to the main street, this left a bar called the

Templar's Well as the only possible location for the premises the Fraules had bought and run.

Expecting a gloomy drinking den with imitation leather seating, stained carpet and an atmosphere choked by cigarette smoke, McCadden was astonished when he went inside. The interior resembled an art gallery more than a rural pub. Spacious and airy, it was decorated and furnished only with lightly varnished wood. A curved bar counter faced the street door. Ten or twelve high stools, most of them occupied by fashionable young drinkers, were placed in front of it. Behind it there were four gleaming copper holding-kegs from which draught beers were served by tap. To the left, there was a raised area behind a low copper railing, dotted with tables and chairs. To the right, there was a row of computer terminals. One of these was being used by a young couple accessing the Internet, another had a long-haired girl sending and receiving emails.

Naune was not so remote, after all.

This was a micro-brewery, McCadden realized, where craft brewers produced and sold their own stouts and beers. It was also a cyber-café. And it was obviously a meeting place for the fashionable young.

While he was there, McCadden decided that the most courteous way of introducing himself was to test the local brew. He tried the wheat beer, reckoning the stout far too heavy and the red ale too light for his mood. By the time he had finished complimenting its pungency and freshness, he was no longer considered a stranger.

Unfortunately, no one in the pub knew anything about the Fraules. Two or three remembered that this was the name of an old woman recently killed in County Cork, but they were baffled by the possibility of a local connection.

The barman, a bearded young guy with a lengthy ponytail and a knowledge of brewing that extended all the way to contempt for the overproduced, overhyped swill that flooded the market, was the most reliable historian. 'The brewery's been here five years now,' he explained. 'Before that the place was owned by a chap from New Ross. A county councillor. He had it maybe fifteen, twenty years. A long time, anyway. Before that . . .'

'None of you were even born,' McCadden sympathized.

'That's right. When did these people run it, anyway?'

'Probably not later than 1950.'

There was a long silence in the bar. Occasionally it was threatened by quiet laughter, but the customers were either too polite, too good-humoured or too reluctant to spoil their own fun to let it rip.

'1950?' the barman echoed. 'That's fucking fifty years ago!'

'I believe it is,' McCadden accepted.

The barman shook his head. 'Not a hope. Unless you ask some of the old-timers. Go back down to Codds. You know Codds? It's the bar on the opposite side of the street.'

'I passed it on the way here.'

'Some of the old lads down there might be able to help you. The beer's crap, though.'

Codds wasn't only on the opposite side of the street. It was on the other side of the technological revolution. A tight, grim little bar, it was inadequately heated by a dying coal fire and half full of dour old men in grimy suits and cloth caps who were sullenly clutching pints of stout. A barely living monument to the joylessness of the good old days.

Clearly, the only thing that really moved inside this poisonous atmosphere was news, because the customers had already been alerted to McCadden's curiosity. And they deeply resented it. To the point of fear.

No one looked up at him as he opened the street door and stooped slightly to avoid the low beam over his head. There was a hostile silence, crackling with menace, as he walked across to the grubby counter.

He managed a pleasant, 'How are you—'

'I'm sorry, sir,' the barman interrupted. A fat man with a sweaty, worried face, his little eyes were unable to rest because of the tension. 'I can't serve you here.'

'I haven't asked for anything,' McCadden pointed out.

'Could you please leave, sir?'

Two musclemen rose from the shadows in an alcove to the right. They seemed to have a talent for synchronized intimidation. Together they adjusted their belts, loosened their shoulder muscles, flexed their biceps and squeezed out between the tables to approach the bar.

McCadden hadn't yet identified himself as a Garda in Naune. And he didn't want to now. He wanted to test how deep these local fears were. Monday morning, if it was necessary, he could always ride back in with the cavalry.

Outside, he found that the news, and the hostility, had spread. Two of the remaining pubs were closed, locking scores of early evening drinkers safely inside, and the last, on the corner site at the end of the village, had installed an impromptu bouncer to block the entrance. The streets were deserted. The shops were closed. All the houses had their blinds down or curtains pulled. McCadden knocked on a few doors, but there was never any response.

Troubled by a sense of unreality, he went back to the Templar's Well, wondering if he'd imagined or distorted the hospitality there. It had the same relaxed scene, the same feel of a different world. The conversation didn't dip when he came in. No one stared at him sullenly. And the barman ambled across to greet him as he approached the counter.

'Well? Did you find what you're looking for?'

McCadden shook his head. 'They didn't seem too keen to talk.'

'They never were,' the barman confided. 'It's a generation thing. I remember asking my grandfather once what he did during the war. The Second World War. We were doing a project on it in school. Personal reminiscences of the war. Something like that. You know what he did? He burned the notebook I was collecting the material in. Thirty-three of us in that class, and not one managed to do that project. The teacher had to forget about the idea. These old guys, they're into secrecy. They spent their lives in the dark. They're still there.'

By the time McCadden had left the Templar's Well again, this turned out to be almost literally true.

Under a broken street light, a small crowd had gathered around McCadden's car, waiting for his return. Among them were the two bodybuilders from Codds, the self-styled bouncer from the other pub and an irritatingly familiar face, under a shaven skull, that McCadden couldn't put a name or a memory to. One of the group was carrying what looked like a wooden baseball bat. As McCadden approached, they shaped themselves into a ragged phalanx behind a powerful fat man who seemed to be their leader. The man was dressed in a blood-stained apron and had obviously come straight from work. He was probably the local butcher.

'Do you have a problem, or what?' this homespun Napoleon addressed McCadden.

McCadden looked closely at their faces, lingering a moment longer on the one in the background that he recognized but couldn't identify, before he stooped to insert his key in the driver's door. They didn't prevent him opening the car, but the fat man placed a hand on top of the door as it swung towards him.

'Just so you know who you're talking to,' he said, 'I'm a public representative for this area. I'm a local councillor here.'

'Which party?' McCadden wondered.

'Does it matter?'

McCadden shrugged. 'Some are more constitutional than others.'

'And some visitors are more law-abiding than others,' the butcher countered. 'So some are more welcome than others. We've had a lot of trouble in this area recently with criminals driving down from Dublin robbing businesses. People are nervous. Sometimes they do rash things when they're nervous. You know what I'm saying? A lot of these criminals are on drugs, too. It would be a terrible thing if the guards found drugs in your car.'

'But not quite as bad as if you found them,' McCadden guessed.

'I wouldn't hang around waiting for that to happen,' the butcher advised. 'You know what I'm saying? That wouldn't be very bright. I was in the six counties there recently and saw what concerned parents did to drug-pushers. Smashed their kneecaps for them. It wasn't very pretty. So take my advice, won't you?'

The village Napoleon released the car door, swung away and marched back down the main street, followed by his scowling bodyguards. As McCadden watched them go back into Codds public house, which seemed to be the headquarters for the local vigilantes, he suddenly remembered who that shaven head and vaguely familiar face in the background belonged to. The man was Pius Eugene Shanahan, the convicted IRA bomber who had been granted early release from prison and who had recently been courting controversy with a series of unrepentant interviews on radio and television. The others crowded around him, eager to obscure him from view. But his own movements drew the eye towards him. He had a distinctive limp.

The welcoming group were almost certainly members of Sinn Fein, of course. Because of its involvement in the politics of Northern Ireland over the last thirty years, the party still had a hankering for trying to solve complex social problems with vigilante crudeness, tapping into a community's fears with the promise of decisive action, particularly where the law was perceived to have failed. Mostly, they overplayed their hand. Like now. They obviously mistook McCadden for a tabloid journalist. But their heavy-handed discouragement merely raised suspicions where there had been only neutral questions before. What did they have to hide? What grisly secrets about the Fraules's time in this village needed to be kept buried with such extreme threats?

McCadden, lost to his thoughts, jumped in alarm as he felt a hand settling from behind on his right shoulder. Already tense, he swivelled sharply, ready to counter with aggression. But even in the dim light under the damaged lamp it was immediately obvious that the thin young man who stepped sharply backwards away from him, gasping with surprise, had no intention of attacking. In fact, the stranger seemed more capable of charity. He was wearing a clerical collar.

'Excuse me,' he apologized. He had a fast, nervous delivery. 'Did I startle you? I'm terribly sorry. I'm Des Wyndham. I'm the Church of Ireland rector. I thought you were a woman.'

Too many quips occurred simultaneously to McCadden for him to locate the best one in time. 'I'm not,' he said simply.

'No, no,' Wyndham protested. 'You misunderstand me. I mean, I expected to find a woman. In some trouble. When I heard that someone in the village was asking about Hannah Fraule.'

McCadden raised his eyebrows. 'News leaks very fast around this area.'

'One of my parishioners was in the Templar's Well, you see. It's very popular. Particularly with the young. And deservedly so. The name is interesting also. The Knights Templar had a castle and a church in this area in the thirteenth century.'

'Right.'

'If you don't mind . . . I don't intend to be rude, but could I ask what the reasons are for your interest in Hannah Fraule?'

McCadden nodded agreeably. It was the most sensible request he'd heard all evening. Showing his ID and introducing himself, he explained, 'Hannah Fraule was murdered in West Cork on New Year's Eve.'

'Yes, yes,' the rector sighed. 'I read about it in the papers and saw the reports on television, of course.'

'I'm trying to fill the gaps in her life. She lived here during the thirties and forties.'

'Long before my time. I was born in 1970.'

'Before mine, too,' McCadden agreed. 'But here we are. And you came looking for me when you heard her name.'

'Yes,' Wyndham accepted. He took a deep breath. 'I wanted to meet you before you left the village, you see. I want to show you something. If you think it's worthwhile. It's too dark now, of course. Too late. But in the morning. Perhaps at ten? There's someone I'd like you to meet also.'

five

When McCadden got back to Dublin a little after nine o'clock, Frank Ryan was waiting for him disconsolately in his flat in Rathmines. Although he'd been trawling through public records until late in the evening, Ryan had been completely out of luck. And now he was so frustrated that even his appetite was off.

'Look,' he said defensively, 'I can't find any references to Harry Fraule or to Emily Fraule.'

'What about Hannah Fraule?' McCadden asked innocently.

'I haven't *looked* for Hannah Fraule,' Ryan exploded. 'I don't have time for *everything*.'

'Okay, Frank.'

'And I'm assuming that Fraule was the surname she took when she married. That's what you said. You asked me for her maiden name. And since, by definition, we don't know her maiden name yet, it wouldn't make any sense to start with her.'

'That sounds reasonable.'

'But look,' Ryan said again. 'What really bothers me is *Emily* Fraule. You gave me a date. January 15th 1927. And you gave me the location, Dublin. But I can tell you now, I'm certain there was no Emily Fraule born on that date. Are you sure of the details?'

McCadden shrugged. 'Her son had no doubts.'

'Maybe she lied to him about it. I mean, according to your notes, she concealed almost everything else. Or . . .' Ryan paused, drawing patterns with his fingers through a sprinkling of breadcrumbs on the surface of the table they were sitting at.

'Or what?' McCadden prompted.

'Or her name wasn't Emily *Fraule*,' it occurred to Ryan. 'Maybe she was fostered. Maybe she wasn't the couple's natural child. Or maybe Fraule wasn't *Harry's* surname. You know what we've got to do?'

'What?'

'I'm not going down to Cork.'

'Any reason why you should?'

'I'll get some of the lads down there to dig us out.'

'On what? I'm not following you, Frank.'

'We've got to start again, Carl,' Ryan insisted. 'Only this time we've got to start with *Siggs's* birth certificate. We know for certain that he was born in Cork, on August 1st 1948. His mother's name and occupation will be on it. And his father's. I guarantee that the woman's name wasn't Emily Fraule when she married. And I'll bet it's because her old man's name wasn't *Harry* Fraule.'

Ryan cheered up at the prospect of this new direction. Suddenly loosening up, he suggested a quick meal in one of the local restaurants and then a visit to a city-centre pub where he'd arranged to meet old friends, Dublin colleagues they'd both worked with in the past.

McCadden was reluctant to join him. Already tired, he had to be on the road by seven the next morning. And before he could even think of sleep, he had to draft a report for Special Branch, requesting information on the former republican prisoner Pius Eugene Shanahan and calling on their assistance in dealing with him. *Ask the limping man with the No. 1 haircut*, he'd remembered on the journey back to Dublin. This was what Ciaran Carthy, the spaced-out, grey-haired hippie in the village in West Cork, had invited him to do. At the time, it had sounded like a derisive throwaway, straight off the top of a clouded head. But possibly it was something more significant than that. He'd have to get one of the local investigating team to take another statement from Carthy. If Shanahan, with his aggressive desire to conceal Hannah Fraule's past, had also been spotted in the village prior to the old woman's murder, he was seriously implicated in the crime.

As he was drafting his report, though, McCadden made the mistake of casually asking Ryan if he fancied joining the new homicide squad and the subsequent discussion brought its own heat and momentum. Countless arguments, a city-centre pub, fifteen former colleagues, seven pints and ten hours later, he slept through the alarm. Eventually woken by Ryan, he showered, dressed quickly and left without breakfast.

Because it was Saturday morning the traffic was light. And the Reverend Wyndham's directions turned out to be remarkably easy to follow. Still, it was already ten-fifteen when he pulled up outside a small country church that was perched at the foot of a mountain, ten kilometres north of Naune.

The place was deserted. Its doors were locked. As the rector had explained, most Church of Ireland parishes had amalgamated in this area because of shrinking congregations, and many of the churches, like this one, were no longer in use.

Checking quickly around and then seeing nothing coming towards him on the approach roads, McCadden guessed that Wyndham had been and left, and was probably angry at himself for foolishly making hopeful appointments. He looked at the display on his mobile phone. He'd given the rector his number. But there were no calls, no messages.

He decided to wait another thirty minutes.

Dehydrated from the previous night's booze, he'd left Dublin without taking any liquid and had been too pushed for time to stop along the way. He wondered if the roadside pump he'd passed on the slight climb to the church was still working. He started walking down towards it, confident that he could keep the church in sight all the time, but he stopped again after a few paces, catching a creaking mechanical noise on the light wind. Seconds later, the Reverend Desmond Wyndham came round the corner by the pump, laboriously pedalling an old bicycle and weaving crazily as he lifted his right hand off the handlebars to wave at McCadden.

The rector was out of breath when he got to the church gates, his delivery even more hurried and broken than usual as a result. Dismounting gracelessly, his long legs skipping along the tarmac as he struggled to pull the bike to a stop, he called, 'Terribly sorry, inspector. I was afraid you'd left. No car. The tyres cut this morning. Couldn't arrange a lift in time. But still, it's a relief . . .'

'Your tyres were slashed?' McCadden asked.

Wyndham nodded briskly, as if it was a frequent but minor inconvenience. 'I'm afraid so.'

'Have you reported it to the local guards?'

'No time. Later.'

'Make sure you do.'

Wyndham released the padlock on the church gates and gestured to his left after entering the grounds, over to the side of the church building. It was a grave he wanted to show, McCadden realized. But whose? Calculating quickly, and giving himself the pleasure of a guess before the actual revelation, McCadden gambled on Harry Fraule. He hadn't quite figured out how a pillar of the local Roman Catholic community might come to be buried in a Protestant cemetery before Wyndham, hurrying excitedly ahead, stopped suddenly by a graveside and beckoned McCadden forward.

The headstone marking the plot had been defaced. Shattered by heavy blows at some stage, it had been carefully repaired and restored, although a small section from the top left-hand corner was still missing. Its surface had also been stained with spray paint. The obscene graffiti was recent, possibly no more than a few days old. Perhaps it was even another of those singular welcomes for the new millennium.

Despite the efforts of the vandals, the carved inscription on the headstone was still clear. It read:

In Loving Memory
of
Capt Albert Siggs MC
2nd Inniskilling Fusiliers
1915–48

His parents, who'd lived into old age and died long after him in the 1980s, were both buried in the same plot and remembered on the same stone.

After silent prayer while McCadden was studying the grave, Wyndham had recovered his breath and his composure.

'You must be confused, inspector,' he apologized. 'I'm terribly sorry. I realize that this can mean nothing to you. You must be wondering if you're wasting your time. And what on earth this has to do with Hannah Fraule.'

'No, I—'

'Please bear with me,' the rector hurried on. 'I did say that I was anxious for you to meet someone. Someone who will put all this into context for you. Far better than I can. In fact, I only know about Hannah Fraule through him. I'm afraid he's in Thomastown, however. It's not a great distance, perhaps thirty kilometres, but as I no longer have transport . . .'

'I'll drive,' McCadden offered.

'And my bicycle . . .'

'We can throw it in the boot.'

'Splendid.'

six

Like a nervous schoolboy on a forbidden outing, Wyndham talked incessantly for the journey. He worked his way feverishly through the local fauna, the bicentennial commemoration two years earlier of the 1798 Rebellion, and the absence of millennium bugs. Anything, in other words, to prevent McCadden asking questions and to avoid spoiling the purpose of the trip with what he considered his own second-hand account. But he got too involved in his own distractions. When they finally reached Thomastown, he was enthusing about the local opera festival and had to be reminded of his function before directing McCadden to a hospice on the outskirts.

The hospital's staff had already prepared a small room where an old man sat by the window in a wheelchair, waiting with his back to the door. He didn't turn when he heard his visitors come in. Thin and sharp-featured, with hard blue eyes, he seemed unfriendly. When Wyndham anxiously made the introductions, he didn't offer his hand. He just nodded sharply.

'This is Richard Etchingham, inspector,' Wyndham explained. 'Like Captain Siggs, he was also an officer in the Inniskilling Fusiliers.'

Etchingham's voice was clipped, lacking in any warmth. 'Merely a lieutenant in my case.'

The rector took this information as a sharp correction, a warning to either tread more precisely through the facts or stay quiet altogether. He smiled apologetically. 'I had better allow Richard . . .'

But an awkward silence followed.

The rector immediately abandoned his own advice. 'We were out to see Albert's grave, Richard.'

'How is it?'

'Fine. Splendid.' The rector was a poor liar. If he fancied himself as a filter between the old man and the cruelties of the world, he was inefficient at it.

Etchingham clearly didn't believe him. Hard-bitten, disillusioned, too old for enthusiasm or outrage, he probably thought Wyndham a fool. He hadn't enough evidence to judge McCadden yet, but he was obviously inclining in the same direction. 'What exactly did you want to know, inspector?'

Since it was pointless trying to run against it, McCadden decided to confirm the old man's jaundiced view of the world. He got the impression that Etchingham had been reduced by the years to two modes: silence and sourness. And his silence was of no use. He asked, 'Were you a close friend of Albert Siggs, Mr Etchingham?'

A lifetime's caution had left the old man with the facility of politely giving nothing away. 'We grew up together.'

'Prior to today, I've heard only one thing about him: that he abandoned his young wife and child.'

'Do you believe that?'

'I know nothing about the man.'

There was another silence, but this time it crackled with tension.

Fretting that things were crashing out of control and splintering in all the wrong directions, Wyndham jumped fussily in. 'What the inspector is really interested in, Richard—'

Etchingham gave him a withering look. 'I'm quite sure the inspector is capable of his own explanations. Are you, inspector?'

McCadden smiled slightly. But he'd already tired of the dance and went for something more disruptive than cool formalities. 'How did Albert Siggs die?'

The old man stared at him, unmoved. 'Why do you ask?'

'The 2nd Inniskillings were evacuated from Dunkirk in 1940, weren't they, when the Belgian Army surrendered and the Germans threatened to overrun the British Expeditionary Force?'

'The rector promised me a policeman. But perhaps you're a military historian.'

'My father was in the Parachute Regiment. He dropped behind enemy lines into France on D-Day and fought later at Arnhem.'

'Did he survive?'

'I hope so. I was born in 1960.'

A slight smile played for a moment on the old man's lips as he realized that his own crustiness had betrayed him, but he didn't seem to advance his mood. He clicked back to his original question, without adding any warmth to the query. 'Why did you ask how Albert died?'

'Partly because it's my job, Mr Etchingham,' McCadden explained. 'Unfortunately, it's one of the first questions that occurs to me. Partly because he obviously survived the war and died so shortly afterwards, which arouses curiosity, and sadness. But partly also because of a vague, uneasy feeling I have. There are no details on his headstone.'

'He drowned. On a stretch of the river that ran through our adjoining estates.'

'In 1948, wasn't it?'

'Yes.'

'What month?'

'Early January. The inquest decided that it was a boating accident.'

'You didn't agree with that?'

'We had mastered that river since we were boys together. We fished it. We swam in it. We boated on it. We knew it intimately, in all its moods, at every hour of the day. Albert could handle a boat as competently and as safely as you can probably handle a car. He enjoyed an occasional drink, but he hadn't taken any on the night of his death. They found no alcohol in his system. He wasn't wounded in the war. He had no disability that might have hindered him. Nevertheless, they maintained that his war experiences were probably a factor. Delayed reaction. What I believe they now call post-traumatic stress. He collapsed, hit his head on the prow of the boat, fell overboard and drowned. They said that he was alone in the boat. But this is something that he never did. We always went together. They hinted that certain circumstances in his life had contributed to making him depressed, and possibly suicidal, at the time. So you see, the verdict of accidental death was really a kindness. To avoid the stigma of suicide.'

'What circumstances?'

'How well do you know your social history, inspector?'

'You mean, as it might apply to Captain Siggs?'

'Naturally.'

'I think as the son of a former British paratrooper living in southern Ireland I'd have some understanding of the life of Protestant landowners in the same society. You were outsiders.'

Etchingham nodded slowly, accepting the point. 'By then the war had ended, of course,' he said. 'But you were right. As you said, the regiment was withdrawn from Dunkirk in 1940. It's where Albert gained his Military Cross, on the retreat to the beaches. For saving my life, actually, and the lives of many others under his command. I sat out the rest of the war in London, recovering from my wounds. Albert went back to liberate mainland Europe. But that was all in the past. We had both resigned our commissions. We were settling down to being the eldest sons of County Wexford farmers again. There were disappointments. Times were difficult. On occasions we were forced to sell to the Land Commission to ensure survival. But there were also times of great joy and the happiest day of all was the one on which Albert and my sister, Penelope, announced their engagement. I'm sure with your comprehensive knowledge of social history, inspector, you'll appreciate that this was more than a romantic occasion. We were Scottish and Welsh and English in origin. We had been here for centuries, and yet were still considered outsiders. We lived in cold, isolated houses, largely hated by the natives. We were colonists still. Our only prospect of community lay with each other. Our only hope of survival was in intermarriage. The engagement of Albert and Penelope gave hope for the future, a sense of securing what we had fought for so tenaciously in the war. And then . . . Then Albert fell in love.'

Etchingham paused. With slow, deliberate movements, his hands as steady as a surgeon's, he searched his pockets, slipped a cigarette from the packet he took out, placed the filter between his lips and closed and returned the packet. He didn't light up. He stared through the window, looking out on the front courtyard of the hospice.

Wyndham thought of moving, perhaps to offer a light, but he managed to restrain himself.

McCadden waited.

After a while, without taking his gaze from the window, Etchingham found a box of matches, struck one and put the flame to the tobacco. He smoked the entire cigarette, down to the filter, in silence, and only seemed to remember his audience when he needed an ashtray afterwards. Wyndham, blessed with an approved role at last, immediately jumped up to be of service. Etchingham crushed the filter tip and stared across at McCadden. His eyes seemed to be resentful.

'At first,' he continued then, 'I thought Albert was worried about the management of the farm, concerned about the family's difficult economic situation. As you'll appreciate, inspector, the symptoms can be somewhat similar. He was distracted. He took little pleasure in the things which had previously entertained him. He had no appetite, for food or for sport. No application. He failed to keep appointments. He discouraged my company. Because I owed my life to him, because my little sister's happiness was at stake – oh, for any number of admirable reasons – I appointed myself a sleuth. I dreamed of being the hero, of repairing what had been broken. I secretly followed Albert. I feared he was in debt, that he was being crushed by some dark financial burden. I wanted to rescue him, as he had once rescued me. As I quickly discovered, however, it wasn't furtive encounters with money-lenders or bailiffs or blackmailers that he was slipping away to. He was meeting a girl.

'I was more astonished than outraged at first. Unfaithfulness was the last vice I would have accused him of. Disloyalty. It was not in his character. He was handsome, yes, but also steadfast. Surprise quickly wears off, however. And *then* I was outraged. It wasn't just the pain that this would cause my sister, the trouble it would create between our respective families. It was also the identity of the girl. She was the daughter of a publican in Naune, from a family of staunch Roman Catholics, a girl whose father was said to have some vaguely disreputable past in Dublin, perhaps with the IRA. Her name was Emily Fraule. From every conceivable perspective, the liaison was impossible. Both families would bitterly oppose it. The girl, at twenty, was far younger than Albert, who was in his early thirties by then. They could not continue living in the area once the relationship was exposed.

'I hoarded my secret through the last month of 1947. The Christmas festivities were a charade for me. As they must have been for Albert. In the New Year, I could tolerate it no longer. I challenged him one night. But as a friend. Because I had prepared and disciplined myself, cautioned myself to be constructive. I challenged him without bitterness or accusation. I told him that I had no idea what attraction, what passion, had first impelled him. I accepted that it must have been strong. I let him know that I was aware of the terrible subterfuge that was forced on him. But I also warned him that this . . . well, this domestic, small-scale attempt at reconciling our two major traditions in Ireland was doomed to failure. The passion would wither. And the attraction, too. If they eloped or married, nothing would be left within a year except regret. And their regret would be so intense that it would turn them against each other, their passion decaying into a tendency to deny what had happened, into a desire to conceal the evidence of a fatal mistake.

'Albert listened to me quietly. He assured me that he understood my motives. And then he informed me that it was too late. The girl was already with child and they had secretly married in a registry office. A great many emotions swirled together inside me. Jealousy. We had been so close and had anticipated remaining so close. Now he belonged to another. Rage. At his indifference to me. At the futility of all my spying and scheming. Despair. Desperation. I've thought about the cocktail many times since that night. If one or other of the elements had been absent, I might not have struck out at him. But I did strike out. We were in his boat, on the river that flowed through both our estates. He ducked to avoid my blow. He was much more the natural fighter than I was. But he slipped on the wet surface of the boat. He lost his footing. He fell back, hitting his head against the prow. He was immediately knocked unconscious. But I didn't go to his aid. I was too angry with him. I slipped over the side of the boat and swam the short distance to the shore. When I left him, he was still lying there, still unconscious. This is why they brought in the verdict of accidental death, you see. There was no evidence of any attack. Nothing but a blow to the back of his head from the prow and the marks where he had slipped. The boat must have lurched afterwards. Hit a bank, perhaps, or a floating log. He clearly slipped over the edge . . .'

Etchingham fell silent again, too lost in his recollections, his remorse, to be even aware of the need for a cigarette.

On the other side of the room, obviously hearing the story for the first time, the rector looked anguished, so drained of life and colour that he seemed ill. His thin face was deathly white. His lower lip was bleeding where one of his teeth had gnawed it. His hands were violently gripping the seat he was sitting on.

'I never admitted my part in Albert's death,' Etchingham went on, in a tired voice now, lower than before. 'They hurried through the inquest. The scandal of the relationship between Albert and Emily Fraule was common knowledge by then. The general opinion, never publicly confessed, was that Albert had actually been killed, probably by the girl's father, Harry Fraule, and some local thugs. But it wasn't only the Fraules who wanted to quickly close the book on the episode. Albert's parents, also. Penelope. My own parents. I couldn't bring myself to speak, to open their wounds even wider with my words. I waited for the police to come and interview me. They never did. No one thought of me in the slightest way in connection with the tragedy. Even when the inquest was concluded and the verdict given, I waited for a summons, a sudden accusation. I saw in the innocent looks of others the knowledge that I possessed only myself. Guilt. It drove me away from home. I travelled restlessly, outwardly easier among strangers who could never guess my secret.

'My parents died almost three decades ago. Penelope passed away in 1995. I came home to see to her estate. Such are the ironies of fate that I suffered an accident while on that visit and I'm now chained here, like Prometheus, longing for death. I still wait for the police to come and interview me. Three years ago, when the rector here told me that a stranger was in Naune, a woman, asking about Hannah Fraule, young Emily's mother, I decided to unburden myself, to tell my story before I died and confess my part before it was buried with me. But I was cheated even of that. The woman never came to see me.'

'Woman?' McCadden echoed. 'What woman?'

Wyndham cleared his throat, but couldn't manage to speak afterwards. His lower jaw trembled when he opened his mouth.

Etchingham looked across at him contemptuously. Obviously, he had no patience with the cleric. Perhaps he'd tried to confide in the young man before and had been awkwardly discouraged.

'You mistook me for a woman last night,' McCadden remembered. 'Is that what you meant?'

Wyndham nodded.

'You thought it was the same woman returning?'

Wyndham nodded again.

'Do you have a name for her?'

'She gave me a card,' the rector explained. 'A card. A business card. I wasn't alone. I mean, she gave it . . . to others, to many people in the village. I brought it along for you.'

His hands shaking, he nervously searched his pockets and eventually found his wallet where it had always been, in the lining of his jacket. He took out a crumpled white business card and offered it to McCadden.

'As Mr Etchingham says, it was . . . well, almost three years ago. I believe she . . . I believe she wanted to locate Hannah Fraule. Some question of a will. Some . . .'

'Right.'

'Perhaps she succeeded. She never returned to discuss the matter with me. I doubt if she ever returned to the village.'

McCadden accepted the card. It read 'Kelly McConnell, Private Investigator', and it had the address of offices in Dorset Street, in the centre of Dublin. It raised an awful lot of questions in his mind, but he put them aside for the moment, along with the card itself, to finish his conversation with Etchingham.

'Do you know what happened to the girl, Mr Etchingham?' he asked. 'Emily Fraule?'

Etchingham shook his head. 'She had already left the area before the inquest was completed. I assume she was spirited away to pass her days in a convent and that her baby was sent to an orphanage. It's what Papists did with erring young women in those days.'

'They weren't unique,' McCadden pointed out. 'I know of Protestants who exiled pregnant daughters to England and never communicated with them again.'

'My knowledge is not as wide as yours, of course.'

'Emily Fraule didn't enter a convent. She went to live in Cork, where she raised her son as a single mother through tough times. You might be interested to know that she also called him Albert. Not Fraule, either. Albert Siggs.'

Etchingham considered this new information for a long time, thinking on lives as they might have been except for one crucial encounter, until he finally gave expression to an old dream once shared by two young army officers. 'Is he a military man?'

McCadden shook his head. 'No.'

'Then it hardly matters, does it? All of it.'

'He's a sphinx,' McCadden offered.

'I have never met one.'

'He set me a riddle, which has baffled him from childhood. His mother is sitting in a room with two other mature women when a young girl passes by the window. "Do you see her?" one woman says. The second asks, "Did you see her yesterday?" And Emily Fraule warns, "Wait until you see her tomorrow." '

Etchingham obviously had a great deal more experience of the bitterness of romance than McCadden would ever accumulate. He solved the riddle almost instantly. With a sour smile playing again on his lips, he looked out of the window into the distance. 'The girl has just taken a lover, inspector,' he explained. 'Today she is flaunting her joy, because yesterday she lay with her man, but tomorrow she'll discover the bitter pain of being abandoned and pregnant in a repressive society.'

'Maybe you could write and explain it to the younger Albert,' McCadden suggested. 'As I said earlier, he believes his father abandoned himself and his mother. A necessary fiction, I suppose. There are probably not many people who would welcome the truth about Captain Siggs, but I'm sure his son is one of them.'

'Perhaps.'

'One more thing, Mr Etchingham. Do you know what happened to Emily's parents, Hannah and Harry Fraule, after the death of Captain Siggs?'

'They left the area shortly afterwards. Their businesses were sold.'

'Do you know why? Or where they went?'

'I didn't enquire,' Etchingham said. 'I had little interest, of course, but no one would have told me, anyway. They belonged to the other side. You'll have to ask one of them. Each tribe tells only its own stories, inspector. The narratives are parallel. So we continue glaring at each other across no-man's-land.'

seven

The address given on the business card was now a shop selling comic books and graphic novels. Kelly McConnell's agency was listed in the Golden Pages, and the size of its display advertisement suggested that it was a large and successful company, but its doors were closed for the weekend and a sweet little voice on the answering service only asked for messages.

This was frustrating enough, but to make matters worse, Frank Ryan had disappeared.

With the weather staying wet and dull, McCadden passed a dead Saturday afternoon working again through the file, vainly searching his notes for an angle he might have missed or a possible direction he'd overlooked. He took nothing from it except a slight headache.

At four-thirty he drove across city for a meeting with a Special Branch inspector named Phelim Bourke on the subject of Pius Eugene Shanahan. According to Bourke, Special Branch had loosely monitored Shanahan's movements since his prison release. Given the political climate close surveillance was unacceptable, but in any case, Shanahan had initially maintained a high profile. In the two weeks either side of Christmas Day, he'd given a series of interviews, fairly triumphant in tone, justifying the campaigns he'd been involved in, particularly the bombing of English seaside resorts and cities throughout the 1980s. Shanahan was an explosives expert. He didn't *plant* bombs – that was left to more dispensable menials within the organization; he designed and constructed them. In the interviews, his attitude to violence mixed pragmatism with what sounded sickeningly like relish.

Most of this material was already familiar to McCadden, but there were two new pieces of information in Bourke's report. Both were significant. Shanahan had been born in County Donegal in 1950 to a staunch republican family, the kind that traced their authenticating lineage with as much neurosis as the English nobility, in this case all the way back to the martyr Eamon Brannigan, who now had a street named after him in central Dublin. Shanahan's mother was Deirdre Rudican, an unusual surname with faint echoes that sent McCadden searching back through his notes, until he happened again on Joseph Mary Rudican, one of the two men arrested for the break-in at Fraules public house in Naune in January 1948.

'Was Rudican an IRA activist, Phelim?' McCadden wondered.

'Yeah, he was interned here during the Second World War. He emigrated to England in the fifties. I'm not sure what happened to him.'

'Was the raid on Fraules pub an IRA operation?'

'That I don't know.'

'Could you check it out for me?'

'Sure.'

A promising connection. But for the moment, this was as far as McCadden was likely to get. Since the New Year, the whereabouts of Pius Shanahan were unknown. Special Branch had lost him. He wasn't at any of the addresses associated with him. He couldn't be contacted through his political party, Sinn Fein. He'd missed two successive appointments for radio interviews. McCadden knew, of course, that Shanahan had been in the village of Naune, co-ordinating the local vigilantes, on the previous night, Friday 14 January. Otherwise, his movements were a mystery.

McCadden had two further questions.

'When did he start shaving his head, Phelim?' he asked.

'A few years ago. I think when he was in prison in England.'

'And how did he come by the limp?'

'When they caught up with him in London, he put up a fight. He was shot in the left hip.'

'Okay. Will you get back to me on the pub raid?'

'As soon as I can.'

And after that, there was nothing for McCadden to do but wait. To kill time, he went to the cinema for an early evening show, successfully avoiding the kids' movies, but ending up instead with the couples, surrounded by crackling sweet wrappings, rustling popcorn, slurping Pepsis and giggling intimacies. The soundtrack on the film offered only intermittent competition.

Driving back to his flat a little after nine, planning a few hours' reading and an early night, he was irritated to find that another car was squatting on his parking space until he pulled alongside it and recognized Frank Ryan's registration plate.

The sergeant was in the small kitchen of McCadden's flat, eating a takeaway he'd just collected. Cantonese beef, with fried rice and prawn crackers. At best, this was an uncertain sign. The big man's appetite could be healthy whether his results were good or bad, his mood elated or downbeat. But since it was unfair to press him for reports while his mouth was still full, McCadden invented a ten-minute errand to the nearby shops for groceries he'd supposedly forgotten.

When he got back, Ryan had tidied away the food, the cartons and the brown paper bags and had a pot of coffee ready to drink. They sat in the living room. McCadden anxiously considered the packet of doughnuts Ryan carried in with him and decided to start before the sergeant's mouth was seduced again.

'Well?' he asked.

Ryan sat in an armchair, holding a mug of coffee. With his free right hand he slipped a notebook from his inside jacket pocket. The pad was already open on the relevant page. 'Albert Siggs's mother,' he said. 'Her name was Emily *Rull*.'

McCadden was astonished. Almost outraged. 'Rull?' he cried. 'Who the hell is Rull? How can it be Rull?'

'There it is on Albert's birth certificate in Cork, Carl. Name and surname and maiden name of mother: Emily Siggs, formerly Rull. Name and surname of father, Captain Albert Siggs, deceased. Emily was born, as we all know, in January 1927. Easy to locate her own birth certificate, now that we have the correct surname. Name and surname of father: Harold Rull. Name and surname and maiden name of mother: Hannah Rull, formerly Fraule. Harry and Hannah – they don't sit too easily together, do they? – married in 1925, two years earlier. They married in a Catholic church in Donnybrook, in Dublin. Very upmarket. Particularly then. Harold Edward Rull's occupation is described as businessman. Hannah May Fraule's occupation is described as businesswoman. There's more.'

While Ryan put away his coffee mug and turned the pages of his notepad, McCadden calmed himself down a little and reflected. From the early 1930s onwards, the couple had used only the surname Fraule for social and business purposes. It meant that the other one – Rull – must have carried some history away with it from Dublin. More than likely, Harry had been a fugitive of some sort.

Ryan settled on a page. Although he was obviously familiar with the details he had written down, he still raised his eyebrows and gave an ironic little laugh before he read them. 'The good news,' he promised, 'is that there's only one registered birth of a Hannah May Fraule for the relevant period. Even better news is that I found it.'

'But the bad news?'

'The bad news, Carl, is that Hannah May Fraule died in infancy.'

'You're joking.'

'No. Three weeks after her birth, on November 7th 1906. Her mother died a few months later, from complications arising out of pleurisy, in the South Dublin Union Hospital, popularly known as a workhouse. The father of Hannah May was unknown. No surviving next of kin. And yet . . . Hannah May Fraule went on to get married in 1925, as we know. She had a daughter of her own in 1927. *And* she was able to present an authenticated birth certificate on each of the occasions it was required. The same details as the dead infant. October 16th 1906. Coombe Hospital. Someone set the woman up with a new identity, Carl. I don't know who did it, but it must have been with the collusion of the authorities. The certificates are not forgeries done by amateurs. They're official documents. And worst of all, I still don't know who the woman was who lived most of her adult life as Hannah May Fraule. I've rattled a lot of cages to get this stuff on a Saturday, but that's it for the moment. The rest is buried. Maybe on Monday I'll go hunting down Harry Rull. I mean, he must've known that the woman he was marrying wasn't Hannah May Fraule. What do you think?'

PART THREE

january, 2000

Travelling south from Dundee to Birmingham about a week earlier, I'd suddenly started shaking with nerves. The rhythm of the train I was on had warned me against making the trip. The more I'd listened to it, the closer I'd come to panic. Other passengers had started looking at me suspiciously. Two kids, running up and down the aisles for most of the journey, had sat opposite me and stared. And an old woman, pretending to read a book, had forgotten to keep turning the pages. Or maybe they'd started looking at me before I'd got the sweats. Maybe their nosiness had rattled my nerves. I couldn't be sure. It was always possible that someone would recognize me from the past. I'd been in Birmingham before. It was a long time ago, almost twenty-six years, but the date and the events had stuck in people's minds. In November 1974, the IRA had blown up some pubs in the city. I hadn't been involved in that operation. I'd been with another unit in England. But I happened to be in Birmingham at the time and I'd got caught up in the security sweep. So travelling south from Dundee last week . . . Well, I hadn't been scared of torture. They'd beaten me badly in the past before they'd finally jailed me. I'd been scared of failure. Scared of leaving the work undone.

Getting off the train and hurrying to find a taxi, I'd kept looking over my shoulders, convinced I was being tailed. But I'd stuck to my plan, as I'd been trained to. I'd gone first to the airport and picked up the return tickets to Dublin I'd already reserved. Then I'd hired a car. Using false documents. Different sets for each. The man I'd been looking for lived in Edgbaston. The place was unfamiliar. And it was posh. You got noticed, if you were a stranger and you didn't have designer clothes. I hadn't fancied it. And yet I'd driven myself on. It was a debt, you see. And the payment of a debt is one of the most honourable and one of the most pleasurable things in life. I'd always respected loyalty. My happiest memory of all is being given the job of topping a snout in Belfast when I was just a raw kid. A republican Judas, who'd grassed to the security forces. No, I shouldn't exaggerate. I didn't top the traitor myself. That was someone else's privilege. I was just part of the unit that snatched the snout. But that was honour enough.

These days I'm working alone, of course. Times have changed. Not everyone can stay active in the field while the political campaign is being fought and victory within grasp. I was alone in West Cork on New Year's Eve. I was alone in Birmingham. And I'd wished I wasn't. My hands shaking, my sweat soaking my clothes and dripping from my face, I'd driven out to the classy estate in Edgbaston. I've never known such bad nerves. But when I'd parked, trying to calm myself by getting my breathing right, it suddenly occurred to me what was wrong. Came to me. Out of nowhere. Would I enjoy doing it to a man? That was the question. Would I get an erection, the way I had with the old woman in West Cork? Would I masturbate afterwards? The thought had disgusted me. Not able to shake it out of my mind, I'd actually got physically sick in the car. And of course I'd known then, for sure, that the sequence wasn't right. The man shouldn't be second. Birmingham was the wrong stop. Accepting this, I'd driven straight back to the airport and taken that flight out to Dublin.

Now, I was at peace again.

To my right, through the open window of the car, I heard church bells tolling for a funeral. I blessed myself and said a silent prayer for the deceased. I didn't bow my head as I should, because I was watching the front door of a house. I knew that I'd be forgiven for this slight omission. Obligation always excuses a lack of strict observance. I'm not a stickler for petty rules. There are more important things in life.

The house I was watching, in Dublin's well-heeled Donnybrook, belonged to a woman called Lucy Cuccini. She lived there with her sidekick, a thug by the name of Christy Sweeney. He was due to leave shortly. Not in response to the bells, of course. He wouldn't be going to church. Every Monday evening, Sweeney goes downtown to a seedy workingmen's club to drink and play darts and plan some fresh scams. He doesn't belong to this respectable neighbourhood. His tart doesn't either. Dirty money has bought them in. Money from whores and drugs and pornography. Even worse, money made in England.

I watched Sweeney slamming the front door as he left the house. I wondered if the gangster was in bad humour. After being scratched by his Lucy, maybe. Sweeney pulled sharply away in his BMW, tyre rubber screeching on the driveway. Although the house was unprotected now, it still wasn't the best time to carry through a raid. It was too early. I would've preferred the middle of the night, when everyone else was sleeping. I could wake her in her bedroom, hand over her wet mouth. That would excite me. The dark. The warmth of the bedroom. Hopefully, just after she'd had a bath. But perfection isn't often possible. Chances have to be taken when they present themselves. She wasn't alone much. Not for certain, so you could predict it. Except for Monday evenings.

My car was parked inside the estate, hidden among a line of others that belonged to outsiders attending the nearby requiem mass. This was clever. It pleased me. When I stepped out of the car, I closed the door and hurried away, as if I was late for the service. There was no one else around. But I kept my head down anyway. All the houses were detached. They were unprotected by walls or fences. Some had low hedges marking the boundaries. Turning off the footpath at Lucy's place, I slipped into the shadows and pulled a balaclava over my face. I was already wearing gloves. Otherwise my dress was appropriate, without being a giveaway. I had on black jeans and a black leather jacket. The balaclava should have been black, too. But I only owned a navy one. The clash of colours annoyed me.

I'd expected Lucy's home to have CCTV cameras at the front and back doors. It had surprised me the first time I'd discovered it hadn't. She had a security light at the rear that was activated by movement underneath it. They were pretty useless. Flying birds sometimes set them off. Prowling cats set them off. But in any case, I had a plan to neutralize it. I had Lucy's telephone number. I had a stolen mobile phone. I rang one with the other. Just for five or six tones. Enough to have her scurrying to answer, either in the front hall or the front upstairs bedroom. While she was there, she wouldn't notice the light clicking on in the rear.

The back door was locked, of course. I expected that. The windows were closed. I expected that. Even though I was caught in the light now, no one would see me. I knew the place wasn't overlooked. Quietly taking an empty wheelie bin with me, I pressed my back against the wall between the door and one of the windows and then violently pushed the bin away from me, so that it toppled and clattered across the concrete path. The noise brought Lucy to the back door. She lifted the blind. She peered out. She couldn't see me. She couldn't see anything, except that something had knocked over her bin and tweaked her light. Not the wind. There was no wind. Dogs? The neighbours' inbred show mutts? She cautiously opened the door to check.

I grabbed the door handle and jerked it towards me, at the same time swinging around the door and bursting right into her. She was too startled to react. She was too off-balance to resist. She started to scream. I stifled that. I punched her hard in the lower stomach, driving the wind out of her. A little gasp. That's all she managed. She doubled up. She was coughing, half gagging. I knocked her unconscious with a blow to the back of her neck. I pushed her inside and closed the door behind us.

We were in the kitchen. I don't like kitchens. They unsettle me. They're too clean. No. I have respect for cleanliness. They're too bright. They're functional. Like robots. Without a soul. The smells irritate me. Holding Lucy up, I opened the double doors in front of me. They led to a dining area. Very impressive. A bit more homely. But not enough. Not my style yet. After that, through more double doors, there was a comfortable sitting room. I dragged Lucy in there. I gagged her with masking tape. I tied her legs with red curtain cord. A nice touch, that. I used the same material to tie her hands behind her back. I propped her against a red leather couch. She was sitting on the carpet.

I settled myself in an armchair opposite her. I sat on its edge, leaning forward, looking at her. She was fifty. I knew that. She'd only been twenty-four back in 1974. She was just eighteen when she hitched up with his High Royalness in 1968. HR. She wasn't good-looking. She thought she was. She'd had a lot of facelifts. Her hair had been dyed a lot of times. At least she was wearing a dress, I saw. Light blue. I prefer that. Not the colour. A dress. With buttons all the way down the front. I don't like trousers on women. I hate jeans. How coarse they are. Under her thin dress, her breasts were swelling with her breathing.

When she started coming round, there was a look of pain on her face, twisting the shape of her lips, and I felt myself getting excited already. She reminded me of Christ's suffering on the cross. The way it's usually painted. Her head resting like that on her left shoulder. Her eyes looking pleadingly upwards. What she saw was the balaclava, the black leather jacket. She didn't see a person. She saw a warrior. An avenger. It scared her. It confused her. Who are you? her eyes asked. I didn't mind talking to her. My voice is pleasant. And I wanted her to understand why she had to suffer. That was important.

But first, I'd printed something out for her. I took two sheets of typing paper from my jacket pocket. I unfolded them. I separated them. I looked at them again. I liked them. Then I turned the first one towards her. My best work. The crucified Amazon. Did it make sense to her? Did she see the connection between herself and the old woman in West Cork? She obviously did. She started crazily shaking her head from side to side. Denying the logical conclusion from the evidence. But they all do that. Who are you? her eyes asked desperately again. I reversed the first sheet of paper and turned the second towards her. I watched her read. Did she understand? 'Sometimes I'm an empress, and sometimes I'm a queen; Simnel is my first name, and Banbury's where I've been.' That's what the note said. Did she understand? If she didn't, I wasn't surprised. The guards hadn't understood my previous notes, either. The crime correspondents don't understand. They've all lost touch. With the past. They have to be reminded. But Lucy understood enough. That was the important thing for now. That was what allowed the ceremony to proceed. I saw the recognition of retribution in her eyes. I saw her own awareness of her sins. And I was kind enough to confirm it with my words.

I slipped from the armchair then and knelt on the carpet in front of her. I reached out to finger the top button on her dress. With my left hand I had to adjust the crotch of my jeans, because I was already getting hard. She shrank away from me. I didn't mind that. She was right to be so scared. But then she started to struggle. That was something I couldn't tolerate. It made my work impossible. I took a flick knife from my jacket. I jerked it open and I held the point of its blade to her neck. After that she stayed still. She started crying. Which was okay. I loosened the buttons on her dress, one by one, until I reached the waist. I never need to go beyond that. I didn't take the dress off her shoulders. I opened the unbuttoned front, exposed the blue brassiere underneath. The look was that of a mother suckling an infant. Tender. I warmed my gloved hands by rubbing them together before putting my left palm against her ribs. Then I slipped upwards, under her brassiere, levering it away, until it popped off the top of her bust. But I saw with disgust that she had unnatural breasts. They'd been enlarged. By silicon. They didn't droop like they should. They stood out, like footballs. I don't really like footballs. They bring back memories of school. Of public parks and games in driving rain. I felt my erection going. And that angered me.

I closed my eyes and brought my face towards her. I didn't touch her. Not yet. I don't fancy caressing plastic. Or whatever it was. I could smell her fear from her armpits. That helped me again. I opened my eyes to locate the nipple of her right breast. I reached for it with my mouth, knowing that at least the nipple couldn't be artificial. I closed my lips around it and sucked. I loved the way it hardened, even though she wasn't enjoying the experience. Her body couldn't help responding. I stroked it gently with my tongue. Just fooling her body. Just until her mind was starting to convince her that this was all I wanted and she relaxed a little, giving it to me. When she was good and loosened out, I took the nipple into my mouth again. I sucked it in, past the teeth. And then released it. Sucked it in. And released it. Sucked it in.

And snapped my teeth together in a savage bite while nicking the flesh with the knife at the same time.

She howled so fiercely that it came back off the gag and almost choked her. Her body recoiled from the pain. But that made the pain worse. Her breast was still tightly clenched in my teeth. Blood spurted from the wound. Into my mouth. Up my nostrils. Across my face. I thought I was going to ejaculate. But that needed a rhythm. A number of strokes. Just as the biting needed a rhythm. A number of strokes. The interesting thing is, you can't really sever anything with human teeth. They're too blunt. They don't puncture. I learned that first from Hannah Fraule and checked it in the manuals afterwards. That's why I use the knife as well, but always at the same time as the bite, so there's no distinction. Anyway. I drank the blood. I opened my mouth. To breathe. To bite again. I wondered how many cuts would be needed. I was slightly put off by the thought that I might be hacking into silicon as well as natural flesh. A lapse in concentration. And I paid for it. I never completed the bite. The breast was torn away from me by her rejection. My teeth snapped painfully together. And I heard a car pulling up outside. Or not directly outside. Next door? I hoped.

I held the knife again to her throat. She was going to die anyway. It didn't matter to me when. No. It did matter. Sequence matters. If I'd learned anything from Birmingham, I'd learned that. First the severed breast, then the death. But my arm jerked so violently when I heard the front door opening that I almost killed her unintentionally. The knife slipped along her shoulder, slashing her dress, the bra strap, the flesh underneath, spurting blood on to the material. I heard her name being called. 'Lucy?' Urgently. Fearfully. It was Sweeney. Back already? Why? I couldn't wait to ask. I couldn't match Sweeney in a fight, not even with a knife. With a gun? Note for future operations.

I pushed off my knees. The double doors I'd come through were still open. Both sets. Back through the dining area. Back through the kitchen. Out the rear door. The light came on, catching me in flight. I sprinted. Around the side. I wondered if I had time to make it back to the car. It was only down the street. But I had to cross by the front of the house again. At least it wasn't awkwardly parked. Unless things had changed. Two teenage girls stepped on to the footpath, coming from a house. They screamed, seeing the balaclava. Maybe the knife, too. I was past them before they figured it out. I was fumbling with the car keys in the driver's door. At least the car was facing in the right direction. Sitting in, firing the engine, I caught a glimpse of a wild pursuing figure in my wing mirror as I slammed the stick into first gear and pulled away. Sweeney. Mad Sweeney. But I was free of him.

I had to force myself to calm down and ease off the accelerator once I was clear of the estate. They would never find me. They didn't know me. I'd even left my notes behind. So what? So what? They couldn't read.

one

Kelly McConnell was a breezy thirty-eight-year-old. She oozed self-confidence. With a staff of fifteen working for her and a business constantly expanding, she was entitled to it. Sections of her operation were still devoted to the staples of the private investigator – sexual infidelity and missing persons – but her own expertise, and a sharp eye for the real openings, had allowed her to corner the market in the more lucrative area of electronic security. The fact was, contemporary businesses were a lot more vulnerable to hackers and pirates than to frenzied guys in balaclavas waving shotguns in the air. She'd made herself an expert in the field. Her enterprise had made her rich. And her wealth had made her confident.

She had a disconcerting style, more common to Americans, of punching through the formalities and getting straight to the point. When her secretary showed McCadden into her high-rise, high-tech personal office in the Financial Services Centre, McConnell nodded at him curtly and demanded 'What the hell took you so long?' before rising to shake his hand. As if she'd been waiting for him all morning. Or all her life.

McCadden dallied with the second possibility. Her self-confidence made the woman attractive. Blonde, brash and sexy, she didn't need much assistance anyway, but her self-assurance added a kind of sheen to the image. And the environment was seductive, too. The glass-walled office, looking out over the river Liffey and the bustling heart of Dublin, was bright and cool. A welcome shift of mood after the gloom of decayed villages, Gallipoli, Dunkirk and rural repression.

But the odd greeting also posed a problem which McCadden had to solve without clumsily exposing his ignorance. She didn't know him personally. She was simply expecting a police officer.

'The standard excuse,' he offered. 'I got here as quickly as I could.'

She had a sense of humour. But not a great deal of time to indulge it. She smiled briefly. 'Would you like a drink?'

'Coffee,' McCadden requested. 'If it's fresh. Not from those awful machines in the corridors.'

'Colombian, Kenyan or Java?' she challenged him.

'The richer the better. Java?'

She buzzed out for a pot, two mugs and a selection of confectioneries. When she lifted her finger off the intercom she said, 'I like people who know what they want, inspector. It saves a hell of a lot of time.' She gestured him into a chair and sat behind her desk, stretching back in the deep leather swivel chair. 'So who's in charge down there?' she asked. 'Foran? Is Pat Foran still stamping the jackboot down there?'

'Do you know him?'

'Would it make a difference?'

McCadden sparred desperately. 'A lot.'

'I suppose it would,' McConnell conceded. 'No, I don't know him. Except by reputation. I was once stationed next door to him. In Cork city.'

'You were a member?'

'Graduated from Templemore College in 1983,' McConnell recited. 'First posted to Cork city. Detective, and transferred to the Missing Persons Bureau in Dublin, 1988. My old man, once the sergeant in a country town, was bursting with pride. But I found I was going nowhere. Two years later I was standing at a station desk between a red-faced lug from the Bog of Allen whose right paw was on my ass and a pale ghost of a git from Dublin's inner city who wouldn't take a woman guard in the patrol car at nights because she was too weak to stand her ground. You know what it's like, inspector. Women in the force. That's when I decided I was out. I could get more of a buzz from private work.'

McCadden used the monologue to make a few connections. Like a good ex-cop, he decided, she'd already reported her previous interest in Hannah Fraule after hearing of the old woman's murder. Although the investigating team in West Cork had done nothing about it, considering her involvement irrelevant, she clearly thought he was following up on this contact.

'Who did you talk to in West Cork?' he risked.

'Who did I talk to? Pine? Sergeant Pine?'

'Right.'

'He sounded confused.'

'Hereditary problem,' McCadden bluffed. 'So you—'

There was a knock on the door and the secretary came in with the coffee. McCadden could smell the aroma long before he saw the pot.

McConnell poured, offered milk and sugar and pastries, and sat back again with her own mug. 'You were saying.'

McCadden stirred a little milk into his coffee, hoping she'd slide into another of the monologues and leave him to enjoy the drink. He said, 'You were in Naune three years ago, making enquiries about Hannah Fraule.'

McConnell frowned. 'I don't think I mentioned Naune, but that's where I was, yeah.'

'I know you'll probably resist telling me who you were representing—'

'I don't have a problem with that, inspector.'

'You don't?'

McConnell put her coffee mug on the desk in front of her. She leaned forward again, looking quizzically at McCadden. 'What is it with you guys?' she asked irritably. 'Don't you talk to each other? I already told this to Pine.'

McCadden shrugged. 'You know how it is. We like to hear it for ourselves. At least twice.'

She didn't answer. She went on staring at him suspiciously. Eventually she cleared her throat and asked, 'Do you have identification on you?'

McCadden produced his wallet and handed it across to her. She didn't just look. She *studied* it.

'Okay,' she said then. 'Sorry. Maybe I'm a little wound up about this.'

McCadden sensed entanglements and searched quickly for the most productive button to tap. 'Personal involvement?'

She smiled. Grimly. 'Maybe you shouldn't accept commissions from old boyfriends. They come with a history.'

'What period was this?'

'Winter, 1996.'

'You were already out of the force?'

'Nearly five years by then. Out on my own. Mostly taking the odd photograph of middle-aged wasters screwing someone other than their wives. All I needed was an unexpected visit from a successful old lover to complete my regrets. And there he was, standing outside the peeling front door of my suburban three-bed semi. Jack Stokes. Flash barrister. Big stable of dubious clients. Jack had a job for me. It was just a one-off, but he was also dangling the carrot of a steady income. His firm needed an associated PI. This was a test. He wanted me to trace someone. This was something I'd become an expert at before leaving the force. But it wasn't a recent disappearance. It was from way back. I wrote this down for you.'

She sat forward in the swivel chair and pulled the keyboard of a computer towards her.

McCadden watched her. Her movements were eager, almost agitated. She was in a hurry to shaft her old lover. Despite her professional success, she nursed a raw personal resentment. It was why she talked so much, and so freely. She was angry. Probably vindictive.

She was a good typist. Her fingers worked rapidly across the keys. She looked only at the screen to her left. Within a minute, two sheets of A4 paper were rolling from the small printer attached to the system. They were copies of the same file. She gave one to McCadden and held the other herself.

'The guy's name was Harry Rull,' she explained. 'Unusual surname, which always makes things simpler. I thought I was on to an easy number. But then Jack told me that he only had two previous records of the subject and I knew I was in trouble. Harry Rull lived in Gloucester Street, in Dublin, up to 1924. 1924? Jesus! I mean, it's not even called Gloucester Street any more. All those inner-city street names were changed when the British pulled out. Typical Irish dream, isn't it? Change the name and you change the identity, the whole fucking history with it.'

Inevitably, McCadden thought of Hannah Fraule. He had no idea what Gloucester Street was known as now, but then he saw that it was listed on the sheet of paper he held in his hand. 'Sean McDermott Street,' he read.

'Harry went to ground after 1924,' Kelly McConnell continued. 'No one knew where he lay his head, what he'd done with himself. But then he surfaced again in 1948. He was in Naune, which is down in County Wexford, as you know. He was a publican, a businessman. His name was Harry Fraule. Like Gloucester Street, he'd reinvented himself.'

'Did you discover that yourself?' McCadden asked.

McConnell shook her head. 'No. Jack already knew. This was the second piece of information he had for me.'

'How did he find it?'

'I don't know. He wouldn't tell.'

'I've been down to Naune. Not a very hospitable place.'

'Maybe not. But I was carrying Jack's introductions. All the doors were open for me.'

'Introductions?' McCadden repeated. 'Who to?'

'The local butcher. Cheevers. He's a county councillor down there.'

'What's Stokes's connection with him?'

McConnell shrugged. 'Like any successful barrister, Jack consorts with politicians. The councillor is from Sinn Fein and Jack does a lot of work for the party. Extradition cases. Defending activists when they step over the line on anti-drug campaigns.'

'Have you ever heard of a pair called Robert Hannifin and Joseph Mary Rudican?'

'No.'

'What about Pius Eugene Shanahan?'

'Shanahan? Well, he's in the news anyway, isn't he? You mean in relation to Jack? You're right. Jack was on Shanahan's legal team.'

'Right,' McCadden muttered. 'Anyway. You set to work looking for Harry Rull.'

McConnell nodded. 'Uh-huh. But the longer I worked, the more I got the impression that Jack was really more interested in Harry's wife, Hannah. Something about the angle of the questions he asked whenever I updated my reports, where he placed the emphasis with his suggestions. The early assumption was that Harry and Hannah left Naune together, probably on the run from something. I followed Harry at first, expecting to find his wife as well. Like an awful lot of people in this country at the time, he emigrated to England in 1948. He went to Birmingham. As Harry Rull, his real name again. But he didn't go to work as a navvy or in a factory, like most Irish emigrants. He didn't work at all. Not officially, anyway, until early 1950. Then he bought a pub. He did well. His wife worked the bar with him. In 1951, they had a son. His mother called him Thomas. He's now a musician, in a radio orchestra.'

'His *mother* called him Thomas?'

'A few months before the birth, Harry turned his back on everything and disappeared again. Wife. Child. Pub. He abandoned the lot.'

'Where did he go?'

'I never found out. Jack hadn't much interest in Harry, except as a lead to Hannah. And she never *went* with him to England. He married someone else over there. Bigamously. Jack only wanted me to find Hannah. I should've asked some questions at that stage, but I didn't. Carry this one off, I thought, and you'll be irresistible to Jack again. Success does make you attractive, don't you think, inspector?'

'Very attractive,' McCadden complimented.

She stopped and looked at him a little warily. 'Thanks,' she accepted. 'But I was going to add, only if you're working for yourself. The talents of the servant only enhance the master's reputation. I didn't understand that then. Idiot that I was, I felt a great sense of achievement when I located Hannah Fraule.'

'How?'

'It was simple, really. It was Hannah, not Harry, who sold the businesses in Naune. Her agent was a solicitor in Wexford town. He was middle-aged then and he's been dead about a decade. His sons took over the practice. They didn't want to talk. As soon as I mentioned Hannah Fraule they got nervous, and fairly rude. They refused to meet me again. I have advantages, though.'

'Your Garda training,' McCadden offered dryly.

She ignored this. 'I discovered that Hannah Fraule was still alive. The firm was still handling her affairs. In fact, she'd actually changed her will a few years earlier. Her address was the village in West Cork where she died. As far as I could tell, she'd been there since 1950.'

'Did you go down there?'

'Yes.'

'When?'

'As soon as I confirmed it. I just left everything and got in the car, as excited as a schoolgirl on a date. Exactly? I don't know. Almost three years ago. Early February 1997.'

'Could you check the precise date for me?'

'Sure.'

'When did you inform Jack Stokes?'

'As soon as I got back here to Dublin, two days later.'

'Did you see Hannah Fraule?'

'I didn't talk to her. I watched her for a couple of days. The village was dying around her then, I could see that. You know the way they go. The local branch of the bank had moved out, the post office had moved out, the shops had started closing. Some of the houses were being used as holiday homes by foreigners. Everybody knew about Hannah, but without even knowing her surname. People thought she was crazy, that she should've been placed in a home twenty or thirty years ago. Hardly anybody talked to her or went to visit her. She discouraged contact. There was a young priest, the health nurse every so often and one of her neighbours who was an artist. That was about it. I've never seen anything like her house. She sat in front of this miserable little fire all day, dressed in a black shawl and dress, doing nothing. Except praying. She prayed a hell of a lot. The smoke from the turf fire came back down the chimney and filled the whole room. She left the front door open all the time to clear it. I've never seen anything like it. My guess is she lived frugally on the capital from the sale of the pub in Naune. All those years. But from her attitude to money, the sort of feverish piety she had, the way she lived, it also struck me that she was guilty about the source of the money she'd come by.'

'In what way?'

'Remember I said her husband Harry lived in Gloucester Street in Dublin until 1924, before he married Hannah?'

'What about it?'

'The house he lived in was a brothel, inspector. Whatever Harry started off as and however respectable he became after his marriage to Hannah, in the early twenties he earned his living as a pimp.'

Baffled by this information and struggling to reconcile the conflicting images he had of Hannah Fraule, McCadden drove slowly to Garda headquarters in Phoenix Park where Inspector Phelim Bourke was waiting to add to his confusion.

'Hannah Fraule's husband,' Bourke opened. 'Harry. You'll obviously be familiar with him already.'

'Getting more so by the minute,' McCadden confirmed.

'You asked me to check if the raid on Fraules pub in 1948 was an IRA operation.'

'And?'

'It was and it wasn't.'

'I could've suggested that myself, Phelim.'

'It's hard to call. Both raiders were certainly IRA activists. Rudican, the older of the two, was an old hand by then, a veteran of the Civil War and of successive IRA campaigns up to the late forties. He didn't talk. But his sidekick, Robert Hannifin, was really only a kid. He worshipped Rudican as a hero, but he fell apart as soon as they were separated. They broke him quickly. According to Hannifin, the pair of them met Harry Fraule at a location in the Wicklow Mountains and they were paid by Fraule to do the job.'

McCadden was dubious. 'Fraule paid to have his own pub robbed?'

Bourke shook his head. 'No, Carl. Fraule paid *to have his wife killed*! Rudican and Hannifin went to the pub that night in January 1948 with the intention of murdering Hannah Fraule.'

'How were they prevented?'

'That I don't know.'

'As far as I can tell, the village didn't even have a resident guard at the time.'

'It's not clear from the files. When the case came to court, the charges were aggravated burglary and possession of illegal weapons. No mention was made of attempted murder. The only evidence we have for that is the interrogation of Robert Hannifin. By then, Harry Fraule had emigrated to England. The authorities subsequently contacted the British police, but nothing ever came of it. Fraule was never returned here for questioning.'

two

Sex.

The more you were exposed to it, McCadden decided, the less appealing it became. But the less access you had to it, the more unattractive you grew. The more it was coupled with commerce, the less you desired the thing itself and the more you craved its own substitutes. Whether it was being sold itself – by prostitutes on the banks of the city's canals, along raunchy chatlines or through calling cards in telephone booths – or whether it was used to sell something else – from talentless girl bands to phallus-shaped ice-pops – its exploitation turned him off. He spent a couple of days looking at it closely. By the end, he was convinced that it wasn't an enjoyable spectacle. And his personal interest in Kelly McConnell had faded.

At two o'clock on Wednesday afternoon, after a hurried lunch with Frank Ryan, he was walking north up O'Connell Street in central Dublin. A century ago, under British rule, it had been known as Sackville Street and was one of the most beautiful in Europe. Now it was as cheap as an ageing hooker. There was too much plastic and too much neon, too many fast-food joints and too many drug addicts closing deals. To add to the existing horrors, its most recently proposed adornment was an elevated spike intended to celebrate the millennium. Because of the extent of the drugs activity around the spot, McCadden privately thought of the proposed sculpture as the Needle Exchange. But even this simplistic monument wasn't the hottest controversy on the street. That was reserved for a proposal to open a sex shop, which local politicians, half of them on the take from dirty planning deals, indignantly rejected as lowering the tone of the capital's main thoroughfare.

Sex.

On McCadden's right as he walked, overlooked now by modern shopping centres and multi-storey car parks, was the area that had once been the most notorious red-light district in Europe. There was nothing left of it these days except its reputation. The sex trade had moved elsewhere. Or it had dispensed with location altogether, doing its business over mobile phones and the Internet. But even that reputation was still a matter for feverish debate, a question of political perspective.

Frank Ryan, chasing a separate line of enquiry but stumbling on the same discovery that Harry Rull had been a pimp, had charmed a couple of local historians and worked himself some invitations to meet survivors from the period, people who'd been born in the area during the first two decades of the twentieth century.

'But I still don't know who Hannah Fraule was before she was given a new identity,' Ryan admitted glumly. 'I just can't get to it. It's gone. It's buried.'

'We could get copies of the photograph Albert Siggs has in Cork,' McCadden suggested. 'How old was she in that? In her thirties? It's less than ten years after Harry was living in a brothel. She can't have changed much.'

Ryan was dubious. 'She might have no connection with his past, no knowledge of what he did, never have been in the streets with the brothels.'

'I'm not so sure,' McCadden objected. 'What bothers me is why *she* had to go undercover, why *she* needed a new identity. I could understand it more if it was Harry. His line of work attracts enemies, from both sides of the law. It would make more sense if he was given a new identity and then married Hannah. But why *her*? Why did Hannah take her new name?'

'I wouldn't be too confident of getting the right answers from the old folks I've met,' Ryan warned. He listed the old-fashioned names. 'May Margery, Stella Douglas, Molly Symons. Not that they have rosy memories of the place. They lived next door to the brothels. They knew what was going on. And they lived in slums. Families of ten or twelve to a room. But their memories are shaped by . . . well, by nostalgia, I suppose. The neighbours were all saints. Not like today. The prostitutes were unfortunate poor girls. The men who used them . . . Well, what else can you expect from men? And the madams and pimps were all scum.'

'Any of them from back then capable of mutilation, would you say?'

'Jesus, Carl, they have trouble lifting a knife and fork. They're mostly in homes, needing constant care. Anyway, the explanation is more likely to be something that happened in Naune in 1948, isn't it? It's a lot more recent. You could imagine someone looking for Hannah Fraule since the

1950s. No joy until the whiz-kid McConnell burgles someone's office to read their papers. That's what she did, isn't it?'

'Probably,' McCadden accepted. 'But she did it more than three years ago. Why wait that length of time? Particularly if you'd been denied revenge for so long.'

'The contact was through Jack Stokes. Maybe Stokes was having a rough time with McConnell. Maybe the woman was holding out on him.'

'There's one other explanation. They had no choice.'

'In what way?'

'Because they were in prison, Frank. Think about it. If they were either already serving a sentence or just convicted when Kelly McConnell passed the file to Stokes, they couldn't do anything about the information. Three years is a long time for a voluntary wait, even if you want to put some distance between the tip-off and the move.'

'They could've been out of the country, not in prison.'

'Too many flights available.'

'With the army on a UN tour of duty, then.'

'Three years is too long for a UN tour.'

'In hospital, seriously ill. On an expedition to the Andes.'

'Okay,' McCadden accepted, 'there are a lot of other reasons, but let's *start* with the prison theme.'

'At least it's familiar ground, I suppose.'

'There's not much point focusing on the period Kelly McConnell got her instructions from Stoke. Our suspect could've been in the middle of a long stretch. Let's concentrate on releases instead. Say, two months prior to the death of Hannah Fraule. I've already asked Special Branch to prepare a list of paramilitaries released. You take the ordinary criminals. Maybe something consistent. A conviction for rape or sexual assault. The other option, of course, is to get Jack Stokes to tell us.'

'He won't talk. Our mystery suspect is a client of his.'

'I'm not so sure. He might be compromised. Is what he did covered by confidentiality? You know something?'

'What?'

'Let's go and ask him.'

McCadden and Ryan had eaten in a noodle house off St Stephen's Green. Stokes's offices were only a ten-minute walk away, back towards the city centre where McCadden was heading anyway.

The building was a Georgian town house off the north quays, close to the Four Courts. It might've been old itself, but it had been restored with new money. Appearances were obviously important to this firm. Impressions vital. The young secretary in the reception lobby was dressed in so classy a business suit that she was hard to distinguish at a glance from the associate lawyers.

'Do you have an appointment, sir?' she asked.

'No,' McCadden admitted.

'Perhaps you could tell me the name and nature of your business?'

'Is it necessary?'

'No one can be seen otherwise, sir.'

'Right.' McCadden accepted. He showed his ID. 'It's Mr Stokes himself I need to talk to.'

The secretary hesitated, the uncertainty obvious on her face. She thought of ringing through, but checked herself as if an old warning echoed through her mind. Finally, she called someone else to take her place at the desk, excused herself to McCadden and hurried into the offices behind her.

When she came back, it was clear that at last she knew what to do. She'd just been told. She said, 'Mr Stokes is out at a business lunch at the moment.'

'You've only found that out now, have you?' McCadden asked.

'I beg your pardon?'

'What time will he be back?'

'I doubt if he'll return to the office today.'

'Long lunch.'

'Perhaps you'd like to make an appointment, sir?'

'When is he free?'

'Not for . . . the next available time is in three weeks.'

'Busy man.'

'Will I put you in the book, sir?'

McCadden looked at the appointments book she'd opened, trying to read the entries upside down. He took a pad from beside her right hand and scribbled his name and the phone number of his temporary office in Harcourt Terrace on it. 'Tell him to contact me here this afternoon,' he instructed. 'Or squeeze me in between Mrs Hunter and Mr Sloane tomorrow morning.'

Outside the barrister's offices, Ryan and McCadden parted. Ryan crossed to the south of the river again, heading back to the regional headquarters and a tedious trawl through the records of prison releases for the previous November and December. McCadden went east along the quays and then turned into O'Connell Street to keep an appointment with a young Trinity College lecturer, Robert Colwell, who'd promised him a guided tour of the early-twentieth-century city. It was two o'clock by then and he was already running late. They'd arranged to meet outside the Savoy cinema at the other end of the street. But they'd never met before and wouldn't recognize each other.

'Tell you what,' Colwell had suggested, sounding boyish and excited. 'Something appropriate. I'll carry either a copy of Oliver St John Gogarty's *As I Was Going Down Sackville Street* or a copy of James Joyce's *Ulysses.* Both writers were frequently visitors to the brothels you're interested in.'

'I tried *Ulysses* once,' McCadden regretted. 'Even though he was paying for it, I hope he gave the whores a better time than he gave his readers. Maybe not. All those masturbatory scenes. Let's have Gogarty.'

So, among the hordes of noisy kids and bedraggled parents queuing for admission to the early showing of *Star Wars – The Phantom Menace*, there was a slight young man with receding hair, animated eyes and a quick, nervous manner carrying an old Penguin edition of *As I Was Going Down Sackville Street.* As they met and introduced themselves, an open-top tour bus, carrying twenty Japanese in pink and purple rain gear, crept past them through the heavy traffic on the street.

'It won't be going in our direction,' Colwell predicted. 'They'll be referred to Brannigan Street behind us here and told it's named after a famous patriot, but nobody will mention it was once Purdon Street, where the most squalid of the brothels thrived. They'll be brought to St Patrick's Cathedral, where Jonathan Swift was dean in the eighteenth century, but they won't hear that he was a savagely disappointed man, sexually and professionally. They'll go to Oscar Wilde's birthplace, but they won't be told about his persecution for homosexuality.'

The historian's complaint in an age addicted to heritage. McCadden sympathized. Drawing on the narrowness of his interest over the last few days, he said, 'Sex seems to be hot for selling everything except the past, then?'

'The past is about consequences. Nobody wants to think about the consequences of sex, inspector. It spoils all the fun.'

They turned right, along Cathal Brugha Street, into Sean McDermott Street, formerly known as Gloucester Street. The contrast with the tawdry prosperity of the main street they'd just left behind was immediate. This was all crumbling old buildings, decaying local authority flats, neglected open spaces and boarded-up business premises.

'Some things don't change that quickly,' Colwell said. 'Or not as easily as mere names. See this?'

He handed McCadden a small folder of photocopied pages. Among them were a 1925 map of inner-city Dublin and a list of official investigations into the area's slum conditions. The list ran all the way from 1882, when 32,000 impoverished families had been surveyed, through 1936, when the figure was 33,000, right up to the heroin and smack epidemics of the eighties and nineties.

While McCadden was still glancing at the sheets and trying to listen and dodge the traffic at the same time, Colwell stopped suddenly outside a derelict building. It had once been used as a computer store. Pieces of the shattered plastic name sign were still visible above the doorway and old stickers advertising accessories, with their grubby corners lifting, were still on the glass behind the metal shutters.

'This is it,' Colwell announced. 'This is where you say your man lived in 1924. This was a brothel. Down to the right, there was a sweet shop, and beyond that a convent with a laundry attached where the nuns put fallen women – unmarried mothers – to work. They had everything on this street.'

McCadden looked at the rotting structure, but he found it impossible to even imagine its heyday. Maybe it was too wet or too cold for thinking about the pleasures of sex. Maybe it was too early in the day. Maybe at night, when the threat of danger moved in with the darkness, it might be easier to visualize the punters slipping furtively through its door, a blowsy madam in the gaslit hall inside, the waiting girls . . .

'Of course,' Colwell explained, 'by 1924 the sex trade was pretty much dead in this area, anyway. It's probably why your Harry Rull moved out. Almost everyone else had moved on by then. You still hear claims that a Catholic organization called the Legion of Mary succeeded in suppressing the sex trade in Dublin where earlier attempts had failed. But there were other historical forces at work. The British Army had withdrawn a few years earlier after the treaty between the two countries. Their barracks, Aldborough, was just around the corner there. Upwards on a hundred thousand willing cocks departing across the Irish Sea like a flotilla of submarine periscopes. No business could survive such a haemorrhage of customers. And then you had the fervent nationalists, of course, coming out of a war of independence and a civil war with an Irish Free State to build, who wanted an image of Ireland Pure, cleansed only by the sacrificial blood of its martyrs. Mostly they denied that prostitution could even exist on Irish soil. Among the Irish establishment, the notion that sex is a foreign import, without native roots, a modern perversion, and in any case technically somewhat beyond the abilities of the Gael, has always been a comforting delusion. And finally you had the fervent Catholics, determined to stamp a religious character on the new state. They also wanted an image of Ireland Pure, but cleansed this time only by the sacrificial blood of the Redeemer. They accepted that prostitution existed, but reckoned they could eliminate it by locking its practitioners away in Magdalene laundries. After Mary Magdalene, the repentant whore in the Bible. Whores are never very popular citizens. Sometimes privately tolerated. But always publicly abhorred. Often identified as the very source of evil in times of national stress.'

'Or personal stress,' McCadden remarked.

'Of course. The victim of choice for many serial killers.'

'When this place was closed,' McCadden asked. 'What year was it?'

'Officially? Only a year after Harry Rull left. 1925.'

'What happened to the people involved in the trade?'

'Most of the prostitutes went on walking the streets elsewhere. The money had moved south of the Liffey by then, anyway. This area was in decline. The only things keeping the trade going had been the port nearby and the military barracks. Now the army was gone and business was poor on the docks. The girls followed the money, obviously. You see, whenever you hear the prostitutes described by contemporaries, or even later commentators, they're always characterized as unfortunates, poor country migrants lost in the big city, trapped by unscrupulous pimps or madams and forced to continue working by threats of violence. There's never any acceptance that they might have *chosen* their trade. They had no free will, according to the zealots. If they had, they would've been virgins or mothers. The only logical development consistent with this myth is that the sex trade vanished from Catholic Ireland once the British, the Protestant administration and the red-light district were all gone. It didn't, of course. Some of the girls actually opted for the way out offered by the missionaries. They were accommodated in those Magdalene laundries, where, as we now know, they were treated so brutally by the nuns that they must've longed at times for their old pimps again. Most continued working as prostitutes, but in the more prosperous south of the city.'

'And the madams?'

'The few remaining in 1925 certainly weren't wealthy. They were struggling. Some had enough to set themselves up as shopkeepers. Most disappeared into the mists.'

'Someone like Harry Rull,' McCadden asked. 'What background?'

Colwell shrugged. He gestured, at first down the street they were standing on and then vaguely around the rest of the area. 'The houses here, Georgian town houses, they were once the most fashionable in the city. But Dublin became *passé.* Society moved to London. The houses were left with agents, who turned them into . . . well, into profit. Whatever made the quickest profit. Tenements. Brothels. Pubs. Some of the agents pimped. But it was a real melting pot here. Ex-army men, veterans of Britain's nineteenth-century wars. Local criminals. Republican gunmen. Corrupt cops. Some were educated, some were stupid. Most were violent. Take your pick. The men were used as enforcers. Bodyguards. Bouncers. Drivers. A few had more intimate relationships with the madams and probably shared in the running of the brothels.'

'You'd have to assume that they stayed in the trade afterwards, wouldn't you?'

'I suppose so.'

'But Harry Rull married a woman who was so respectable that she was part of the local organizing committee for the Eucharistic Congress in 1932 and was introduced to the papal legate when he came to Ireland.'

'Was she a missionary? Maybe she saved Harry's soul.'

'I don't know. But it doesn't fit, does it?'

'Not the accepted patterns, no. But the more you study the details of history, the more exceptions you find to the accepted patterns, until you question the patterns themselves.'

'Right.'

Colwell lightly rattled the shutters outside the derelict shop. 'Do you need to get access to here? I'm sure you could arrange it.'

'No, it's not necessary.'

'Will we do the rest of the area, then?'

'Right.'

The end of Sean McDermott Street marked the perimeter of the old red-light district. They turned right, then worked their way through a warren of tight lanes and littered courtyards. Colwell enthusiastically identified relevant landmarks. A stone eagle that had once been mounted over the entrance to a pub where most of the prostitutes picked up clients. The spot where a crucifix was erected by the missionaries during a blessing of the stained streets after the closure of the brothels.

But McCadden had lost interest. He had enough background. The strange life choices of Hannah Fraule still nagged at him. And he knew that no amount of location work here was going to offer him an insight into them. He stayed with the tour out of politeness, because the young lecturer had put so much effort into it, but he was relieved when they finally came back into O'Connell Street and said goodbye.

three

Jack Stokes didn't telephone McCadden. Another call to the barrister's office early next morning unearthed only the unsurprising news that Stokes was unavailable and the unreliable promise that a message would be dealt with promptly.

'Right.'

'*Do* you wish to leave a message, sir?'

'I'm thinking about it.' And he was still thinking about it a minute later, when Frank Ryan opened the door of the office and came noisily in, waving sheets of typewritten paper. McCadden covered the mouthpiece before replacing the receiver. 'You any good at accents, Frank?' he wondered.

Ryan sat in the chair on the opposite side of the desk. 'Identifying them?'

McCadden shook his head. 'Imitating them.'

'No. One of those kids outside does it. Drive you crazy. I don't know how good he is.'

'Send him in when you're ready, will you?'

'Okay.' Ryan spread the pages on the desk in front of him and ran the index finger of his right hand across the row of sheets. 'We've finally got that second statement you asked for from Ciaran Carthy about the limping man with the No. 1 haircut.'

'What does he say?'

'That it was a joke. Something the boy who discovered the body, Darragh Cole, had pestered him about during the previous week. The boy himself was questioned again and admitted that he made the story up to try and scare his mother into staying at home with him at weekends.'

A suspiciously neat dead end, McCadden thought. But he couldn't do anything about it for the moment. 'I don't know.'

'Well, it does really sound like something out of *Treasure Island*, doesn't it? "The limping man with the No. 1 haircut."'

'What else have you got?'

'Suspects. We've gone through the prison releases for November and December last year and Special Branch has given us a separate report on paramilitaries.'

'Let's hear what Phelim Bourke has to say first.'

'Apart from Pius Shanahan, he's recommending three others for a closer look. Peter Desmond, Bobby Tee and Eddie Boyce. Know anything about them?'

'No.'

'Desmond is from Belfast. Convictions for robbery and assault before being recruited by the IRA. Jailed for a mortar attack on an RUC station. He was serving a twenty-year sentence. Bobby Tee is from Donegal. Ran into trouble there as a tearaway teenager. Convictions for joyriding, car theft, housebreaking and indecent assault. Jailed for car bombs in London. He served time in Wandsworth prison with Shanahan. Boyce is from Dublin. Convictions for armed robbery and sex offences as a teenager. Jailed for holding up a security van. Shanahan, Desmond and Tee have all disappeared since they were released. Boyce is living and working in Dublin.'

'Any of them represented by Jack Stokes?'

'Only Shanahan. None of the others.'

'What about your own crowd?'

'I've narrowed it down to two. Both have convictions for sexual assault. Both were represented by Stokes at their trials. One was also convicted of laundering money for a prostitution ring. The other went down for armed robbery of a country pub. The interesting thing about the second guy is that he held his last victims hostage overnight and took to a little torture with a knife to get the information he needed from the publican's wife. What do you think? Do we pay them a visit?'

Somehow, McCadden wasn't enthusiastic. 'Do we have alternatives?'

'Not particularly. Special Branch are searching for their own fugitives, Shanahan, Desmond and Tee. They'll let us know.'

'Right,' McCadden accepted. 'We'll head out in about an hour, then. Okay? Send in that uniform first, will you?'

The uniformed guard with a talent for impersonation, a young redheaded Dubliner named Mason, went suddenly dry-throated in the presence of his inspector. 'It's like at the medical, sir, trying to give a urine sample to the doctor,' he apologized. 'You get too self-conscious.'

McCadden gave him a glass of water and some reassurance. 'It's nothing elaborate,' he explained. 'Can you do a middle-class Dublin accent?'

'No problem, sir.'

'Someone on about thirty grand a year,' McCadden couldn't help teasing. 'With the tastes of a speculator, the talents of a plagiarist and the mentality of a servant.'

'Ah . . . I'll do my best, sir.'

'Right.' McCadden wrote a telephone number on a pad and pushed it across the desk. 'I want you to ring that number. It's a barrister's office, Stokes and Partners. You're ringing from the office of a Mr Sloane. Your boss, Mr Sloane, has an appointment with Mr Stokes at ten. You need to reach him urgently, but his mobile is switched off. You might be able to get a message to him through Mr Stokes. Can you manage that?'

'Maybe if I could practise a little first?'

'Good idea,' McCadden approved.

He watched the young guard slowly getting to grips with his lines and only interrupted to remind him that there was a time limit to his rehearsal. Mr Sloane was due in town at ten.

The performance itself went well at first. Mason grew in confidence when it finally dawned on him that the receptionist on the other end of the telephone couldn't actually *see* how nervous he was. But gradually he became confused again, and then uncomfortable. When he eventually replaced the receiver, he did it hurriedly, anxious to break the connection.

'Well?' McCadden demanded.

'She got suspicious, I think,' the guard admitted. 'I had to point out that I wasn't Mr Sloane's *personal* secretary.'

'I heard that.'

'She said they'd already contacted Mr Sloane's office. Mr Stokes cancelled all appointments for the remainder of this week and next week. He's indisposed. And I should already have known that.'

'Good man,' McCadden applauded. 'That's all I wanted to know. Now, give Aer Lingus a ring, will you, and book me on a flight to Birmingham for Monday morning.'

'Which accent, sir?'

'What?'

'What voice do you want me to use?'

'No, this is just a normal reservation . . .'

Jack Stokes lived in a three-storey late Victorian house in the wealthy inner suburb of Rathgar. Mason was elected to drive there, while

McCadden and Ryan sat in the rear seat of the car, discussing strategy. They didn't expect instant co-operation from Stokes – it was already too late for that – but they did hope to rattle the barrister a little by making him fully aware of his position. Stokes wasn't foolish. And certainly not altruistic. He was a tough criminal lawyer, with the minimum affection for the police and the courts and a lot of contacts in the criminal underworld, but he wouldn't carry the can for someone else's mistakes or misdemeanours. Maybe after a few days' reflection, gnawing on the problem, something might loosen with him. Or maybe he was already debating the issues with himself.

McCadden didn't think the lawyer was ill, of course. More likely, Stokes was buying time and space while contemplating how to deal with the pressure. So McCadden didn't expect a stunning nurse or a matronly home help to respond when Ryan rang the doorbell that morning. He expected Stokes's wife, maybe one of his kids, or – with a bit of luck – even Stokes himself. Instead he was confronted by what looked like a rugby front-row forward squeezed into a dark suit, the jacket of which was several sizes too small for his massive torso. Obviously, a hired security guard.

McCadden immediately showed his ID. It was the only thing that softened these mountains, although it rarely shifted them. This one stayed blocking the doorway, admirably mute except for murdering the line he'd been coached in. 'Mr Stokes is not at home.'

It wasn't true, of course. The curtains were closed. A restless child, kept home from school – presumably for the same reasons a bodyguard was employed – made a squealing noise inside before being harshly silenced by a tense adult. The family's third car – judging by its condition and the age of the registration plate, anyway – was parked in the open driveway, suggesting that the rest of the fleet was safely away in the locked garage.

But McCadden had no warrant, no authority to push it further. 'Right,' he accepted. He left his name and telephone number again, along with the reminder that he'd tried before. 'Tell him it's important, will you?' he instructed the security man, but without too much optimism.

As they were driving away, he ordered Mason to stop around the first corner, out of sight of the house. 'I want you to stay here,' he said. 'Watch the house. Try not to be seen yourself. I know it's not easy when you're in uniform, so don't worry if you're spotted. We'll be back to you within a couple of hours. If anything moves before that, contact us.'

McCadden had given himself two hours, but actually neither of the suspects on Frank Ryan's list delayed him for more than five minutes. The first had emigrated to Spain before Christmas, to join his pals by the poolside. The second had broken a leg playing football on 30 December and had celebrated the New Year from a hospital bed. Frustrated by so many successive dead ends, McCadden suggested calling on the paramilitary, Edward Boyce, who lived in a north inner-city flat, close to the area McCadden had toured the previous day.

Boyce had never married. It was his mother – a shuffling, careworn woman who couldn't have been much more than fifty, but who had the pained movements of someone twenty years on from that – who answered the bell.

'Can't you leave him alone, for God's sake,' she pleaded immediately. 'He's got himself a job now. He's out of all that.'

'Where is he working?'

'You'll only go in there to give him a bad name and get him sacked.'

'No,' McCadden promised. 'We won't do that.'

Boyce worked in a scrappage yard nearby. The trade-off was that if McCadden and Ryan waited until lunch and agreed to meet in a pub, Boyce's younger brother would carry the message to him.

Thirty minutes later, McCadden was toying with a glass of dire white wine in the pub, watching Ryan do justice to the bar menu, when an excited Mason – forgotten about until then – suddenly burst across McCadden's mobile phone, offering a feverish commentary on movements in and around Jack Stokes's house out in Rathgar.

'It looks like only Mr Stokes himself, sir. I mean, I don't know him. So I'm not sure. I mean, I wouldn't recognize—'

'What's happening?' McCadden interrupted.

'The security man who opened the door to you, sir, he's driving what I think is Mr Stokes away in the car that was in the driveway. Do I follow them?'

'How are you going to manage that?' McCadden wondered.

'Well, I could call for a squad car, sir. It'll only take a minute.'

'No, stay put. Contact me again if there are any other developments, or when they return.'

For an armed robber with a bad reputation, Boyce was a small man, not particularly threatening in appearance. He was said to have an explosive temper. Expecting cops, he was already resentful when he came into the pub.

'You're interrupting me lunch,' he accused. 'What do you want? I don't have to talk to you.'

He looked like a man who was too fiery, too impetuous to be carrying guilt around with him, McCadden thought. 'How did you spend the New Year, Ted?' he asked anyway.

As he sat, Boyce ducked and weaved, like a boxer warming up. 'What are you trying to pin on me now? Every time there's something, you're on me back again. I told the Branch. I'm finished with politics.'

McCadden had some sympathy. But not much. 'Where were you on New Year's Eve, through the night, and then on New Year's Day?'

'I was in London. With the job. The boss, he organized this weekend for everyone. 'Cause of the millennium, like.'

'Can you prove it?'

'Ask at the job, if you want. Why? What's the story?'

McCadden and Ryan exchanged a look and stood up from the table.

'Nothing, Ted,' McCadden told him. 'Thanks, anyway. And good luck.'

Back in Rathgar, Mason was still standing sentry around the corner from Jack Stokes's house. Without any natural camouflage for the blue of his uniform, he'd felt exposed and uncomfortable the last few hours. The strain was starting to tell. He slumped into the back seat of the car to make his report.

Stokes and his bodyguard hadn't returned yet, he explained. And there was at least one other security guard with the rest of Stokes's family inside the house.

'What are they so scared of?' Ryan wondered. 'Of course, if we stay watching long enough, we might find out for ourselves.'

'Not with that level of protection,' McCadden disagreed. 'Nobody's going to make a move until it eases off.'

There were only two approaches to the house, from north and south along the same street. McCadden told Mason to take the car to one end of the street and asked Ryan to walk to the other. He was going to stand, out of sight, near the front entrance to the house.

He waited for forty minutes. Getting bored. His legs tiring. His concentration drifting. Then a hurried call from Ryan and a speeding car with Stokes in the front passenger seat came at him almost simultaneously.

The car swung in through the open gates of Stokes's house. McCadden pushed away from the wall he'd been leaning against and walked after it.

The big security guard came quickly out from behind the wheel and was moving to block him, until he recognized who it was.

Unaware of all this, Stokes was struggling to open the passenger door and lift himself out of the seat. 'Martin!' he shouted at the security man. 'Where the hell are you?'

He was still huddled, still trying to straighten himself, when McCadden called his name.

'Mr Stokes?'

The lawyer started, lost his footing on the gravel, and reached out for the bodyguard who'd finally come round to support him. He jerked his head to see who'd summoned him. There was probably fear on his face, but it was difficult to be certain. He'd been badly beaten recently. With more than a bare fist. With a cosh or a knuckleduster. And his features were too bruised for the subtleties of expression. Under his jacket, his left arm was out of the sleeve, crooked in a sling.

McCadden held up his ID. 'I'm Detective Inspector McCadden, Mr Stokes. I've been trying to contact you at your office.'

'You're trespassing, inspector,' Stokes snapped. 'Unless you have a warrant.'

He didn't wait for an answer. He turned away and struggled towards the house.

The bodyguard closed the car door and offered a quick apologetic gesture before following his boss.

McCadden watched them enter the house and shut the door.

four

McCadden had been in Birmingham only once before. A woman colleague of his with a weekend package for two, a couple of stand tickets to Villa Park and a recently unfaithful fiancé had invited him to help her cope with her losses on a short holiday. He'd seen little of the city and his memories of it were mostly grey. The Aston Villa match had been a dull scoreless draw. The shopping expedition in the tatty Bull Ring had been a drag. And the jilted woman had been inconsolable anyway.

He wasn't really hopeful of giving the city much of a chance to add some colour and character to his memories on his second visit. His focus was too narrow and his schedule too tight. A morning flight into the airport at Elmdon, contact with British liaison officers, and then immediately on to the genteel suburb of Edgbaston, where Thomas Rull lived.

The liaison officers, a detective sergeant named Jones and a detective constable named Heald, weren't locals. Jones was Welsh, a sharply dressed young man with a soft, undulating accent. It immediately struck McCadden that he was more likely to work in intelligence than in CID. But he wasn't surprised. He'd come to accept the shadowy presence of spooks and terrorists hovering around the corpse of Hannah Fraule.

'I suppose the late forties wasn't the best of times for co-operation between our countries,' Jones remarked as they drove towards Edgbaston. 'After the tensions from the war, I mean. But there was always some exchange of information. Scotland Yard interviewed Harry Rull in 1951, in connection with the attempted murder of his wife and his links with the IRA.'

'Why so late?' McCadden wondered. 'They were told three years earlier.'

Jones dodged the question by ignoring it. 'To be honest, the Yard were probably more interested in Rull's links with the IRA. He owned a licensed premises here in Birmingham at the time. Six months after

Scotland Yard located him, he disappeared. Do you know if he's still alive, sir?'

McCadden shook his head. 'I don't know. It's possible, I suppose, although he'd be in his nineties. Are you still interested in him?'

'London Metropolitan would certainly like to talk to him. Among other things, there's the murder of two young prostitutes in Harlesden in the late seventies.'

'Anything I should know about the victims?'

'They weren't mutilated, sir, if that's what you mean. But they were knifed.'

'How did Harry come to be involved?'

'He controlled the prostitution ring they worked for. He was once a major player in the London sex trade. He'd been sent down twice in the sixties, once for assault and once for living off immoral earnings. It was always suspected, though, that he maintained his links with the IRA while living here. This became of particular interest when the IRA relaunched its campaign in England with the car bombs in London in 1973.'

'Were the murdered prostitutes working for the security forces, by any chance?'

'No, not in any regular sense.'

'So what became of Harry?'

'After a lifetime hiding behind innumerable aliases, he disappeared completely in 1977. No one has heard of him since.'

'Is his son aware of Harry's record?'

'The only thing that will surprise him is that you're an Irish police officer, not an English one.'

Thomas Rull wasn't a bit-player in a radio orchestra, as Kelly McConnell had reported. He was something much more accomplished than that: first violin with the City of Birmingham Symphony Orchestra. He had late afternoon and evening rehearsals that day, preparing for a concert in the International Convention Centre the following week, hence the tight schedule. Although he seemed strained and subdued, he wasn't unwelcoming. Like most people who live alone, he was slightly awkward in informal social situations. He had too little experience of them. He needed a familiar structure, a rehearsal or a dinner party, with its practised moves and formal safety nets, to put him at his ease.

He brought McCadden and Jones into a bright living room at the front of the house. The room was stylish, but it was also cold. Its bare wood and minimalist furniture gave the impression of a sparse lifestyle. There was colour without emotion and light without energy. Perhaps the expression of feeling was reserved for the music, for that curious tension between restraint and passion that a performer manages.

Rull was almost forty-nine years old. He had a tossed, careless appearance, with unruly hair and unfashionable clothes that were dated but comfortable. His attitude was polite. 'Have you had anything to eat, gentlemen?'

Left with Jones while Rull went to the kitchen, McCadden found nothing much in the room to linger on. It had been stripped back to form a space that was a little alienating. There was a range of small bronze sculptures on themes from German mythology, suggesting that the collector might be a fan of Wagner. And apart from the few items of steel and glass furniture, that was it.

When Rull came back, he was carrying a silver tray with a pot of coffee, a plate of biscuits and a cheeseboard of Stilton, Brie and Cheddar. As he poured the coffee, he explained that he had no childhood memories of his father. 'He left when I was an infant. Because of the closeness of the two events and the constant reminders that they were inseparable, perhaps I've always associated his departure with my own arrival. My mother had no contact from him for many years afterwards. She continued to manage the public house, at least until 1974, when the IRA exploded their bombs in Birmingham and killed twenty-one people.'

'Was your mother Irish?' McCadden asked.

Rull shook his head. 'No, she was English. But it was known that my father was Irish. In the aftermath of the bombings, the public house was boycotted by many, including those who had once called themselves our friends. You can hardly blame those who reacted. When you're under attack, particularly from hidden agents within your own society, it can be difficult to distinguish. My mother sold the licence in 1975.'

'Was it originally in her name?'

'No. My father transferred it.'

'Before he left?'

'In 1969, when he suddenly materialized on our doorstep after an absence of almost eighteen years.'

'What brought him back?'

'He had recently been released from prison. I had just won a prestigious music award. I was eighteen years old. I assumed that he was attempting to gain credit from the reflection of my success, having contributed nothing to it, and I rejected him.'

'Did you meet him subsequently?'

'My mother saw him intermittently over the following decade. She always remained curiously loyal to him. I always disliked him. We didn't see him again after 1977. When my mother died in 1991, he didn't attend the funeral.'

'You don't know whether he's still alive or not?'

'No.'

McCadden looked down at the neglected cheeseboard. He was hungry and the display was appetizing, but it would have been crass to divert his attention to food. He poured fresh coffee into his cup and stirred a little milk into it. He asked, 'Did he ever talk to you about his past in Ireland?'

Rull frowned and played distractedly with a coffee spoon for a few moments. 'No. We never talked at all. After his disappearance in 1951, the police told my mother that he was already married in Ireland and that he was associated with the IRA. To be quite honest, I felt cheated when I later discovered this.'

'You never asked him about it?'

'I had no interest.'

'On the other hand,' McCadden pointed out, 'he was obviously anxious to ensure that you and your mother were financially provided for.'

'Merely a guilty conscience in his case.'

'Why would a man as self-interested as the one you describe be burdened with a conscience?'

'In one of the few honest exchanges my mother ever had with him, he confessed that he had already abandoned a child to its fate.'

'Did you take that to refer to his past in Ireland?'

'My mother was of the opinion that it happened before he came to Birmingham.'

'Did she mention any details?'

'I didn't ask. I interpreted his confession as a calculated play for sympathy.'

'Right.' McCadden wondered if the man was somehow uneasy with the notion that his talent had blossomed from mud and that his education was secured by dirty money. Perhaps it explained the neurotic sparseness of his home.

Rull silently put the coffee spoon back on the tray. He lifted the cup he'd been drinking from and replaced that as well. He found the milk jug and sugar bowl and placed them beside the mug. 'Once,' he said then, 'he persuaded my mother to ask me to play "Love's Old Sweet Song". Do you know it?'

McCadden nodded. 'I've heard of it. Did you oblige?'

'No.'

'Right. So I suppose he never got round to explaining what it meant to him?'

'No.'

'Did your mother ever explain to you how she met your father, Mr Rull?'

Rull suddenly stood up, as if to clear the coffee table. But he didn't take the tidied cutlery and crockery with him. He turned away from it. He said, 'Would you excuse me a minute, gentlemen?' And then he left the room again.

Coming back, in probably less than the literal minute he'd asked for, he was carrying one of those small paper wallets that processed photographs are usually delivered in. He took a batch of coloured snaps from it and put the empty wallet on the coffee table beside the tray. He sat back in his seat. 'My mother never discussed my father,' he said, 'apart from the vague and impractical request not to think badly of him. She suffered greatly because of him. In her personal life. In her domestic life. In her social life. By mere association. Even when he turned up, unannounced, after all those years of neglect, he actually had another woman with him. I found this quite disgusting. Inexplicably, my mother accommodated her. When my mother died in 1991, I discovered these photographs among her papers. I don't remember them. They must have been taken without my knowledge.'

McCadden accepted the offered photographs, passing each one across to Jones after he'd looked at it. They showed paired combinations of the same trio, but at two different dates, one in late 1970 and the other in early 1973. Harry Rull, still a big, muscular man, but white-haired now and heavily lined in the face, was as old as the century in both of them. The middle-aged woman, still soft-faced, still beautiful, and obviously once an English rose in her youth, must have been Thomas's mother. The third was a dark-complexioned, striking young woman, who had long black hair in the earlier photographs and short blonde hair in the later ones. McCadden could sympathize with Thomas Rull's bewilderment. Given the circumstances of their meetings, the three looked remarkably cheerful.

'Who's the younger woman?' McCadden asked.

Rull grimaced. 'My father's mistress.'

'Do you know her name?'

'No.'

'Three years ago, Mr Rull,' McCadden said then, 'someone in Ireland hired a private detective to trace your father and his first wife. Did you talk to anyone at that time?'

'I have always refused to discuss my father with anyone other than the police.'

'Did anyone contact you?'

Rull nodded. 'They tried. It wasn't a private detective, however. It was a lawyer. A rather ostentatious individual, whose sense of dress and personal jewellery reminded me of the excesses of certain football managers. His name escapes me.'

'Jack Stokes?' McCadden supplied.

'Yes, I believe it was,' Rull confirmed. 'Stokes. I refused to assist him.'

McCadden looked again through the photographs Jones had handed back to him. 'Would you mind,' he requested, 'if I made coloured photocopies of these to take back to Ireland? You've been extremely kind, and more than helpful, and I don't want to impose, but I think I'll find these valuable.'

Rull opened his arms in a generous, almost pleading gesture. 'Take them,' he pressed. 'Take them. There are several other prints. And negatives. When my father deserted her in 1951, my mother destroyed all the family snapshots, including those of my own first six months. In the end, I suppose these were all she had left of him. I've never understood why she agreed to pose for them. I've never understood why she welcomed my father and his mistress, or why she was disappointed when I refused to be civil to them. But there you are. I believe that human relationships can be rather baffling at times, inspector . . .'

Disappointed after the meeting with Thomas Rull, McCadden turned down an invitation to lunch with the two English detectives and asked instead to be dropped in the city centre. He had nothing particular in mind before his flight home. No shopping. No sightseeing. He just wanted to be alone.

Heald drove. Jones sat with McCadden in the rear seat, rambling on with implausible idleness about the nearby Quaker village of Bournville, where the Cadburys had founded their famous chocolate factory. It was only when they'd pulled into a multi-storey car park and McCadden was on the point of leaving that Jones finally changed his tone and suddenly asked, 'Have you ever come across a woman named Lucy Cuccini, sir?'

'Cuccini?' McCadden repeated. 'No.'

'You might know a man named Christy Sweeney, however. Also, for some reason, known as Sweet Sweeney. Perhaps because of an addiction to Cadburys. I believe he lives in Dublin.'

'I haven't worked in Dublin for about seven years,' McCadden explained. 'I've heard of Sweeney. All I know of him is that he's an enforcer for a drugs gang.'

'He's also Lucy Cuccini's partner.'

McCadden was becoming impatient. 'So?'

'That's who the young woman with Harry Rull in those photographs is,' Jones said. 'Lucy Cuccini. She's a Londoner, of Italian origin, born in 1950. Originally she worked as a prostitute in Soho. In 1968 she started a permanent relationship with Harry Rull. She was eighteen. Rull was in his late sixties. But it seems to have survived until Rull disappeared in 1977. After that she lived here with Sweeney, until he ran into trouble with a turf war in London and was lucky to escape with his life.'

'And now they're in Dublin?'

'Yes.'

'Thanks.'

'That's not the point I'm making, though. You see, however unpredictable he might have been otherwise, Harry Rull's taste in women was always consistent. He preferred prostitutes. Wild rebels, as he put it himself. Too romantically for my liking. But he seems to have wasted a better education than I had. Wild rebels. Sexually free in a stifling society.'

'As he put it?' McCadden echoed. 'Are you quoting him?'

'I believe there may be a document in existence, sir, in which he used the phrases.'

For the moment, floundering in unfamiliar territory, McCadden was reduced to a mere sounding board. '*May* be?' But in the silence that followed, he slowly worked his way through the implications of Jones's carefully released disclosures. The existence of a statement by Harry Rull, his sudden disappearance from Birmingham and his continued links with the IRA when he resurfaced in London, all wrapped together by Jones's knowing manner, could only lead to one plausible conclusion. 'You recruited him,' McCadden realized. 'When you caught up with him, instead of charging him or sending him back to Ireland, you recruited him as a double agent, a mole within the IRA in England.'

'Rull wasn't an IRA activist,' Jones said. 'In fact, he had no time for the militant nationalists. But his dealings with the terrorist named Rudican made him acceptable to them and useful to us.'

'In what way?'

'When Rudican had completed his prison sentence in Ireland in 1951, he came over here. His mission was to analyse the feasibility of a renewed IRA campaign on the mainland. He was based in London.'

'So that's why Rull was interrogated in '51 rather than '48 and why he left Birmingham.'

'He was, I believe, already tiring of domestic bliss. Another pattern in his life.'

'Did the IRA finally uncover him?'

'They may have.'

'Is that why he disappeared in 1977?'

'It's possible, I suppose.'

'So all that earlier stuff about his criminal record and his status in the London sex trade was just smoke in my eyes?'

'No. That's how he lived his life. He took his chances. Nothing to do with us.'

'Right,' McCadden said dubiously. 'And this *may be* document of Harry Rull's. What's in it?'

'An account of the attempt on his wife's life in 1948. Otherwise, Rull's personal history. His dispute with his parents as a young man. His attraction to Dublin's red-light district. His first meeting there with his wife, the woman you call Hannah Fraule, who was working as a sixteen-year-old prostitute in one of the brothels.'

McCadden was overtaken by astonishment again. '*Prostitute?*'

'As I said, sir, he always had the same taste in women.'

'Have you any proof?'

'Oh, yes.'

McCadden took some time to recover. Then, desperately trying to figure out what was being offered and what was being asked in return, he struggled to keep his responses as non-committal as possible. 'What are you interested in?' he wondered. 'An interview with Lucy Cuccini in Dublin? Confirmation of what happened to Harry Rull?'

'That,' Jones accepted. 'But also the lawyer you mentioned earlier.'

'Jack Stokes?'

'I'm curious about him. He's over here very frequently and I'm not quite sure precisely what his business is.'

McCadden gave it some thought. 'Look,' he said, 'I have no intention of ending up being shafted as a dupe of British Intelligence. If we're going to do this, let's do it officially. You get your boss to release a copy of Rull's statement to my commissioner. I'll get the commissioner to exchange what we have on Stokes and Lucy Cuccini. Where did you have in mind for lunch, by the way . . . ?'

five

On the return flight from Birmingham that evening, McCadden conceded his window seat to a Young Flyer who spent the time setting new records in a number of disciplines in International Track and Field on his Game-Boy. The kid glanced out once at the aerial views. Otherwise, the generosity was wasted on him. Young or not, he was already too experienced to be impressed by flying.

When I was your age, son . . .

The constant bleeping of the console, the boy's frantic movements as he repeatedly negotiated virtual sprints and long jumps and his mother's insistence on keeping her original seat while passing her offspring what might have been anabolic steroids across McCadden were all a little irritating. But purely as distractions, they were welcome as well. McCadden didn't want to brood too lengthily, or too hopefully, on the jigsaw he was putting together.

That Jack Stokes had failed to squeeze any information from Thomas Rull was not in itself significant. Stokes was a persistent, resourceful investigator with wide contacts among the police and criminal underworld, and there were other paths to the discovery of Harry Rull's colourful record once you had established that Harry had emigrated to England. What *was* certain was that, when he first approached Kelly McConnell, Stokes already knew about the attempt on Hannah Fraule's life in 1948. He knew that Harry and Hannah had lived in Naune in County Wexford until then. And he knew that Robert Hannifin and Joseph Mary Rudican came there to murder Hannah. Whoever employed him to trace the Fraules gave him this information. Whoever employed him, therefore, was more than likely in the same camp as Hannifin and Rudican. More than likely, they intended killing Hannah Fraule once she was located again. Why? To complete the contract that Harry had taken out on his wife in 1948? Why had Jack Stokes allowed Kelly McConnell to continue searching for Hannah and prevented her from pursuing Harry, supposedly the original object of the search, and then paid a perfunctory visit to Birmingham himself, to be easily fobbed off at the first attempt by a retiring violinist? Was Stokes's visit a smokescreen? Was he afraid that McConnell might discover that Harry Rull was *still alive*?

Holding off a frantic javelin thrower on his right, McCadden took the envelope of Thomas Rull's photographs from his pocket and studied its contents again. It was the old man who interested him. Harry Rull at seventy, and again at seventy-three. The white hair. The structure of his face. He thought of that photograph taken in Naune in 1937, of Harry and Hannah and little Emily, and he tried to imagine the *manner* of Harry's ageing, tried to use that formula to project an image of Harry as he might be now if he was still alive. He thought of the old man in the motorized wheelchair, seen three times in West Cork, twice in the village, outside Hannah's house, and again at the graveyard after Hannah's lonely burial. And he wondered. Wondered if Harry could have survived. Or wondered if it was true, as the Irish poet Patrick Kavanagh once claimed while writing about the haunting gap left by his own father's death, that every old man looked the same.

As the plane descended through heavy cloud over Dublin, McCadden thought also of the photograph of the Eucharistic Congress mass hanging on the wall of the hovel where Hannah Fraule had spent her last years as a recluse. It was the memory she treasured the most, the image she most wanted to portray. When she looked into the mirror of the past, that was the reflection she wanted to see. He wondered about the other photograph that had hung beside it at some stage. Wondered if it could be, again, that family portrait outside their pub in Naune. He'd probably never know, he accepted. Just as he'd never know precisely what Hannah did after she survived the attempt on her life in 1948, or why the IRA pair, Hannifin and Rudican, were so easily intercepted and arrested when there wasn't even a resident policeman in the village of Naune.

But it was Hannah who most absorbed him. A prostitute at sixteen. A pillar of church and society at thirty. A fugitive at forty. Did she flee directly to West Cork after the attack? Or did she look for a revival of the old life in Dublin? Did she repent? Did she become genuinely spiritual, rather than just socially religious? She lived another fifty-two years. And the extraordinary thing was, the second part of her life seemed to have been as bleak and repetitive, as one-dimensional and empty of incident as the first had been outrageously colourful and varied to the point of contradiction.

A game of two halves . . .

McCadden was in a taxi on the way home to his flat in Rathmines when he found two AA batteries in his jacket pocket. He had a faint recollection of accepting them on the plane, either as exhausted duds from the kid's Game-Boy or as replacements from the kid's mother, but he couldn't remember which.

He wasn't looking forward to settling back.

The flat he was renting was in the basement of an ugly Victorian building, without natural light and with cramped rooms full of cheap furniture and morose carpets and grubby wallpaper. He'd have to change soon. Get somewhere decent. A permanent home in Dublin. Bring his gear up from Waterford. It was a question of time.

He was relieved to find that Frank Ryan was still staying over in the spare room.

'Hey, Frank!' he said cheerfully, after locating his notebook from West Cork and checking the registration number of a red Mercedes driven by a middle-aged woman and carrying a toothless old man and his motorized wheelchair. 'You're a man of surprising interests, full of arcane titbits. Perfect material for the more demanding TV quiz shows, like *Fifteen-to-One* and *Mastermind.* Tell me this. Is the following registration number likely to be on a car driven by a woman called Lucy Cuccini, still devoted to a centenarian Harry Rull, who is sentimentally crooning "Love's Old Sweet Song" on the rear seat while sharpening his dentures?'

Ryan was reading a newspaper and not particularly listening. 'See this, Carl,' he countered. 'The wheelie bins in the south county have the local authority coat of arms on them. Their motto – on a bin of rubbish! – is "This We Hold In Trust". And someone has written underneath, "Corrupt Politicians Have Taken Everything Else."'

'Dublin wit,' McCadden remarked. 'You can't beat it, can you? Any developments while I was away?'

'Yeah,' Ryan remembered. 'Phelim Bourke left a message for you. Your elusive political scientist, Pius Shanahan, was spotted in Cork last Thursday night. He was mooching around an estate in Douglas. Isn't that where Albert Siggs lives?'

'It is. Was Shanahan picked up?'

'No. One of the Branch lads recognized him and tailed him to Douglas, but then lost him before the back-up arrived. Shanahan must've noticed he was being followed.'

'Was he by himself?'

'Apparently.'

'Did he make contact with Albert Siggs?'

'No. But it's too much of a coincidence, isn't it?'

'Any news of the other two, Desmond and Tee?'

'Nothing.'

Shadows, McCadden thought. Dancing with the ghosts of Hannah Fraule and Harry Rull. If Rull was even dead.

No longer in the mood for banter, he glanced at his watch and closed the notebook without calling out the registration number of the red Mercedes. 'Right,' he said wearily. 'Let's go for a drink, will we?'

PART FOUR

january, 1948

When they first came for Hannah, on the night of 11 April 1924, they called her by her family name.

'Hannah Buckley!' they cried. 'Which of you is Hannah Buckley?'

At first, I didn't even know who they were looking for. Although we'd been lovers for almost a year, I'd never heard her mother's name. I never knew her as anything other than Hannah Rose.

I was standing at the head of the stairs on the first-floor landing. I saw them rush the front door and push quickly past the man on guard there. There were three of them. Young men in cloth caps and belted raincoats.

I thought they were religious zealots. There was now a native government in power. Its politicians were largely Catholic prudes, embarrassed by sex and then enraged by their own embarrassment. Its police officers, the same fervent republican madmen I'd first met in this area six years earlier, were already on the streets, trying to intimidate the prostitutes. There was a new Catholic organization called the Legion of Mary. Its missionaries held prayer meetings near the brothels and tried to force the girls into shame. We had been expecting some form of attack.

Lately, our friends in high places had been advising us to pull out. The tide of opinion was turning. They could no longer continue protecting us if we persisted in openly trading as a brothel. What was needed, they argued, was to take our trade underground, to live above like respectable citizens while secretly satisfying the baser desires below. The old hypocrisy.

I imagined that this was the reason for the attack on our house in Gloucester Street that night.

But I was quickly disillusioned.

Our man guarding the front door was now slumped inside the hallway, disabled by knife wounds to his arms and hands. One of the intruders had grabbed a girl by the hair and was pulling her head backwards, examining her face as she screamed.

'That's not her, lads! It's not her!'

These were no crazed missionaries drunk on the Lord's commandments. These were dedicated assassins searching for a specific target.

At that moment, alerted by the commotion, Hannah came from a bedroom on the first floor and stood behind me, calling anxiously. 'What is it, Harry?' One of the young men, his attention drawn to the movement and the voice, looked up and pointed jubilantly.

'There she is, lads! You're Hannah Buckley, aren't you?'

Without waiting for his companions, he rushed up the stairs. I didn't wait for him, either. Before he had time to steady himself and bring the knife he was carrying into play, I stepped down and swung a fist into his face. He more or less hurried into the blow and was stunned. But the others were close behind him. One was tugging what seemed like a revolver from the pocket of his raincoat. I threw myself down at him. It was the only chance I had. When we collided we tumbled back down the stairs. He was on his feet before me. His helpers were also closing in. But luckily our doorman, although wounded, had raised the alarm outside. Others came rushing to help. The three attackers were quickly outnumbered and only managed to escape by brandishing their weapons to clear a path and then fleeing into the darkened lanes once they were on the street outside.

No one had recognized them.

And yet they knew who Hannah Buckley was.

I asked her about this afterwards. She confirmed that this had been her mother's name. But she could not name anyone, apart from Sarah Cunningham, the former owner of our brothel, who could be aware of it.

Some days later, we were told by a police inspector that the leader of the gang who had attacked our house was a republican fugitive named Joseph Mary Rudican and that Hannah's name was on a hit list. The confused politics of the period are almost impossible to understand, even for the Irish. Enough to mention that after the withdrawal of the English and the inevitable bloody civil war, there were gunmen everywhere. It never occurred to me at the time to ask why Hannah was on a hit list, and no one offered an explanation. I assumed it was because she ran a brothel that had once been popular with the old administration. After all, the IRA were burning splendid old houses about the countryside, and for no better reason than the religion of the owners. Why should they spare a mere kip house in the slums of Dublin?

We had to get out.

More difficult still, we had to disappear.

But I must admit, nothing seemed to give our patrons more childish pleasure than the prospect of providing Hannah with a new identity. Among the nationalist politicians of the time there was an intense passion for renaming things. Streets were renamed, torn away from the old English heroes they once commemorated and given to the new Irish heroes. Parks were renamed. Monuments. People hastily abandoned the Anglo-Saxon forms of their own names and invented Gaelicisms to take their place. New identities were quite the rage, and not at all a problem.

The only difficulty lay in Hannah's insistence on retaining her forename. I expect it offered her a sense of continuity, a thread she was reluctant to sever, but it made things slightly more awkward than they might have been. Finally, however, even this was resolved, when it was decreed that a pauper's child had not, after all, died in vain in 1906 after struggling for breath for a mere three days.

The child had been christened Hannah May Fraule. And she had no surviving relatives.

Hannah and I resettled in Donnybrook, on the south side of Dublin city.

I don't know who bought our expensive house. I didn't ask. I didn't enquire into the source of Hannah's considerable personal wealth.

When Hannah and I completed our transformation by marrying in 1925, she was still only nineteen years old. Although the official records show that Harold Rull married Hannah Fraule, we took to using the titles Mr and Mrs Fraule afterwards. My own surname was too well known to our pursuers, too easily traced and recognized.

But with the loss of my name, the excitement also went from my life.

I wasn't alone in this. As I've already mentioned, many others were also intent on disguising the past. Within a short space of time, the brothels in Monto closed, scattering prostitutes about the city. Our old haunt, Gloucester Street, was changed to Sean McDermott Street, after some demented patriot. Even Montgomery Street, which had given the area its nickname, was replaced by Foley Street. The red lights went out. And a melancholy, breast-beating gloom descended on the whole nation.

The same man who desires a whore to enliven his bed longs for an angel to rest in his cradle. The wild revolutionary who wants only blood on his hands becomes obsessed with cleanliness after gaining power. It's one of the great ironies of life.

I was compromised by the birth of our daughter, Emily, in 1927.

We had never discussed either starting or raising a family. Until it was unavoidably obvious, I wasn't even aware that Hannah was pregnant.

A child, I think, was the final adornment for Hannah, the last accessory to a new look she had embraced. She had settled into respectability with surprising enthusiasm. And talent. I thought she might miss the old freedoms and excitements. She didn't. Or she preferred the newer ones.

Our home in Donnybrook was spacious, and yet, for a period from the mid- to the late twenties, it always seemed to be crowded, either with farmers and shopkeepers whose sons were Catholic clergymen, or else with Catholic clergymen whose fathers were shopkeepers and farmers. These were the inheritors of the new Ireland, these celibate young men or sexually deprived old men, and they swarmed around Hannah, like flies attracted to jam. She kept them mercilessly in thrall. She was everything to them. She was twenty-one years old, extraordinarily beautiful, wealthy, witty, pious, and yet crackling with sexual energy.

I imagined I had no role in this repulsive charade. I was wrong. And Hannah knew that I was wrong long before I discovered it myself. In fact, I was essential. A deserted wife, abandoned by her husband, no matter how wise or wealthy or benevolent, could not be elevated by a nation of priests and farmers and shopkeepers to a central status. Illusion, while elastic, does have its breaking points. Even hypocrisy has parameters.

As a free agent, of course – a loose cannon, so to speak – I was also a threat to Hannah. The young men who had come to murder her in Gloucester Street in 1924 had now gone underground, defeated in a civil war and afterwards suppressed, but they were still eager to locate her, anxious to discover her new identity.

On the other hand, if I was betrayed by her, I might well meet a bullet myself in some of the darker alleys of the city.

We were bound by mutual distrust.

Hannah never advanced these arguments to me. She never made the case for staying together as a couple. She noted my growing restlessness. She watched my preparations for departure. By then, I had exhausted my own money, most of it on Hannah herself. Barely a decade on from my escape from my parents and I was again reduced to stealing and pawning. I had no future. Having nothing to protect, I had never built.

It was Hannah who gave me my future. Hannah, more devious and more resourceful than the rest of us, more aware of the precise lines of courtship between sex and power. It wasn't merely that she became pregnant. Since our marriage, for all her theatrical display, she had remained faithful.

Whatever else I was uncertain about, I knew that the child she was about to bear was my own.

In an age of revolutions, I was never a revolutionary. I was only a rebel.

A revolutionary would have quickly strangled the child at birth or slowly strangled it with neglect. But when I first held Emily in my arms, shortly after her delivery, I felt confused by an unfamiliar bond, trapped by the sudden awareness that I couldn't either abandon my daughter or force her to endure a childhood as constrained and arid as my own had been.

For the moment, it didn't even matter to me that Hannah had anticipated my response and set this snare for me.

But only for the moment.

Some time after her confinement, in the autumn of 1927, following the general election of that year – and I think she waited until the consequences of the ballot were clear – Hannah chose a lover. I say 'chose', because that's exactly what she did. The moves in the game of hypocrisy at that time were very precise. She could not be promiscuous; that would lead to notoriety. She could not have sex with anyone without influence; he wouldn't be powerful enough to shield her from exposure. She needed an individual whose position was secure enough to guarantee her protection, but whose age and virility were not fearsome enough to discourage all the others who desired her.

She chose well. Her lover was a government minister, a senior member of the cabinet that had ruled the country for the previous five years and which would continue to do so for the next five.

From that time our movements were perfectly synchronized, but in different circles. For the most part, I lost sight of her manoeuvres. I know that they were always sure-footed. I believe she changed horses, for instance, along with the rest of the country, in the general election of 1932, which saw the defeat of the sitting government. She took a new lover. A new government minister.

Nothing illustrates our separation more vividly than the Eucharistic Congress of that same year, 1932. This was the great celebration of Irish Catholic nationalism, that bauble which had been won by a century of struggle against the might of the British Empire and which was now on display to the whole world. While Hannah, whose influence with the bishops was considerable by now, served on numerous organizing committees, squeezing forward to kiss the hand of the papal legate and the hems of many sanctified garments, I took Emily, then a lively and inquisitive five-year-old, on a tour of my old haunts in Monto, where there were no brothels, no prostitutes and no drinking dens any more, but where the poor people of the slums, now more numerous than ever, had decked their streets with bunting, painted their houses green and white and brought out the few tables and chairs they had to serve tea and sandwiches to the foreign visitors who were in town for the Congress.

However, early in 1934 there was a second crisis, another reminder that the past wouldn't be so easily manipulated and might even have a momentum of its own.

In January that year, word was passed to Hannah that a murder squad, led by Joseph Mary Rudican, was edging uncomfortably close to discovering her. Since she was warned by her lover, it had to be assumed that the information came directly from army or police intelligence and was reliable. We were advised to move again, and preferably away from Dublin.

Hannah chose to dismiss the threat and the advice. It was mere rumour, she insisted. There was no proof, no evidence that she was being watched or followed. Perhaps she felt immune. Perhaps she had convinced herself that she was now too powerful, too important, to be touched by menials. Success had made her arrogant. She had forgotten the source of it. Above all, she did not seem to understand any more that she was still a whore, that her services, and her position, were at the command of another.

In February, she was brutally reminded of the truth.

She was travelling through St Stephen's Green in her open carriage. Apart from her driver, she was alone. She did this tour of the city every morning, granting its citizens a rare glimpse of class, before visiting or meeting acquaintances for lunch. She saw no reason to alter her routine.

Close to the Shelbourne Hotel, a young man jumped from the pavement into the carriage. Before Hannah had time to alert her driver with a cry for help, the young man produced a revolver. He didn't shoot with the weapon, however. He viciously clubbed her across the face with its butt and then quickly vanished into the crowds again as she slumped on the seat, bleeding profusely.

Although there was no permanent disfigurement, she did need extensive treatment in hospital. And while she was there, her influence rapidly dissipated, like an unstable shape formed by smoke that is suddenly blown away by a puff of wind. It had no more substance than that.

Without her face, the surface appearance she had invested so much faith in, Hannah was nothing. Her former admirers turned away from her, unable to look on her bruised and ugly features. And of all those Christian gentlemen, monsignors and bishops who had swarmed about her before, not one came to comfort her in hospital. Her political patrons abandoned her as well, of course. And even the wives of the nation's farmers and shopkeepers, who had previously envied her grace and beauty, came only to gloat.

The incident, and its consequences, made our departure from Dublin inevitable.

I have always mistrusted the official account of the attack on Hannah at St Stephen's Green.

Whether or not they were actively searching for her at that time, I don't doubt that gunmen would have paid her a visit if they had been told where she was, but I believe that, having found and isolated her, they would simply have executed her. These were not squeamish or half-hearted people. Among other atrocities from this period, they shot and murdered a seventy-two-year-old Admiral in his own drawing room.

But I have another reason for my scepticism.

It is surely inconceivable that we could have retained our names if an assassin was so close. Hannah Fraule was too easily traced. And yet, there was never any proposal to further conceal ourselves with aliases or pseudonyms. Quite the opposite. When we established a business, we were encouraged to trade as Fraules.

I have always believed, therefore, that the young man who assaulted Hannah was an agent working for Hannah's lover.

The minister wanted to free himself of her.

Perhaps he had simply tired of her and she wouldn't take the more gentle hints or else responded with a counter-threat. But perhaps it was something more severe than this. It may have been the austerity of the times, the sexual puritanism exacerbated by economic gloom. A rather retentive Catholic Church kept a painful grip on the country's vitals. At the very least, with the army and police intelligence now aware of Hannah's background and enemies all too eager to promote leaks of information, the minister risked being compromised. It was also true that the minister's party colleagues were former missionary gunmen themselves and had only lately come to constitutional politics as a means of repressing sexuality. The fanatical rump they had left behind with this move were those same madmen who slaughtered retired sailors in their homes, those same zealots hunting the minister's mistress. Such confused intimacies, bordering on incest, were becoming intolerable.

Having failed to talk Hannah into leaving Dublin, I believe the minister intimidated her into doing so.

I don't think he was harsh, except in the sharpness of the lesson. He certainly wasn't ungrateful. Had Hannah been reasonable, she would have accepted that she was generously provided for. But Hannah's intoxicating decade close to the reins of power had corrupted her judgement.

Life might have been different if responsibility had ever come naturally to me. But it didn't. Self-restraint was always a tortuous struggle. Nevertheless, our new home, in the remote village of Naune in County Wexford, probably suited myself and Emily far more than it suited Hannah.

I compromised by balancing a double existence. In my youth, rejecting my parents' shrivelled hypocrisy, I had swapped the day for the night and the glare of labouring in the sun for the pleasures of carousing in the dark. Now I drove myself to live both day and night. I had my pleasures, my drinking companions, my mistresses. But I kept them concealed from view. As I kept my resentment and my thirst for revenge concealed. And I always ensured that I was smiling for my daughter when she woke each morning.

By then, Emily was almost eight years old. For the first time, she had real friends to play with. She was at the very beginning of the journey towards an independent life. For her, the country was actually a release from confinement. She had fields and lanes to roam, farms to visit, animals to discover and love.

By contrast, Hannah during these early years in Naune was a rather pathetic figure. I believe she was slightly insane, driven mad by bitterness and resentment and frustration. Frustration of ambition, which can be as devastating as sexual frustration. She had recovered her looks, of course. She was as bewitchingly beautiful as before. But she had carried with her all her grand airs and pretensions, and they were sadly out of place among the haystacks and the muddied lanes.

I don't pretend that the locals weren't impressed by her. Of course they were. Immensely. Recognizing these as simple, devout people, Hannah quickly advertised her significant role in the Eucharistic Congress, her familiarity with the personal names of cardinals and bishops. She kept her own name constantly before her tiny public by commandeering every local committee and charitable organization. She swiftly seduced some besotted provincial hack, who lavished a small fortune in newsprint on her. She rarely presented herself as a wife, and never as a mother. Such was the intensity of her lustre that others could not share her light and survive. But even this triumph had its galling denial. Terrified that exposure from her role in the Eucharistic Congress really had alerted her pursuers, she could not allow her photograph to be published.

Such was her public character during the early years in Naune.

Privately, she raged.

She swung violently between accepting the official explanation for the attack on her in Dublin and savagely accusing me of betraying her.

I hadn't betrayed her, of course, but the accusation put the idea into my head.

The truth is, I needed some defence, some weaponry of my own. Particularly when Hannah's megalomania started to threaten Emily as well. She ranted about preventing the child from associating with lower classes. She rambled on about saving her for a triumphant return to Dublin society. This was a dangerous new direction in Hannah's obsession with status. And I had to take steps to prevent it.

First, as proof of our identities and location, I hired a local photographer to take a family portrait outside our public house in Naune. I had to do this covertly, duping Hannah into the pose. With this in my possession, I set about the rest of my strategy.

I already knew a great deal about the organization whose gunmen hunted Hannah. I reminded her how easy it would be to contact them. And this in itself was enough to gain some power over her. Faced with the choice of relinquishing her daughter or her own lingering ambitions, she let Emily go.

Part of our agreement was financial. Since the child's future was at issue, I insisted on taking control of our main business activities.

After this battle, concluded in the summer of 1937, Hannah spent an increasing amount of time in Dublin again, particularly during the Second World War, when for a time the city became a rather Bohemian oasis in the midst of international carnage. What she gained from these visits, I'm not sure. Very little, I imagine. She had been too long away from the sheets of men of influence.

And by and large, this is how things remained until Christmas 1947.

By then, Emily was twenty years old. A young woman. Although she had inherited more of my own looks than Hannah's, she was pretty and attractive. The previous eight or nine years she had spent more time away from home than in Naune, at first at her boarding school in Wexford and then in London. She had a talent for dress designing, the focus of her studies in England, and an ambition to establish her own couture business.

Although she had planned to travel in the summer of '47, specifically to the fashion houses of Paris and Rome, she changed her mind at the last moment and returned to Naune. The resumption of her studies in the autumn was again punctuated by frequent weekends back in Ireland. She seemed unusually restless. I imagined she was having doubts about her choice of career. Or perhaps she was worried about her performance, her results.

But of course I was merely a victim of the usual blindness of parents.

It never occurred to me that Emily had a lover.

That Christmas, however, she gathered all her news together into one startling bundle and finally told me, not only her lover's name, but also the date of their secret marriage, the first names they had chosen for the child she was pregnant with and their intention of emigrating to America.

I was enraged. Not because her husband was a recently demobilized British Army captain and a Protestant by birth. I had no objection to soldiers or to Protestants. I was enraged because I felt betrayed. I gave expression to my anger. And after almost twenty years of self-denial and duplicity and frustrated self-discipline, my anger had accumulated a great deal of bitterness and my rejection was harsh.

When Emily left the house that night, she had no intention of ever returning. She travelled earlier than she had planned to Cork, from where they had booked their passage to America, and she waited there for the arrival of her husband.

From that moment, I considered myself released from every obligation. I contacted the village butcher, Francis Cheevers, whose political sympathies I was well aware of. His fanatical father, also the local butcher in his time, had once led a half-hearted attack on the ancestral home of the Protestant family Emily had married into.

On the morning of 3 January 1948, having bled our bank accounts and business and secretly transferred the money to England, I left the village of Naune, driving the short distance east to New Ross and connecting there with the early bus to Dublin. As I remember it, I was carrying only a small brown suitcase.

They were waiting for me at the junction we had agreed on, about twenty miles south of Dublin city, Cheevers, still as coarse and bloated as when he'd terrorized the other children as a boy, and a slight, redheaded youth who was introduced as Robert Hannifin.

It was Hannifin who drove us afterwards, although the black Ford, a familiar sight in the village, actually belonged to Cheevers. I had little interest in our destination, although Cheevers fretted beside me in the rear seat every time I peered too obviously through the windows. As far as I could judge, the small cottage we finally pulled up outside was a few miles north of Glencree in County Wicklow. Another car was already parked by the front door. Hannifin didn't cut the engine when he stopped, he left it idling. When he stepped out and opened the rear door for me, Cheevers climbed into the driver's seat, quickly circled the farmyard and left again through the muddied entrance.

Inside the cottage, sitting behind a rough deal table that had a revolver resting on its surface, there was a haggard, middle-aged man. His head was uncovered. He was wearing a heavy trench coat and had a thick woollen scarf wrapped around his neck for warmth. His face had once been plump but had lost its tone over the years, and the flesh was now slack and flabby. He hadn't shaved for several days and his rough beard was greying. His brown eyes were piercing and distrustful. Behind his table, he looked like an interrogator waiting with sour relish for his next victim.

This was Joseph Mary Rudican.

I recognized him immediately as the man with the knife I had confronted on the stairs in Gloucester Street in 1924.

It was obvious, though, that Rudican didn't make the same connections and had no idea who I was. He was sharp enough to catch the flash of recognition in my eyes, but he had no understanding of its source. Unsettled by suddenly finding himself on weaker ground, he fingered the revolver and suspiciously demanded to know what information I was carrying and why I had asked to see him. When I wondered if he was still anxious to trace the whereabouts of a former prostitute named Hannah Buckley, otherwise known as Hannah Rose, he was even more startled. Once he recovered, however, he coyly admitted that he might be interested. His eyes betrayed more bloodlust than mere interest, though. I told him that there were conditions. I asked him to confirm that he had attacked the brothel in Gloucester Street in 1924 and that he had no involvement in the assault on Hannah ten years later in Stephen's Green. I insisted on knowing why he hunted Hannah Buckley. He was greatly amused by my obvious assumption that his organization would show such dedication to the pursuit of a mere whore who had opened her legs for high-ranking British Army officers and officials. He had no hesitation in telling me the real reason for the death sentence on her. In fact, he gained by publicizing it.

Hannah was an informer.

In 1921, as a sixteen-year-old, she had lured a high-ranking IRA volunteer named Eamon Brannigan into an ambush set for him by British agents in a lane off Gloucester Street, where he was brutally murdered. It was also believed that she was responsible for the arrest and torture of other local republicans living or hiding in the slums around the brothels.

All missionary revolutionary organizations have long memories for the deeds of their martyrs, but they reserve their most perfect recall for their own Judases.

I left that meeting with Joseph Mary Rudican and Robert Hannifin, after accepting a lift to Dublin and then arranging to tell them where Hannah Buckley, or Hannah Fraule, could now be found, and I travelled directly by mail boat to England and then by train to Birmingham.

one

Lucy Cuccini had an exclusive address in Donnybrook where she lived in one of the plusher estates with Christy Sweeney, a well-known figure in the criminal underworld; and the owner of the red Mercedes that had put in an appearance after Hannah Fraule's funeral in West Cork, recorded promisingly as Helen Troy, owned a house in the nearby suburb of Rathmines. Checking the locations on a street map, McCadden found that they were equidistant from where he was sitting in his temporary offices in Harcourt Street. He was childishly undecided about which to visit first. Lucy Cuccini might offer him an explanation of what had happened to Harry Rull since his last disappearance in 1977. Helen Troy might bring him to the old improviser himself. He flipped a coin. It settled on his desk in favour of the woman with the legendary name.

The house was in a quiet corner of a residential square. In one of its upstairs rooms, behind a window that had been stripped of its curtains, a middle-aged woman was frantically shaking out linen while making the beds. McCadden recognized her immediately, noting that he'd seen her twice now and on both occasions she was behind glass and nervously absorbed. Pulling up, he couldn't spot the red Mercedes among the cars parked by the footpath. He noticed, however, that some of the approaches to the house had been adapted for wheelchair access. Although the stone steps leading up to the main front door were still in place, those to the basement had been replaced by a gently sloping ramp.

He parked and walked to the house, still unseen by the domesticated maenad in the upstairs bedroom. As he turned back to close the front gate behind him, he heard the sudden growl of a low capacity engine. Simultaneously, the old man in the motorized wheelchair buzzed up from the basement flat and the woman above, alerted by all the noise, threw open a bedroom window and craned her head out to look down. The old man, with childish glee, skilfully manoeuvred the wheelchair so that it blocked McCadden's access to the front steps. He said nothing. He stared aggressively, sucking his cheeks inside his mouth so that his face was distorted. A death's head, mounted by lips that were pursed for a kiss.

McCadden felt ridiculous. 'Looks like it might rain again,' he offered. But with no conviction. The absurdity of discussing the weather with a mechanized watchdog was too uncomfortable for him.

Ironically, the woman in the upstairs window seemed to share his view. 'Granddad!' she yelped as if she was calling a frisky mongrel to heel. 'Granddad! Back!'

It might have been illusion, but as the unspoken encouragement *Good boy!* echoed inside McCadden's head, the old man seemed to snarl to himself before spinning away and retreating to his kennel.

Reaching the front door as the flustered housewife opened it for him, McCadden already had his ID and a calming opening line at the ready. 'We're just making a few enquiries in the area.'

Invited inside, he was showered with nervous apologies. 'You mustn't mind granddad. I'm sorry, my husband isn't here. Please ignore the state of the place. My cleaning lady. Last night I had the most awful nightmare. Somehow or other she was my dentist and she started drilling my teeth with her usual incompetence. I always think they set me on edge for the day. Nightmares.'

They ended up in a neurotically tidy breakfast room, the woman still desperately working off her nervous energy, McCadden slightly dizzy from the irrelevant assault. He asked, 'Are you Ms Helen Troy?'

'I'm married, inspector.'

'Yes, but—'

'*Mrs* Helen Troy.'

'Right. Do you own a red Mercedes with a '98 Dublin registration?'

Her raised right hand flapped against her agitated breast, fanning cooling air to her flushed face at the same time. 'Oh, my God! It's Harold, isn't it?'

McCadden knew that it was too good to be true, but a mild spasm of hope still gripped him. 'Who's Harold?'

'My husband. He took my car this morning. I did tell him about the left wing mirror. Unfortunately, the flow of traffic at the junction of—'

'It's not your husband,' McCadden interrupted.

'And the problem with the clutch. Well, you know what mechanics are like, inspector. I'm sure you do. I've been back three times with that—'

'There's no problem with the car. Not today. We're investigating a crime and we're simply eliminating people from our enquiries.'

'What an odd idea.'

'Which?'

'Eliminating.'

'Right. What I need to know, Mrs Troy, is whether you were in West Cork over the New Year and if you were driving the Mercedes while you were there.'

The question brought on another flutter of nerves. She slumped, melodramatically, into the nearest armchair. 'Oh, my gosh! I knew he wouldn't be satisfied. I said to Harold, I said, you can never trust a farmer. Not that Harold was with me. When I came back.'

'So you were in West Cork?'

'I'm not at all convinced he wasn't trying to pull the wool over our eyes.'

'Mrs Troy—'

She suddenly gripped the arms of the chair and pulled herself forward to perch excitedly on the edge. 'Now, don't tell me,' she pleaded. 'Don't tell me. West Cork. I knew it immediately. It's a real giveaway. You must be investigating that murder down there. The old lady. No, don't tell me her name. Don't tell me. Hannah Fraule! That's it, isn't it? I must tell granddad. He'll be so excited. We were there, you see.'

'Where?'

She sprang up, intending to contact the old man, but then, like an animal sensing danger on the wind, she stuck her nose in the air and gave three or four hurried sniffs. 'The cakes!' she cried. 'Quick, man! Quick! What time is it?' She hurried off. In the doorway, she half turned again, torn between domesticity and hospitality. 'You must think me very rude. I'm not usually like this, you know. You're probably better off if you just follow me. Ignore all the rest. Go with the flow, as they say.'

McCadden trundled after the impossible woman, evilly imagining useful professions her husband might be skilled at. Chemist. Butcher. Gunsmith. When he caught up with her again, she was on her knees in front of an electric cooker in the kitchen, her hands protected by oven gloves, lifting out a tray of perfectly browned cakes. 'These are queen cakes,' she announced proudly. 'Quite simple little things, but quite delicious. They're for granddad. I prefer the larger cakes myself. Don't you? Dundee. Dundee cakes are my favourite.'

'Dundee?' McCadden echoed. Now and then, the clutter threw up sounds that seemed to have maddeningly elusive significance. If only he could grasp the connections before they were swamped again. But his head was spinning.

'Do you have a sweet tooth, inspector?'

'My sergeant—'

'Oh, now, that's what all the men say. I'll only take this for my little boy. I know you.'

McCadden desperately tried to row back to the island of sanity his own interests represented. While the woman obsessively arranged her cakes on a tiered serving tray – she wouldn't give him any, he realized then, because the removal of even one would ruin that perfect pyramid – he silently rehearsed the sequence of questions he needed her to answer. But as he waited, trying to time the delivery of his first query to coincide with a quiet moment in the woman's crowded schedule, his mobile phone rang. It was McCadden's contact in Special Branch, Phelim Bourke.

'How far away are you from the Pine Forest, Carl?' Bourke wanted to know.

'I'm in Rathmines,' McCadden told him.

'Well, it might be worth your while making the journey out. We've finally found Pius Shanahan for you.'

'Is he talking?'

'Are you alone there?'

'No, not particularly.'

'Okay. He's not even moving, Carl. He's dead.'

'How?'

'Gunshot.'

McCadden jotted Bourke's directions in his notebook and contacted Frank Ryan, arranging to meet him at the scene. When he disconnected the second call, Helen Troy was standing patiently in front of him. 'Bad news?' she enquired.

'Confusing,' McCadden admitted. 'Do you mind if we hurry things along a little?'

'Oh, not at all. I hate wasting time. Harold, my husband, is always trying to convince me—'

'Your grandfather, Mrs Troy. What's his full name?'

'Granddad? Peter. Peter Michael. Troy, of course. Silly me. I almost forgot the most important part. Sometimes, because you're so familiar with a thing yourself—'

'Has he ever lived in England?'

'Not that I know of, no. I think I'd know if he had.'

'How old is he?'

'I don't think we'll ever see his age, will we? They say that people's life expectancy is increasing. But I don't know. Those old folks from that generation. He's eighty-nine, believe it or not.'

'Was he with you when you were touring in West Cork over the New Year?'

'I brought him. Sure, that's what we went for.'

'What?'

'I beg your pardon?'

'What was your reason for visiting the area?'

She gazed at him with soft, maternal indulgence. 'We went down to see where the old woman had been murdered, inspector. I thought I had already made that clear.'

'You went to visit the scene of the crime?'

'Yes.'

'Why?'

'It's granddad's hobby. He's like Sherlock Holmes. Whenever he sees a murder reported in the papers, he has to solve it. I do feel sorry for him, you know. He has very few interests since all his friends have died. Although he did enjoy their funerals. I will say that for him. It gets him out of the house, you see. The murders. And he could be wasting his time on a lot worse things. It's a bit of a drag for me, of course, having to drive him places down the country. But that old woman in West Cork really got her hooks into him. They're about the same age, you see. Now, you'll be interested in this. Do you know who he thinks did it? . . .'

two

The Pine Forest, stretching across the slopes of the Dublin Mountains a few kilometres south of the city, was a popular spot with walkers and day trippers. From its approach, the visitor could look back down over the spread of the capital city, from Dublin Bay in the east to the satellite towns and grim housing estates in the west. Its proximity to the city and its quiet seclusion made it attractive to many types. Lovers. Families. Fitness freaks. And murderers. It was the most popular location in the country for concealing bodies.

At the scene, a uniformed sergeant was on duty on the main road trying to keep the unusually heavy traffic moving smoothly. News of the killing had obviously travelled fast. So fast that McCadden half expected to see a motorized wheelchair whizzing past him when he got stuck in the jam for a few minutes. Beyond the sergeant was one of the access routes to the forest. A small car park, now crowded with police vehicles, and a pedestrian exit from that, protected by two heavy iron barriers, led to approved walking trails.

At first, McCadden thought that Shanahan must have driven here and been shot while he sat in his car. A silver Mitsubishi Lancer, cordoned off by crime-scene tape and surrounded by Garda technicians, was sitting in a far corner of the car park. But as he pulled in, guided to a space by another uniform, he noticed Frank Ryan waving at him frantically from another direction, gesturing him away from the silver Mitsubishi.

Ryan was standing by himself on the pathway behind the barrier at the exit from the car park. Dressed in wellington boots, a padded ski jacket and an incongruous grey trilby, he was keeping himself warm with a polystyrene cup full of steaming liquid. His urgency and his isolated position suggested only further difficulties, but they came from a totally unexpected source.

'Albert Siggs was attacked in Cork last night, Carl,' he explained. 'I just got the report before I left the office. He wants to see you.'

McCadden had no heavy clothing with him. The leather jacket he was wearing wasn't really efficient enough. He was cold and wanted to keep moving, but the news made him pull up sharply. 'Anything to do with Hannah Fraule?' he wondered.

'He seems to think so. And I'd have to agree with him. It looks like someone made an attempt to cut and bite off his right nipple.'

'Is he okay?'

'Stable. Off the critical list, but still serious. He'll recover.'

'Does he know who it was?'

'No, I don't think so.'

'When was he attacked?'

'About eight o'clock, apparently.'

'When did Shanahan die?'

'That I don't know. I haven't been there yet. I just got here before you and I was waiting until you arrived.'

'Was he shot in the car?'

'No.' Ryan pointed through the trees. 'Down the trail, somewhere into the forest. Haven't you got any boots in the car? The ground is soft. You're going to ruin your shoes if you go like that.'

McCadden borrowed equipment from a squad car and followed Ryan along the beaten path into the forest. About half a kilometre on, the path forked, rising into the mountains on their right and dipping towards a stream to their left.

Shanahan had been killed on the near bank of the shallow stream. His body was now concealed behind a white plastic partition. The tall assistant state pathologist, Hugh Craig, dressed in white overalls, could just be seen on the other side of the screen. In the immediate vicinity, within a cordon of yellow tape, scene-of-crime officers were also busy.

Phelim Bourke, the Special Branch inspector, was standing to one side talking to some of his officers. 'Any news?' he greeted McCadden hopefully.

McCadden shook his head. 'No. What happened?'

'Well, we estimate about midnight last night, Shanahan drove up here, into the car park. He must've arranged to meet someone. He locked the car, walked along the path down to here. There's a torch he used close to the body. He walked up and down a bit to keep himself warm. Footprints in the soft ground. Someone joined him. Two sets of prints. They stood together for a while. Then the contact drew a gun. No idea of the make or model yet. Shot him once in the chest. When he fell, finished him off with a second bullet to the back of the head.'

'Professional hit?'

'Looks like it.'

'What do you reckon?'

'I reckon we're in the shit, Carl, unless we quickly figure this out. He's a couple of months out of jail – released as a gesture of our acceptance that peace is descending on us all – puts in some quality time with the media idealizing his own murders, disappears for three weeks and ends up face down in the mud of the Dublin mountains with a couple of slugs in him. Who do I think did it? Take your pick. Could've been taken out by loyalist paramilitaries to settle an old grudge, by his own side because his loud mouth was threatening the peace process, or by vindictive relatives of one of his victims who couldn't stomach his gloating any more. Who knows? The word is, he disappeared for the last three weeks because he was searching for someone. There's a guy over there I want you to meet about that.'

'Why was Shanahan called *Baker*, Phelim?' McCadden wondered.

Bourke shrugged. 'Is it relevant?'

'I don't know. Something just occurred to me. Dundee. Eccles. They're confectioneries.'

'So's a fruitcake,' Ryan chipped in unhelpfully.

'The only legitimate job Shanahan ever had was as a baker,' Bourke explained. 'He did his apprenticeship in Belfast, got a job in Hastings, in the south of England, and from there co-ordinated the bombing campaign of seaside resorts in the seventies and eighties until he was picked up and convicted. Most of his time was done in the high-security section of Wandsworth Prison in England. It was said he used to bake political cartoons while he was there. Decorative cakes. He was transferred back to Northern Ireland to complete his sentence as part of the ongoing peace negotiations. That any help?'

'No,' McCadden admitted. 'What about the other two released prisoners you suggested, Peter Desmond and Bobby Tee?'

'Nothing.'

'They don't want to be found, do they?'

'Obviously not.'

'What's the drill here?'

'We'll wait for the pathologist's preliminary report and some early indications from the technical lads. There's a conference this afternoon.

High-level stuff. Because of the political implications, this has them worried all the way to the top. We'll be sitting at the lower tables. You're expected to be there, to explain your interest in Shanahan.'

'Frank can fill in for me,' McCadden offered. 'I've got to go to Cork. Who did you want me to see?'

On drier ground above the sodden bank they'd established a small field canteen using a tent and its canopy. There was nothing on offer except dire coffee, strong tea and watery soup, all of them steaming hot and all more beneficial as hand warmers than as drinks. Inside the tent a slight middle-aged man was sitting alone, nursing a polystyrene cup. He was introduced to McCadden as Philip Crowe, a Sinn Fein councillor from one of Dublin's city-centre wards.

On the walk from the crime scene to the tent, Bourke had explained that Crowe was also a former political prisoner and that he seemed to have some role within his party that involved integrating and debriefing the recently released activists. He'd come there that morning to identify Shanahan's body. It was impossible to be certain, but his presence seemed to indicate that the man hadn't been killed as a result of any internal disputes within his own organization. In fact, Crowe seemed as anxious as everybody else to quickly find the killer and defuse the situation. The potential damage to the peace process was considerable.

Essentially, Crowe merely repeated to McCadden what he'd already told Bourke. But the fact that he did so eagerly, without complaint, indicated his anxiety. He said, 'I know you were looking for Baker the last two weeks or so since you met him down in County Wexford. I haven't seen him. I don't know anyone who has. I've heard, though, that he was asking to find someone himself.'

'Do you know who?'

Crowe shook his head. 'No.'

'It wouldn't be Peter Desmond, would it?'

'I doubt it.'

'Or Bobby Tee?'

Crowe transferred the polystyrene cup to his left hand and lifted his right to demonstrate. The first two fingers were crossed and stuck tightly together. 'Baker and Bobby Tee were like that,' he explained. 'Like father and son. Bobby Tee worshipped the ground he walked on. If he thought Baker needed to see him he'd go through hell and high water to get there.'

'Any idea what he's been doing with himself since his release?'

'He's a nice quiet lad, Bobby is. Keeps himself to himself. Apart from Baker, no one ever got very close to him. I'm sure he just wants to get out of the glare, get down to putting his life back together again.'

'Right. Any other suggestions?'

Crowe looked into his cup, and decided against tasting the contents. He asked, 'The name Banbury mean anything to you?'

McCadden shook his head. 'No. Isn't it a town in England? In Oxfordshire?'

'It's also a cake,' Frank Ryan pointed out. The others looked at him with varying degrees of indulgence. 'Well, it is,' he defended himself.

'Do you think Shanahan found whoever he was looking for?' McCadden asked.

'Doubt it,' Crowe said. 'I think if he'd found him, the guy would probably be lying down there now, not Baker.'

'Maybe the quarry found him first.'

'Maybe.'

'Any idea *why* he was looking for someone?'

'None.'

'Do you know anyone called Harry Rull, Mr Crowe?'

'Harry Rull? Can't say I do, no. Not ringing any bells.'

'Joseph Mary Rudican? Or Robert Hannifin?'

'Names from the past,' Crowe mused. 'Rudican goes all the way back to the War of Independence, the Civil War. He was only a kid at the time. He was interned in the twenties. Sentenced to be executed, then pardoned. He stayed active in the IRA. He was jailed again some time in the late forties, for fund-raising.'

'Armed robbery,' Bourke translated.

Crowe ignored him. 'He died in England in the early eighties. He was seventy-five or seventy-six years old.'

'And Hannifin?'

'He was Rudican's sidekick at one stage. But they gave him early parole for the armed robberies and kept Rudican in for the full term. Hannifin died in a car accident shortly after his release. He was only in his twenties. Why do you ask?'

'Wasn't Shanahan Rudican's nephew?'

'That's right. Rudican's sister was Baker's mother. Baker stayed with Rudican when he went over to England first. Why do you ask?'

'I don't know,' McCadden admitted. 'I thought you might be able to throw some light on it.'

three

Albert Siggs was recovering in a private ward in Cork's regional hospital. A young uniformed guard was sitting in the corridor outside, under instructions to prevent any visitors who weren't accompanied by another officer.

According to the doctors, Siggs had suffered a particularly brutal assault. Blows to his face and upper body had broken his nose and caused extensive bruising. A number of cuts on his shoulders, neck and chest had been made with the point and blade of a sharp knife. On his right breast there was an oval wound identified as a bite mark. Unfortunately, this wound had been cleaned prior to treatment and no one had thought to either sketch or photograph the bite mark or to take saliva swabs. It was already too late to rectify the oversight. And although McCadden had instructed the scene to be preserved as part of an ongoing murder investigation, it was also possible that the local guards, treating it as a violent break-in, had muddied the evidence.

Despite his injuries, Siggs was sitting up in bed, waiting eagerly for McCadden. He'd obviously polished and rehearsed his opening line. He said, 'Have you solved my childhood riddle yet, inspector? The one where yesterday, today and tomorrow bring such contrasting fortunes to a young woman.'

McCadden shook hands and sat on a chair by the bedside. 'The girl was pregnant,' he said. 'And alone.'

Siggs nodded. 'Very good.'

'Actually, I had it solved for me,' McCadden admitted. 'If I was quicker at solving puzzles, you mightn't be lying here.'

Siggs shrugged, groaning with pain from the slight, involuntary movement. 'I did predict that it was my past you were about to alter, but even I didn't expect such consequences. Still, you can't shift so much earth without also unsettling some resentful creatures that have made it their home. Do you have an explanation for the attack?'

'Partial,' McCadden confessed. 'Maybe if you could tell me what happened first, I can fill you in later.'

'Yes, okay.'

'What time did the attack take place?'

'I didn't get a chance to check, really. But certainly after midnight.'

'The impression we had in Dublin from the early reports suggested it was around eight o'clock.'

'No. I was sleeping. I fell asleep after watching a television programme that finished a few minutes before midnight.'

It pushed Shanahan out of the frame. Even if he'd travelled by helicopter, he couldn't have made it from Cork in time to meet his killer in the Dublin mountains. And yet, among the items collected from the scene of the attack on Albert Siggs and preserved for forensic examination was a printed note left behind by the intruder. As far as McCadden could remember, it employed the same format as the jeering notes previously sent to the journalists. It had the same font and type size, the same starting position on the page, the same line-spacing, the same margins and the same jibing style. The only difference – although it wasn't printed as verse – was that it rhymed. It read, 'Sometimes you'll find me in a flap, Jack. Sometimes I'm done for Yorkshire parkin. When chocolate creams come back to back, your cheery buns are ripe for markin.' Amazon Man was really a misnomer. The stream of bizarre images led directly to the nickname that Shanahan had made his own. Baker.

'The time of the attack eliminates someone I had in mind,' McCadden explained to Siggs now. 'That's why it's significant. Tell me what happened.'

Siggs drew a breath. 'I was sleeping, as I said. I was woken by a noise. I learned later that this was the intruder knocking glass out of the back door to force an entry. I listened for a while. You're not always certain at night whether it's a dream or not. I fell back asleep without investigating. When I woke again there was someone in the room. It was dark. There was only a shadow, stooping over me. He was holding a knife to my throat.'

'Did you see anything of him?'

'He was wearing a balaclava.'

'Impressions?'

'Young. Fit. Well built.'

'Did he say anything?'

'He ordered me to keep still and quiet.'

'Accent?'

'Irish. Somewhere in the north-west of the country. Probably County Donegal.'

'You didn't get the impression it was false?'

'No. It was without variation. And he talked a lot. Too much for a burglar. He had no intention of letting me live to repeat it, I suppose. And like most people who talk a lot, he didn't want to listen. The first thing he did was to place tape over my mouth. I got the impression that he then had a problem with my position. I think he would've preferred it if I was unconscious. He told me to turn over in the bed. I really thought at this stage that his intention was rape, but he merely wanted to bind my hands. He made a mistake. When I brought my hands together behind my back I turned the palms away from each other, so that the tape was loose when I twisted them back. He turned me over again afterwards. He dazzled me with torchlight in my eyes. And then he started talking.'

'How much do you remember? The more detail the better, obviously.'

'I can paraphrase. I couldn't vouch for exact reproduction.'

'As much as you can.'

'Perhaps the first thing he said was actually the most significant, because I remember that distinctly. He told me that he knew that Hannah Fraule was my grandmother. Since I'm still not absolutely certain of that myself and I doubt if he could have established it independently . . .'

McCadden nodded. 'Yes, I've been to Naune.'

'Then the lunatic came from there?'

'I don't think so,' McCadden said. 'He got the *information* from there. If I can trace the source, I'll also find him. Another mistake.'

'But only because I survived,' Siggs pointed out. 'Apparently, he has a death list of people connected to Hannah Fraule and a man she married.'

'Rull.'

'Rull, yes. This is why he insisted on knowing if I had any children. I suffered because at first he didn't believe my denials. It's some sort of grotesque vendetta. He listed the victims for me. Hannah Fraule. Myself, as her only grandchild. Rull's son in Birmingham. A woman in Dublin who was Rull's mistress, named . . . Puccini?'

'Cuccini,' McCadden realized. 'Lucy Cuccini.'

'Yes, that's it. Is she dead?'

'Why?'

'He boasted that he had already dealt with her. Given the whore her penance, was the way he put it. He had a peculiar fondness for religious imagery, combined with a twisted patriotic fervour. I thought that particular union had mostly gone from Irish life. Then he showed me that absurd drivel he had printed, shining the torch on it for me to read. Have you seen it?'

'Yes.'

'It seemed to have intense significance for him. He wanted me to understand. He was frustrated at my obvious bewilderment. He decided finally that I was faking it and he lost his temper. He beat me with his gloved fists. I lost consciousness. When I came to, he had stripped me to the waist, cutting away the top of my pyjamas. I thought again that his real intention was sexual assault. He was manipulating my right nipple, making it firm, squeezing it painfully. But I also sensed that he was extremely uneasy, as if he was disgusted. Steeling himself, he suddenly dipped his head and bit my chest, while at the same time slicing it with the knife. The pain was intense. But while his head was down, I slipped my hands from the tape. The only thing I could find nearby was a coffee mug on the locker. I grabbed that and smashed it against him. The blow itself didn't do much damage, I suppose, but the mug shattered and I used the jagged edge as a blade, cutting across his face. He dropped the knife and recoiled. He also lost the torch. And, of course, his limp restricted him.'

McCadden was suddenly alert. 'Limp?'

'While he was moving around the bed, I noticed that he had a pronounced limp.'

'Which leg?'

Siggs thought about it. 'Left,' he said.

'Did he follow you?'

'I was more familiar with the layout of the house than he was. When I swung out of the bed, I managed to get through the bedroom door, down the stairs and on to the street, where I raised the alarm. He was gone by the time help arrived.'

'Did you hear him following you?'

'On the stairs, yes.'

'Was he limping?'

Siggs creased his forehead, went to answer immediately, but then checked the response. 'Actually,' he said finally, 'he wasn't, no. He was pounding after me.'

'An amateur,' was McCadden's thoughtful judgement.

'Do you know why he's pursuing this insane vendetta against Hannah Fraule?'

'She's supposed to have worked as an informer for British Intelligence in the 1920s,' McCadden explained, 'betraying republicans to the authorities. I know the IRA has a long memory and a long arm for informers, but from what I've learned so far I think now that this is the perception of a disturbed individual, not the programme of any organization.'

'The Nazis were disturbed individuals, inspector,' Siggs pointed out. 'Their organization gave them the licence to practise. Where do you draw the distinction? If violence becomes the primary virtue for a military organization, it will inevitably attract psychopaths to its ranks.'

McCadden accepted the points, but repeated, 'I think he's an amateur, Mr Siggs, untrained in combat skills. As you describe it, his attempts to subdue a captive are incompetent.'

An hour later, after working again over the details of the attack and then carrying through on his own pledge by describing most of what he had learned in Naune and from the statement by Harry Rull to the English police, McCadden left Albert Siggs with the promise to return. He liked the man. Siggs's calm approach to the violent upheavals in his own sense of identity contrasted with the usual idiotic hysteria the subject generated. His resilience indicated a strength that drew its source from his own character and from his mother's courageous struggle rather than from any fanciful notions of roots and heritage.

It was past six in the evening before McCadden cleared the city's rush-hour traffic and left Cork. Despite a message on his mobile phone and a brisk reminder as soon as he activated the car radio, both warning him that the commissioner urgently needed to talk to him, he didn't return to Dublin. He drove east along the coast, through his old stamping grounds in Waterford, on to New Ross, and from there across to the village of Naune. The journey took him almost three hours. By then, Cheevers' butcher shop in the village square was closed for business. The butcher wasn't at home in his spacious bungalow on the northern outskirts of the village. He wasn't in Codds public house, either. No one seemed to have seen him all day. No one knew where he was.

It took McCadden another hour, and another welcome visit to the micro-brewery at the Templar's Well, to discover exactly where the Reverend Des Wyndham actually lived. As it turned out, the young cleric was still beavering away in his study, putting the finishing touches to a sermon devoted to the themes of loyalty and denial. His reaction to seeing McCadden on the doorstep of his presbytery wobbled dramatically from surprise, through pleasure, and on to worry.

'Since I was down here almost a fortnight ago,' McCadden asked him when they'd settled inside, 'has anyone else been asking about Captain Siggs and his son in Cork?'

Wyndham was astonished. 'But of course,' he exclaimed. 'Albert Siggs's lawyer. Albert junior, that is, the Captain's son. Enquiring about legal rights to the family property and such things. He came with your warm recommendation.'

'Right. Did he give a name?'

'Pitt.'

'Not Brad, was it? Or William, maybe. Elder or Younger.'

'No, I don't quite think it was . . .'

'Big man. Handsome. Dark hair. Flashy dresser. Lots of jewellery.'

'The very same. You have him exactly.'

Jack Stokes, McCadden confirmed to himself. Again. 'What day was this?' he enquired.

'You were down here on . . .'

'Friday night and Saturday morning, the 14th and 15th of this month.'

'The following Monday, then. That would make it the 17th, wouldn't it?'

'Odd question, I know,' McCadden warned. 'But did he show signs of recently being in a fight?'

'Not at all.'

'After I told you and Mr Etchingham about the existence of Captain Siggs's son,' McCadden asked then, 'did you or Mr Etchingham discuss this information with anyone else?'

The confirmation came in the form of contrite confusion. 'Oh dear! Shouldn't I have, inspector?'

'There's no reason why you shouldn't. I didn't specifically ask you to keep quiet about it. I just want to establish something, that's all.'

'There are a great many people in this area, inspector, Church of Ireland parishioners, who have a natural interest in the fortunes of one of our oldest families, and such was the astonishing nature of the revelations you brought us . . .'

By Saturday evening, McCadden calculated, before he had even reached Dublin, news of Albert Siggs's existence had spread like wildfire through the Church of Ireland community. By Sunday morning, it had reached the Roman Catholic community as well. Probably by Sunday afternoon, and probably through the local butcher, Jack Stokes was made aware of it. The only thing missing, because it was the sort of detail that gossip discarded in its haste, was Albert Siggs's address, which McCadden had left with Des Wyndham and Richard Etchingham. So the next day, Monday the 17th, Jack Stokes had travelled down to personally winkle this out.

four

On Friday 28 January, five hours before a warrant to search his home and his offices was executed, Jack Stokes turned up at the Garda's regional headquarters in Harcourt Terrace asking to talk to McCadden. Off the record. He came without back-up, but two of the bodyguards he'd hired to protect himself and his family insisted on keeping him wedged between their massive frames until they were ordered to ease off.

Stokes had made an effort in front of the mirror that morning. Someone had softened the heavy bruising on his face with considerable make-up. His crippled left arm, still protected by a sling, was hidden underneath a Rocca overcoat, with the empty sleeve, neatly inserted in the side pocket, managing to look mysterious and debonair instead of deficient. But the image, and the expensive scent he wore, couldn't disguise his decline. He smelt of fear. And his body, coiled by apprehension, twisted itself into ugly postures at every stray sound or movement.

Stokes was scared because the murder of Pius Shanahan had spooked him. He thought he knew who had lured Shanahan to the Dublin mountains and blasted two slugs from a Walther 9mm into him. And he was convinced that the killer's next target would be Stokes himself.

Stokes was wrong, however.

A search of Lucy Cuccini's house in Donnybrook the previous day had turned up confirmation of the story McCadden had brought back from Albert Siggs in Cork. Lucy Cuccini had been attacked on the night of Monday 17 January. A prescription for painkillers from her doctor, who had treated the wounds to her breast, and the neatly folded page on which her assailant had printed his verse were both recovered from her bedroom. 'Sometimes I'm an empress, and sometimes I'm a queen; Simnel is my first name, and Banbury's where I've been.' Neither Cuccini nor Christy Sweeney admitted anything, but it was a simple exercise to imagine the fallout from that attack. For two decades, Dublin criminals like Sweeney had feuded with republican paramilitaries. They knew each other intimately. In itself, the note would probably have suggested the involvement of Baker Shanahan, but if Amazon Man had given Cuccini half the earbashing he'd inflicted on Albert Siggs then the connection would be obvious. Sweeney, with his reputation at stake and his honour tainted, had immediately lashed out in revenge, taking out a contract on Shanahan's life. Whether the investigating team would ever locate who had pulled the trigger was questionable. Whether the Serious Crime Squad could find enough evidence to link Sweeney to the assassination before a republican hit man widened the feud by taking out Sweeney and Cuccini was the real problem.

In the circumstances, faced with an escalating blood feud and a deranged murderer still on the loose, McCadden had no objection to talking to Jack Stokes off the record. The only secure vacant space they could find, though, was an interview room at headquarters. McCadden carefully demonstrated that he was disconnecting the microphones and video recorder before opening the session.

He said, 'Why don't I establish a few things first for my own satisfaction, so that I know where we're going. Is that okay?'

Placing a bulging manila folder on the table between them, Stokes nodded curtly. 'Okay.'

'In November 1996,' McCadden said, 'you retained a private investigator named Kelly McConnell and instructed her to locate the whereabouts of Hannah Fraule. Correct me if any of the following conclusions are incorrect. At that time, you already knew that a two-man IRA unit, Joseph Mary Rudican and Robert Hannifin, had tried to murder her in 1948. You knew that she had worked as a prostitute before embracing respectability in the village of Naune. You knew that her husband, Harry, had deserted her, had set her up for the IRA pair and had emigrated to Birmingham. All right so far?'

Stokes nodded again. 'Yes.'

'Right. Who hired you to find Hannah Fraule?'

'Pius Shanahan.'

'Shanahan was in prison in England at the time.'

'I was a member of the legal team representing that group of prisoners and had access to him.'

'Look,' McCadden stressed, 'I know that Shanahan didn't kill Hannah Fraule. I doubt if he ever had any intention of harming her. So what was his purpose in trying to trace her?'

'Wait,' Stokes requested. He opened the flap of the manila folder in front of him, took a sheet from the stack of papers inside and handed it to McCadden. 'Read it.'

It was a reduced photocopy of the letters page from the *Irish Times* newspaper, dated February 1996. A small item had been circled in red marker.

Sir,

I am currently researching a biography of the Irish patriot Eamon Brannigan, 1895–1921. I would be grateful for any contact from any of your readers with personal reminiscences or documentary or photographic records of the subject.

Yours,
Pius Eugene Shanahan,
c/o Stokes & Partners.

'On the level?' McCadden asked.

Stokes gestured. 'His notes, early drafts, all the research material . . . That's what's in this folder.'

'Give me a synopsis.'

'Of what?'

'The biography. Brannigan's life.'

Stokes sighed. 'Most of it is common knowledge, inspector. He joined the uprising in 1916 and was interned in England afterwards. When he was released, he immediately went back to guerrilla activities. He used the red-light district in the centre of Dublin as a refuge. He was notorious, but he was also elusive. The authorities could never find him, never trace or anticipate his movements. His lieutenant at the time was a resourceful sixteen-year-old you'll be familiar with. Joseph Mary Rudican.'

'The acolyte,' McCadden observed.

'It was really during this period, 1918 to 21, that Brannigan's reputation was made. As an organizer. A romantic outsider. A bandit in the tradition of the old legends. He was reputed to be untouchable. So his betrayal and killing were all the more grubby and despicable. He befriended and helped some of the young prostitutes in the red-light district. He was a devout man, a missionary in his way. One of the prostitutes, Hannah Fraule, under the guise of needing his assistance, lured him into an ambush where he was killed by Crown forces.'

‘I think I get it,’ McCadden said. ‘Shanahan couldn’t publish this without establishing that Hannah Fraule was dead, for fear of libel.’

‘Partly,’ Stokes confirmed. ‘No one expected her to be found alive. She was born in 1906. I expected Kelly McConnell to find confirmation of her death.’

‘Don’t you think it’s odd,’ McCadden asked, ‘that the same dodgy relationship keeps recurring in this story? High priest and acolyte. Mentor and pupil. Hardened old gunman and fervent young devotee. Brannigan and Rudican in the early 1920s. Rudican and Hannifin in 1948. But Hannifin became an apostate, a Judas, a betrayer of the sacred cause. So he had to be replaced. By Rudican and *Shanahan* in the early 1960s. And for the new millennium? Pius Eugene Shanahan and . . .’

There was a hint of mockery in McCadden’s catalogue that made Stokes stare at him, his eyes burning with resentment. Securing the flap inside the research folder – a useless gesture of exclusion – he said bitterly, ‘You already know who Amazon Man is, don’t you?’

‘Only since last night,’ McCadden admitted. It had come to him when he’d finally accepted that the killer must have been born or reared near Shanahan’s birthplace in County Donegal. They had similar accents. Albert Siggs had described it to McCadden. Lucy Cuccini had obviously described it to Christy Sweeney. The north-west of Ireland. County Donegal. Apart from that, the killer was almost certainly much younger than Shanahan, had obviously spent enough time imprisoned with the older man to grow to worship him, to school himself in the ancient wrongs his hero’s family had supposedly suffered and to dedicate himself to the task of avenging the injustices. Wildly impressionable, mentally unstable and capable of extreme violence for the cause he perceived himself as serving, he also had to be released from prison in late December. Only one name fitted this profile. ‘Bobby Tee,’ McCadden said. ‘His name is Bobby Tee.’

Stokes snorted irritably. ‘You didn’t need to talk to me at all, did you?’

‘I did,’ McCadden corrected. ‘Where is he?’

‘I don’t know.’

‘You don’t know?’

‘Don’t you believe me?’

‘Maybe. You’re probably too vulnerable to play any more games of hide and seek. Where’s he *likely* to be?’

‘Do you think we haven’t checked every possible location, every known associate?’

'We?'

'When Hannah Fraule was killed, Shanahan guessed immediately that Tee was responsible and went looking for him.'

'Instead of informing us.'

'Don't be naive. You know the attitude of militant republicans to the police force.'

'Well, I used *informing* deliberately. However, you must have made contact with Tee. At least once.'

Stokes glared at him again, the resentment welling up once more. 'What makes you so sure?'

'On Monday 17th you were in Naune, where you acquired Albert Siggs's address. The night before last, Tee attacked Albert Siggs in his home. Unless he got the information from you, Tee couldn't be aware of Albert Siggs's existence, his relationship to Hannah Fraule or his address in Cork.'

Stokes sulked and played with a jewelled ring on his right hand. 'We thought of using the information on Albert Siggs as bait to lure Tee into a meeting.'

'How did you contact him?'

'There are recognized modes of communication through republican newsletters, which he reads.'

'But don't tell me,' McCadden pleaded sarcastically. 'Tee didn't trust you. He got to you before the scheduled meeting and beat the information out of you. That must have been what? Tuesday or Wednesday, the 18th or 19th? When I saw you on Thursday that week, you were already in bad shape.'

'Something like that,' Stokes conceded.

'And you still didn't inform us. You let Albert Siggs out to dry, without even warning him. Didn't you realize, for Christ's sake, that Tee intended murdering him?'

'Shanahan watched Siggs's house for a while. We didn't have the resources. Nobody wanted to drag other people into this, and particularly not the political party, the organization. It wasn't on.'

'Has Tee shaved his head, by the way?'

'Yes.'

'In imitation of his hero?'

'I suppose so.'

'Since when?'

'He started when he was released from prison. He didn't show any such *obvious* signs of emulation while they were imprisoned together.'

'Do you know that his bizarre identification with Shanahan also extended to limping on his left leg while he was killing and maiming?'

'He never showed that to me, no.'

McCadden gestured his disgust and sat back in the chair. 'This mutilation of the breasts,' he said then. 'Is that just a peculiar twist to Tee's sick mind, or does it have some wider significance?'

Stokes sneered. 'You really don't know much about Eamon Brannigan, do you?'

'I know nothing at all about the man, apart from the fact that they named a street after him, and the stuff you told me earlier.'

'When Hannah Fraule led him into that ambush, his murderers mutilated his body by cutting off his right nipple and leaving it in the alleyway beside the corpse.'

Fact or myth? McCadden wondered. Propaganda or history? Reality or adornment of the legend? He was dubious. 'Who's supposed to have done this?'

'The special forces of the Crown, the dregs of the British Army, sent to Ireland to subdue republicans by a reign of terror.'

'Why did they do it?'

'Are you one of those, inspector, who think that the English are incapable of atrocities?'

'Everyone is capable of atrocity, Mr Stokes. But I'm trained to consider certain questions. Why did the military mutilate Brannigan's body? Were there similar incidents? Why the breast? Why *only* the breast? Why leave it lying beside the corpse?'

'Barbarity, inspector!' Stokes shouted angrily. 'Sheer barbarity!'

five

Depending on how you looked at it, Eamon Brannigan was either a Catholic nationalist icon, brave and resourceful, principled and determined, and therefore a hero who had sacrificed his youth for Ireland, or else he was an addictive personality whose half-baked notions of purity and virtue attained through sacrifice led to a feverish confusion in his mind between assassination and baptism, a zealot who referred to women only as the moulders of the next generation and who believed in the existence of a mythical creature called the Gael, which lived for eight hundred years, ate only potatoes, uttered only oracles, knelt only to pray and would have mastered the universe if he hadn't been downtrodden by the English. But McCadden was pressed for time and didn't bother to look long enough for his natural sympathies to land him in the latter camp. Lamenting a job where the life was almost always of little significance and the death almost everything, he hurried on to Brannigan's final hours.

The investigation into Brannigan's killing, by the Dublin Metropolitan Police, had been patchy. Because of the vicious war between republicans and the British Army, the military commander in Ireland had the authority at the time to hold a military enquiry into a violent death and dispense with a coroner's inquest. This is what he did with Brannigan. But something made the army uncertain of its ground. They called in detectives from the DMP. And cops being cops, regardless of what political masters they happen to be serving, the detectives carried through an investigation consistent with the procedures of the time, until they were pulled off the case again by the military.

Brannigan had died behind the yard of a tenement house in a lane off Gloucester Street. According to neighbours, he'd been staying in the house for the previous two weeks. They claimed not to have known that he was an IRA man.

On the night of 2 March 1921, Brannigan was seen by a number of prostitutes who were standing outside Jack Maher's pub in Purdon Street. He was talking to a well-dressed young woman. She was described as good-looking, with long black hair, aged anything from fifteen to twenty. Two nights later, the same young woman called to the tenement room where Brannigan was hiding. The pair were seen leaving the tenement together and entering the lane behind its yard. It was a place where prostitutes frequently had sex with clients. Another prostitute gave evidence of taking a client down there a short time earlier and finding three threatening figures already lurking in the shadows. Big men. 'Of military bearing,' as the whore was supposed to have testified. They'd scared the hell out of her and she'd brought her client elsewhere.

Brannigan was now led into what was obviously an ambush. The indications were that he fought, but was quickly overpowered. Like most IRA men on the run, he probably carried a revolver. No weapon was ever found. And it wasn't known why he didn't attempt to use it to defend himself. Nor was it known where his attackers went afterwards. They didn't stay with the body, suggesting that it wasn't an official military operation, or, if special forces were involved, that there was something questionable about their presence.

The body wasn't discovered for another two hours. Word had passed around about the potential danger in the lane and the place had been avoided until a prostitute desperate for a quick trick had decided to try it again. And that was as far as the detectives from the DMP had managed to get. From there, a military enquiry took over. What the soldiers made of it was a matter of guesswork. The files were inaccessible.

Within four months of Brannigan's death, there was a truce between the IRA and the British Army. Inside a year a provisional Irish government had taken over and the DMP was replaced by the force McCadden was now a member of. Some things had been lost for ever in the transfer of power, deliberately or accidentally. But the reason why the military had been spooked enough to call in civic detectives had actually survived. The original of the police doctor's report after the autopsy on Brannigan had apparently ended up in the military file, but a copy of his preliminary examination had stayed with the DMP's records. Brannigan hadn't been shot. This in itself was surprising. The fatalities in the war between the IRA and the British Army at this time were almost invariably the result of firefights. Brannigan had been stabbed with a broad-bladed weapon or weapons. These might have been bayonets, or they might have been knives. The preliminary examination was understandably uncertain.

There were wounds to both his hands, consistent with trying to ward off an attack. The fatal ones were to his neck, his stomach and his chest. He died from internal bleeding. But the most significant detail was contained in the final sentence of the doctor's preliminary report: 'In addition, several unsuccessful attempts have been made to sever the victim's genitalia, resulting in profuse loss of blood, and the victim's right nipple, along with a portion of surrounding flesh, has been severed from the breast and placed beside the body.'

Brannigan, McCadden was now convinced, hadn't been killed by the military. Official version or no official version. History. Folk legend. Republican hagiography. The weight of these was nothing against McCadden's certainty. The DMP detectives in their time would have made an instinctive judgement. And McCadden shared it with them now. There was a significance to the cuts on Brannigan's body that couldn't be explained even by the savagery of a bloody guerrilla war. He hadn't been killed in an official military operation. It just suited everyone to pretend afterwards that he had. Another hit for the splendid security forces. Another martyr for old Ireland.

In more relaxed circumstances McCadden would have enjoyed pursuing this case, but he doubted now that even its resolution would bring him any closer to finding Bobby Tee before the man attacked again. For all the obvious similarities between the killings of Eamon Brannigan and Hannah Fraule – who was surely the dark-haired young woman luring Brannigan to his death – there was no *logical* connection between them. The fact was, Bobby Tee was simply fooling himself. He liked to think that he was serving a broader cause, that he was avenging the stained honour of his hero, Pius Eugene Shanahan. This was what had given him the licence to maim and kill initially. As with so many other psychopaths, the sacred notion of service had released his latent cruelty. In reality, of course, Bobby Tee was merely gratifying a twisted individual craving. His failure to make contact with Shanahan, his obvious dread of being restrained by his hero and his attack on Shanahan's representative, Jack Stokes, all illustrated this.

But for the moment, McCadden guessed, Bobby Tee would also remain faithful to the original justification for his cruelty. He wouldn't yet attack and kill at random. He wasn't ready to sever the comforting argument he'd started out with. That would take another major shift inside his unbalanced mind. So far, therefore, there was a recognizable pattern to his assaults. Even more significantly, his victims could be narrowly described. Hannah Fraule and Harry Rull and their descendants, either through blood or through marriage. Harry Rull had presumably died in 1977. Hannah herself was now also dead. The security surrounding her grandson, Albert Siggs, had been discreetly intensified. The British police had been alerted to the threat to Thomas Rull in Birmingham and had come back with reports, relevant or not, of a suspicious character casing the estate in Edgbaston in mid-January. Lucy Cuccini and Christy Sweeney were still in custody, and safe for the moment.

Cuccini, however, it occurred to McCadden, was something of an exception. Neither blood relative nor relative by marriage, she had merely benefited from Harry Rull's wealth, through his will, a qualification that considerably broadened the range of possible victims. Were there other beneficiaries of Harry's will? Could Bobby Tee know about them? Or what of those in the distant past who might have financially helped or benefited from Hannah Fraule's rise to respectability?

At one o'clock on Sunday morning, 30 January, after falling asleep in his gloomy basement flat while worrying about the daunting list of possibilities this new qualification offered, McCadden was woken again by a memory. A distracting memory, he thought initially, of a private investigator's shapely legs and short skirt, a versatile desk in an air-conditioned office and an opportunity he had foolishly ignored. It's possible, of course, that policemen only dream of sex to stimulate their deductive powers. Before McCadden could either fall back into the dream or advance to fantasy, he suddenly recalled that Kelly McConnell had discovered Hannah Fraule's address in West Cork through the old woman's solicitor.

Without noticing the time, he got out of bed, checked through his notebook and rang Kelly McConnell. He didn't know the solicitor's name. A solicitor who was dead now, of course. A solicitor whose sons, he remembered, had inherited the practice in Wexford town and who had been instructed to alter Hannah Fraule's will some years ago.

He managed to reach only an answering machine at Kelly McConnell's home number. He left a message. And rang her office. Where another answering machine responded.

Hanging up, he nervously drummed a pencil on the surface of the bedside locker and tried to think of alternatives. He still had an investigating team in West Cork, he recalled. Someone would be on duty at the station in Bandon. They'd know if the will had been read. Who had benefited. If the details had been publicized.

But no. He didn't trust them. Either to understand his needs or to comply with his orders if they did understand.

He thought of Curtis then. The young black detective with the justifiable chip on his shoulder. Couldn't remember his first name. But there it was, in an early page of his notebook. Joseph. Opposite the man's home, mobile and work numbers.

McCadden rang the home number, concerned for a moment that Curtis might be living there with nervous parents. But it was Curtis himself who answered.

'It's Inspector McCadden, Curtis. In Dublin.'

Curtis groaned. Understandably. But he didn't descend to the obvious. He didn't complain that it was past one in the morning, that he was off duty and had just been sleeping. All good points in his favour when it came to assessing his value as an assistant.

'Are you awake enough, Curtis?'

'Yeah, I'm okay.'

'This is important. Do you know if Hannah Fraule's will has been read yet?'

'It has, yes.'

'Do you know the provisions?'

'She left everything . . . She still had quite a decent amount in stocks and shares. Nine or ten thousand pounds. She left it all to Elizabeth Cole.'

'Elizabeth Cole?' McCadden echoed. It sounded familiar. But he couldn't place it immediately. 'Who's Elizabeth Cole?'

'You remember. The mother of the boy in the village who discovered her corpse. She looked after the old woman.'

'Right. I remember. I suppose this would be common knowledge down there by now?'

'Big local news story, sir.'

'Get yourself out of bed, son,' McCadden instructed. 'Get a couple of uniforms from the nearest station and get them to guard the woman's house in the village. My orders. Get yourself out there as well. Take your mobile with you and keep in touch with me. I'm heading down there myself.'

PART FIVE

january, 2000

The money should've gone to the descendants of Eamon Brannigan. I told her that. She didn't even understand. I showed her the poem and all she did was shake her head at it. 'Inspectoral midgets and probing gnomes, Can't find the street of Sherlock Holmes.' She just shook her head. This was my problem with her. Things had been different with Hannah Fraule herself. Even with Siggs and with Lucy. I saw the recognition of retribution in their eyes. She was ignorant. She was like a lot of people in this country today, because she had no time for the past, no idea of where she came from or what sacrifices others had made to put her where she was. But ignorance is no defence. Whether she knew it or not, she inherited the sins with the money. She wasn't stainless.

Stainless? I laughed when I thought of that. I paid for her time. I paid for her penance. I bought her.

Ever since I saw in the news, around the middle of January, that Hannah Fraule had left her the money, I'd planned to watch her movements. I should've made time for her then, only that Jack Stokes came good with the story on Siggs and I needed to clean that up first. Blood has priority. I watched her over a couple of weekends anyway. She thought she was good-looking and stylish. I could tell that. But I don't like brunettes. I don't like women who cut their hair short in that unnatural way. She wore a black leather overcoat. It's not a good colour for a mother. It's not soft enough. And anyway, underneath the look there was just the usual grubbiness. She was working as an escort. At least two nights every week, on Fridays and Saturdays, a man called Michael Slade picked her up at the village in his Jaguar. She always left the boy alone in the cottage whenever she went with Slade. She always went to Kinsale or to Bandon, to one of the hotels in those towns. Different hotels on different nights. Slade would have a man waiting for her. Sometimes she stayed the night with this one man. Sometimes she left earlier to go to another one.

One night I waited for her, parked on the road outside the hotel. She was with a Jap that time. I nearly got sick. It's the way they smell so much of fish. The fishy smell from her breasts if he touched them with his mouth. I hoped she was hygienic, took frequent baths and all that.

Maybe I could've captured her more easily at the cottage, when she was sleeping in the dead of night. But I knew that she'd deny everything. What could I prove? The boy would see me as an ordinary criminal. She wouldn't confess her sins. I wouldn't see the recognition of retribution in her eyes. And everything would be pointless without that.

I rang Michael Slade. I was clever. I'd followed that Jap enough to discover his name and his workplace and now I pretended that he'd recommended the service to me. I booked a room in a hotel in Kinsale. I met Slade to discuss the arrangements. I couldn't have taken him in a straight fight. He was too big, too powerful. I was frightened he might recognize me from the television coverage of the prison releases before Christmas, but he was really only interested in checking that the money I offered him was genuine. That's the way the country has gone now. It's the only standard the Irish still have. Whether the banknotes are good or not. I still nearly made a mistake, though. I nearly sneered when he quoted me the rates. Two hundred pounds for an hour. Two hundred an hour? For a whore? I know volunteers, maimed in the struggle for liberation, working now to keep body and soul together for maybe five or six pounds an hour. But in one way, I didn't mind handing over the money. I knew I was going to take it all back again.

She definitely sensed something when she came into the hotel bedroom. She was uneasy. She had to force herself to look happy about it all. I suppose I'd built myself up to a different kind of action from the one she was used to and she'd noticed that. It's possible that my dislike of her showed through as well. This is why I prefer the balaclava. Basically, it's cleaner when they can't see you. You can be yourself behind the mask. You don't have to disguise your feelings, put on a false expression. That's important. I've always hated having to lie. It's why I nearly lost it with her in the hotel. Also, it was so late by then, just after one in the morning, that I knew she'd been with another man before she came to me. The thought of that, particularly if she hadn't washed well, made me tense. She probably thought I was nervous about sex. She probably remembered she was being overpaid to relax me. But when she touched me, putting her hand to my face, I acted before I'd intended to. Reacted, I suppose. I wasn't certain yet if Slade had gone from the hotel or was waiting for her outside. She had a mobile phone. If I'd given her the slightest opening, she would've called him and ruined everything. I was clever, though. I might've moved too soon, but I kept a cool head. I pulled her towards me with my left hand. When she pressed against me I took the knife in my right and flicked it open. She gasped when she felt the cold steel against her neck. I like that sound. I like the way the whole body shrinks inwards, away from danger. Except a woman's breasts, funnily. They expand. Coming to smother the trouble. I got my palm over her mouth before she could scream. And then I told her how we were going to do this. She had to put her black leather coat back on. I had to put my arm around her waist underneath the coat, as if we were romantic, but with the point of the knife pressed into her ribcage on the other side. All that was difficult. And getting out without trouble needed a bit of luck. Only a bit. I'd planned it well, picking a room close to the stairway that led all the way down to a service entrance at the rear of the hotel, into a lane where I'd parked. We met no one on the way.

I opened the passenger door of the car and pushed her through, all the way across until she was sitting in the driver's seat, behind the wheel. I told her to drive. She was going to pretend that she wasn't able to, but I'd tipped out the contents of her bag and there it was, along with a nasty little stun gun, her ten-year licence. She obviously couldn't be trusted. It made the journey tricky. But I got some compensation. The way I held the knife against her ribcage, I could feel the softness of her breast against the back of my hand. I told her to drive home, all the way to the village. That really surprised her. It knocked her back, the fact that I knew where she lived. She went quiet after that, trying to figure it out. At first I didn't mind. She concentrated on the driving. But afterwards I got annoyed. I don't like people who can't talk, who create really awkward silences.

She didn't give me any real problems on the journey back to the village. She thought a couple of times about making a play. I could always tell. She'd get chattier. Friendlier. She'd pretend to understand me a bit more. Lies again. Once, going through Clonakilty, she saw a couple of guards walking the beat and wondered about creating an incident, maybe rear-ending the car in front or swerving over to the footpath. But I kept the knife biting into her flesh. And the guards turned a corner anyway just as we got near them.

The crazy village she lived in was deserted when we got there. There was still Garda tape across the front door and the windows of Hannah Fraule's house. I think I got an erection just passing the scene again, remembering the good work on New Year's Eve, and not because the car hit a pothole and jolted my hand hard against her breast or because her gasp of pain reminded me of how close we were to the end. I told her to pull up outside her cottage. She went to switch off the ignition, but it was so cold I told her to leave the engine running, driving the heater in the car. It struck me that the cold would make her nipples erect. I opened her leather coat. Cold? She was sweating underneath. Beads of it were on her bare neck, over the low-cut blue dress she had on, trickling down into the darkness between her breasts. That excited me. I cut away the shoulder straps of the dress. She had on a soft brassiere underneath, a nice light-blue, without wires or bones or anything hard and unfeminine. And then she ruined it all. She started crying. She pleaded with me not to hurt her. She offered to do anything I wanted. It really irritated me. It really annoys me, that. They always assume you only want to have sex with them. They can never think of anything nobler. I was feeling tense. Her voice was driving me mad, nagging at me. And what started bothering me also was that her left breast was the one closer to me and I couldn't reach across to the right without risking losing control. But just in time, I remembered that she didn't understand anyway. It didn't matter. She had no sense of history.

I cut away her brassiere, exposing the breasts. They looked good. Full, with nice firm nipples. Not like a model's. Like a mother's. I badly needed to suck on them, to bite a little just as a taster. But after what had happened with Siggs, I had to be more careful. I clapped my hand over her mouth again and cut into the quivering breast, the way a cook pierces a roasted chicken to ensure it's done properly, with the juices running clear. She tried to yelp. That was stifled. But the pain couldn't have been that bad. Only a starter. The nice thing was that some of the blood trickled down the blade of the knife, over the hilt and on to my hand, from where I could quickly lick it clean.

I was really into it at this stage, really enjoying it. I thought I was actually going to ejaculate. But out of the corner of my eye I suddenly caught a glimpse of the curtains being lifted in one of the cottage's windows. I was fairly startled, obviously. When I turned to check, though, I saw it was only the boy, rubbing the mist from the glass and sticking his face against the pane to peer out. It must have been his bedroom. He must have been woken by the sound of the car idling outside. He probably thought I was Michael Slade. I caught a little hatred in his eyes. So I told her immediately. Right, we were going inside. We were going into the cottage. Because there was always the danger that the boy would get worried enough or get confused enough to actually call someone on the phone. I told her to cover herself with the leather coat, not to let the boy see her like that, half-naked in public, even if it was the middle of the night. She was crying by then, pleading with me again. But as I said to her, she really should've thought of all that before she got herself mixed up with an informer like Hannah Fraule.

one

It was all over by the time McCadden reached the village. Entering from the east along Main Street, his headlights picked out a uniformed guard who was on duty outside the door of the cottage, slapping his hands and stamping his feet to keep the blood circulating against the cold of the dawn. The blue Astra that Bobby Tee had used was still parked against the footpath.

The guard didn't recognize McCadden until he was shown identification. Stiff, and raw-faced from the rain and biting wind, he managed only a ragged salute.

McCadden gestured towards the darkened cottage. 'Anyone in there?'

'No, sir. It's empty. The officers from the Technical Bureau haven't arrived yet.'

'Is it open?'

'Yes, sir.'

McCadden covered his shoes with protective plastic and pulled on a pair of surgical gloves. He lit a torch as he opened the front door of the cottage, but then quickly found a switch and turned on the electric light instead. From Curtis's description, he knew that the bedrooms were on his right and the living and kitchen areas to his left. Beyond the tiny hallway, he turned left. For the moment, he was interested only in a single item in the cottage's interior. Guided again by Curtis's directions, he passed the open fireplace on his right and stopped in front of a photograph that was hanging in the alcove beyond. A monochrome photograph inside a heavy wooden frame that was too ornate and too large for the size of the print. It showed a group of five young women standing on the front steps of a red-brick Georgian house. All of them were dressed for summer, in the style of the 1920s, in bright floral dresses and straw hats. In the centre, framed by the ornamental arch of the doorway behind her and instantly recognizable, was a youthful Hannah Fraule, hardly out of her teens it seemed, but dark-haired and already strikingly beautiful. Her companions, ranging in age from early twenties to mid-thirties, were unknown to McCadden. But he had no doubt that the splendid old Georgian house was in Dublin's red-light district and that the women were prostitutes.

As Curtis had deduced, and reported to McCadden, this was clearly the companion piece that had once hung beside the photograph of the Eucharistic Congress in Hannah Fraule's house a little further along Main Street.

McCadden eagerly reached out and lifted the photograph, releasing its cord from the hook that had been set into the alcove. He studied the faces for a few moments, and then turned the frame over. The backing on the rear was of brown paper, old and discoloured and long stuck to the wood with adhesive. Nodding with satisfaction, he took a large evidence bag from his pocket, carefully placed the heavy photograph inside, sealed the Ziploc and carried it with him as he left.

Outside, the uniformed guard was now pacing briskly and executing parade-ground turns at the gables of the cottage.

'Where's Detective Curtis?' McCadden asked him.

'In hospital, sir.'

'I know. Which one?'

'I'm not sure.'

'Where's Bobby Tee?'

'They took him back up to Bandon to the station there.'

two

He was a stocky, muscular young man. His head had been recently shaved again. The bald white skull gave the effect of lengthening his pale forehead and of deepening the two caverns where his dead blue eyes had concealed themselves. There was a bruise on his crown and a fresh scar along his left cheek where Albert Siggs had hit him with a coffee mug and then cut him with a broken shard. When they brought him up from the holding cell to meet McCadden, he limped into the interview room, favouring his right leg. Sitting in the chair on the opposite side of the table, he manipulated his supposedly damaged left leg with his hands before settling into a position. The doctors called to examine him had found no evidence of any physical injury to his hip. He hadn't spoken when he was arrested. He hadn't spoken while he was being taken under armed guard to Bandon or during the preliminary interrogation. And he didn't respond now, as McCadden introduced himself and opened with a few formal questions. He stared at a point on the wall a little to the right of McCadden's shoulder, and never even parted his lips. It was impossible to know what was happening behind those misted blue eyes. Forced to guess, McCadden would have said that Bobby Tee was trapped inside the bizarre world of a republican martyr who hadn't yet died. It was pointless trying to reason with him.

If he had a weakness, McCadden thought, it wasn't that he was drawing his inspiration from a dead man – the whole republican movement sustained itself on the dead – but that he didn't seem to be aware of Shanahan's murder. So after rambling through a number of vague queries, unrelated to the incidents of the previous night, McCadden suddenly asked, 'You don't happen to know who shot Pius Shanahan, do you, Bobby?'

It got a response. But an unexpected one. Tee's blue eyes darted towards his questioner and for a second the faintest of knowing smiles flickered around the corners of his lips. There were two possible explanations for this extraordinary show of superiority, McCadden realized. Either Tee didn't accept the news reports of Shanahan's death, dismissing them as fabrications, a ruse to lure him into a trap, or else, convinced that *he* was Shanahan and aware that he was still alive, he *knew* that McCadden was telling lies.

McCadden, with little experience of interviewing either political fanatics or the criminally insane, quickly conceded that he was wasting his time. He knew, of course, that a result wasn't needed from the interrogation. Bobby Tee would be charged with the crimes of the previous night. The first judge he appeared in front of would immediately send him for psychiatric assessment. And the chances were – the *hope* was – that he'd never come back.

When Bobby Tee had struggled to his feet and limped from the interview room, McCadden asked a detective the same question he'd put to the uniformed guard outside Elizabeth Cole's cottage in the village.

'Where's Detective Garda Curtis?'

'He's in hospital, sir.'

'I know, I know. But which one?'

'They took them all back to Cork. Curtis and Nolan and . . .'

McCadden grunted. Another thirty kilometres in the rain, back along the route he'd already travelled, on the hour's sleep he'd managed to grab the previous night. At least it was early Sunday morning. The traffic would be negligible. And Cork's regional hospital, where he'd visited Albert Siggs on Wednesday, was in the western suburbs of the city.

Dispensing with the car's heater, which always sucked the moisture out of the air and left him torn between drowsiness and a searing headache, McCadden grew progressively colder the closer he got to Cork. By the time he pulled into the hospital car park, his feet were icy, his hands were almost numb on the steering wheel and the wound in his shoulder was aching again. By contrast, Joe Curtis had a snug little arrangement. Propped up in a comfortable bed in a nicely heated room, he was surrounded by admiring young nurses and enjoying all the benefits of the flip side to Ireland's complex attitude to black people. Compassion. McCadden didn't begrudge the young detective his rewards. Apart from anything else, Curtis had a knife wound across his chest that had taken innumerable stitches to close. But he did have to scatter the fan club before talking to him.

When the room was clear, he sat at the bedside, held up the Ziploc bag and its contents and said, 'I got the photograph.'

Curtis's eyes mixed eagerness and caution. 'Was I right, sir?'

'Yes, you were right. I thought you weren't listening to me when I was talking about the other photograph in Hannah Fraule's house.'

'Only a pose, I'm afraid.'

'It has its uses,' McCadden conceded. 'But listen. You'd better tell me what happened, before those nurses come back.'

McCadden already knew that a uniformed guard from Clonakilty had reached the cottage within ten minutes of his own phone call from Dublin and that Curtis, travelling from Bandon, had joined the guard about twenty minutes later. At first, satisfied that the cottage was secure and assuming that its occupants were asleep, they'd waited outside. But the boy had woken and repeatedly looked out of his bedroom window, suggesting that he was alone, and Curtis had asked McCadden's permission to check this out. From inside, thirty minutes later, Curtis had reported on the arrival of the blue Astra. And then he'd suddenly broken off the contact.

Curtis enthusiastically pulled himself upright in the bed now to finish the story, forgetting that every movement brought him pain and threatened to tear the stitching on his wound. He groaned angrily. 'The boy thought it was a man called Michael Slade,' he said then. 'A friend of his mother's. But he wasn't sure. Slade always drove off immediately after dropping his mother, apparently. I asked the boy to look out of the window again, but to keep calm if he saw anything unusual. He did well. As soon as Bobby Tee noticed him, he forced Mrs Cole out of the car and towards the cottage. I had no option but to take him as they came through the door.'

'Did you see the knife?'

'No, sir.'

'He might've had a gun, Curtis.'

'I figured he wouldn't, given his record. But I was ready for it, anyway.'

'Right.'

'Whatever he held on her, a knife or a gun, I knew he had to place her in front of him as he entered. I told the uniform – his name is Nolan, sir, and he did really well – I told him to grab Mrs Cole as soon as she came in and drag her to safety. When he did, I confronted Tee. I warned him that I was an armed Garda and ordered him to lie on the floor. He must've been surprised, but he recovered pretty quickly. He lunged at me with the knife, catching me across the chest, as you can see. I couldn't risk a shot with so many of us in that confined space, but I managed to club him with the revolver. By then, Nolan had pushed Mrs Cole and the boy to one side and was able to attack Tee from behind. Between us we subdued him fairly quickly and held him there until back-up arrived.'

'Where's Mrs Cole now?'

'He cut her breast, sir, while they were sitting in the car. She was treated by the paramedics and they brought her here for observation. She's in the women's section. One other thing you need to know, sir. Mrs Cole works as an escort at weekends.'

'Escort? I thought she was an artist.'

'She is. But her work doesn't sell.'

'Right.'

'That's how Bobby Tee picked her up. The other character, Michael Slade, is her, ah, manager. The lads in Cork have a file on him. There's nothing on Mrs Cole. I don't think the boy knows yet about his mother's real occupation, but he's bright enough to figure it out before long.'

'Right,' McCadden muttered again. A little taken aback, he stood up and offered a handshake as confirmation of his approval. 'Don't go away, Curtis,' he cautioned. 'I'll be back.'

'Yes, sir.'

Staff always hurry in hospitals, scurrying from ward to ward, from patient to patient, driven by a sense of urgency and by an awareness of the preciousness of time. McCadden wanted to linger on his way to Mrs Cole, to absorb the implications of what he'd just heard and to adjust his approach to the woman, but the nurse escorting him dragged him along at a hectic pace. Luckily, Mrs Cole was still with her son, sitting up in bed, holding the boy's hand and talking intently to him. Left alone when the nurse returned to her duties, McCadden watched them for a while through the open door. She was a nice-looking woman, he thought. Her short hair and gentle face made her look younger than thirty-two. And her intensity, her obvious concern for the boy, made her even more attractive.

She was still nervous, though. She looked sharply across at him as he knocked and entered and she watched him with anxiety until he introduced himself.

'Excuse me, Mrs Cole. I'm Detective Inspector Carl McCadden, from Dublin. Would it be convenient to talk to you for a few minutes?'

'McCadden?' she repeated. The expression in her eyes shifted from fear to curiosity. 'The black detective – Curtis – said that you were the one who figured out that I was in danger.'

'A little late. A day earlier would've saved you a lot of trouble.'

'Nobody's perfect, inspector,' she remarked, with a quiet insistence. She squeezed the boy's hand and asked him to leave them alone for ten minutes. He went, but reluctantly, glowering at McCadden. 'I'm sorry,' she apologized. 'He's not usually surly.'

'Nothing much is usual at the moment,' McCadden reassured her. He sat in the chair the boy had just vacated. He'd intended telling her that he'd just learned how she earned her living, that he knew her son was successful in school and well adjusted, apart from a dislike of their remote village, and that her occupation would soon be exposed, probably by the tabloid press, who never saw any point in giving sympathetic column inches to a victim unless it increased their suffering. But somehow, despite her son's performance, he had expected someone less capable, less intelligent, less educated. His advice seemed suddenly redundant. Instead, in a spontaneous gesture, he placed his hand over hers and pressed it gently, promising support. 'Listen,' he said then, removing the framed photograph from the evidence bag he'd been carrying with him. 'I took something from your home. It will probably be used as evidence in the investigation into Hannah Fraule's death, but I'll make sure you get it back when we're finished. I know a lot about Hannah Fraule's life at this stage, Mrs Cole. What I'd like to hear is why she gave this to you.'

'Because we understood each other, inspector,' Elizabeth Cole said simply. 'It's probably why she also left me the money.'

'Pity it wasn't more.'

'Enough to buy a little space. I think maybe that was her intention.'

'Did she ever talk to you about the old days?'

'Only in a general way. What still amused her was the descriptions the newspapers always used. They were unhappy girls of the unfortunate class. And the men were setting forth on a night of adventure. She never tired of repeating those phrases to me.'

'Did she ever mention a character named Eamon Brannigan?'

'Brannigan?' She thought about it carefully, but shook her head. 'No. Why?'

'He was murdered in 1921. I think she lured him into an ambush. But I don't know what he did to deserve it.'

'I can guess,' Elizabeth Cole said knowingly.

McCadden nodded, suddenly reminded of something the young historian, Robert Colwell, had said to him about the fervent nationalists of the period. They wanted an image of Ireland Pure, cleansed only by the sacrificial blood of its martyrs. Mostly they denied that prostitution could even exist on Irish soil. He said, 'So could I, Mrs Cole, if the courts were satisfied with guesses. But they're not. So . . .' Suddenly extrovert, almost with the flamboyance of a magician on stage in front of a hushed audience, he twirled over the framed photograph. He plucked a pen from his jacket pocket and held it poised over the brown paper backing, ready to pierce its surface. 'If you don't mind, I'm going to look inside this frame.'

Elizabeth Cole frowned at him. 'Why?'

'Why? Because peculiarities run in families, Mrs Cole. Hannah Fraule had a daughter. Did you know that?'

'No.'

'She's dead now. But when the child was ten, she cut a clipping from a newspaper and hid it inside a framed photograph. More than likely, she was copying the practice of an adult. Do you mind?'

'Go ahead. I'm intrigued.'

McCadden didn't hesitate. Plunging downwards with his pen, he punctured the brown paper and tore it away. The crisp, desiccated material crumpled in his hands. He eagerly searched inside, across the rough surface of the mounting board, along the smoother edges of the inner frame and found . . . absolutely nothing. For a moment, he was paralysed by astonishment. 'Wait,' he said. Fumbling anxiously, he quickly took the thing apart, separating mounting and print and glass and frame, and laying the pieces on the bed beside him. When he still found nothing, he slowly raised his eyes to stare at Elizabeth Cole. 'I was sure . . .'

'What did you expect?' she asked him.

McCadden was too bewildered to answer. But he looked so childishly crestfallen, so like a little boy who had ripped open a sweet packet to find only pebbles inside, that she started laughing at him, gasping with pain every time her shaking ribcage pinched at the wound to her breast, but still unable to control her amusement. The tears streamed from her eyes. It was part joy, part relief, part the suppressed mirth of almost seven years of silently enduring men's absurd certainties and deadly expectations. 'I'm sorry,' she tried to apologize. 'I'm sorry.'

Half-flattered that a woman could feel safe while laughing at him, half-mortified by his naive lapse, McCadden stoically endured it. 'It's all right, Mrs Cole.'